THE BOAT HOUSE

KERI BEEVIS

Boldwood

First published in Great Britain in 2023 by Boldwood Books Ltd.

Cover Design by 12 Orchards Ltd

Cover Photography: Shutterstock

A CIP catalogue record for this book is available from the British Library.

Paperback ISBN 978-1-80415-141-9

Large Print ISBN 978-1-80415-142-6

Hardback ISBN 978-1-80415-140-2

Ebook ISBN 978-1-80415-144-0

Kindle ISBN 978-1-80415-143-3

Audio CD ISBN 978-1-80415-135-8

MP3 CD ISBN 978-1-80415-136-5

Digital audio download ISBN 978-1-80415-138-9

Boldwood Books Ltd
23 Bowerdean Street
London SW6 3TN
www.boldwoodbooks.com

To everyone in Team Beev.
Thank you all for continuing to support me.

PROLOGUE

Call Handler: Norfolk Constabulary. What's your emergency?

Caller: Please help me. He's going to kill me. You need to come now.

Call Handler: Where are you?

Caller: Wroxham. Or near it. We're out in the countryside.

Call Handler: Are you at a house?

Caller: Yes, we rented it.

Call Handler: Do you know the address?

Caller: The Stone Boat House. It's down a country lane, but I can't remember the name of the road.

Call Handler: Can you describe where you are?

Caller: There are woods and there's a jetty and an abandoned cottage on the opposite side of the river. You have to come quickly. He's going to kill me. Please just help me!

Call Handler: Okay, help is on the way. Are you hurt?

Caller: Please hurry. I'm scared.

Call Handler: What's your name?

Caller: Emily.

Call Handler: Emily, I need you to stay calm and talk to me. Help is coming. Is there somewhere you can hide?

Caller: I am hiding. I managed to get down in the storage room.

Call Handler: That's good. Stay there and wait for the police to arrive. Do you know where this man is right now?

Caller: I don't know. He was upstairs, but I think he might have gone outside.

Call Handler: Do you know who he is?

Silence.

Call Handler: Emily? Are you okay? Are you still there?

Silence.

Caller: (Sobbing) My boyfriend, Max. He's got a knife—

Piercing scream.

Call Handler: Emily?

Line goes dead.

1

THREE DAYS EARLIER – SUNDAY

If you asked Emily Worth what the first thing was she had noticed about Max Hunter, she would say, without hesitation, it had been his smile.

They had met by chance in a busy Leeds city-centre street as she was delivering a tray of cupcakes to a pub ahead of a hen party, as a favour for her friend, Francesca. A series of Mr Bean-style calamities, involving a jammed heel caught in a pavement crack and a distracted cyclist who Max had to jump out of the way of, putting the pair of them on a collision course, which ended up with tangled limbs and both of them sprawled on the pavement, Emily sitting in Max's lap.

She had expected him to be annoyed, especially when he glanced down and realised the butter cream icing of several phallic-shaped cakes had covered his T-shirt, but instead she'd heard the rumble of laughter, saw one dimple crack, pulling the corner of his mouth up with it, as he'd looked at her with a charmingly crooked grin.

'Did you just splatter me with willies?'

He had sounded both intrigued and amused. His eyes twinkling.

That was the second thing she had noticed. She was sitting close enough to see the flecks of silver in his light blue irises; the creases fanning out from the corners of his eyes suggesting that he laughed a lot.

Emily didn't believe in love at first sight and had put her moment of flustered silence, the air feeling as if it had literally been knocked out of her, down to the adrenaline rush of the fall.

'Are you okay?' His smile had slipped a bit. 'Are you hurt?'

That was when she'd realised she was just sitting there in the busy street, still on his lap, and staring at him open-mouthed like some kind of gormless fool.

Embarrassment kicking in at her lack of good manners, she had almost leapt to her feet. 'I'm so sorry. Your T-shirt is ruined.'

'Forget about it, it's fine.' He'd hesitated, seeming amused at her attempts to brush the cream off his chest. 'Though this is nice.'

Emily had frozen, realising that what she was doing was actually quite inappropriate. She should have asked first before touching him. Her palm had heated against his chest. 'I'm sorry.'

'So you keep saying.' He'd glanced at the cake box, where the name of Francesca's little cake shop, The Sweeter Side, was printed in sugar pink letters. 'I take it these are for a hen do.'

'They were.' Emily had grimaced, looking at the ruined cupcakes.

'Will you be able to replace them?'

'I hope so. My friend made them. Hopefully there's time to make another batch.' She had closed the lid, taking a step back. If there was any way to salvage this, she had to get back to the cake shop quickly. 'Look, I really am so sorry,' she'd apologised once more as she retreated. 'I've got to go.'

Max had started to say something else, but she was already in the thick of the crowd and his words were lost.

Back at the shop, Francesca had rolled her eyes, teasing Emily about being a klutz, but quickly set about making a fresh batch of willy cakes as she'd grilled her friend about the hot stranger whose lap she had landed in.

'You didn't even get his name?' she'd questioned, dismayed.

'There wasn't time. And I was flustered,' Emily had admitted. She had already been kicking herself in disappointment at the missed opportunity. 'It was just a brief encounter.'

She didn't expect to see Max again, certainly didn't count on him showing up at the cake shop her best friend owned. It seemed she had made quite an impression, Francesca had told her with a smug smile, handing over the note with his number scribbled beneath the words,

For Willy Girl

Fast-forward three years and they now lived together and co-owned a beautiful border collie, Scout.

The last few months had been awful, though.

Not Max's fault, Emily reminded herself. Well, mostly not. Her dad had died and then her life had fallen apart. Everything that had happened had been beyond her control, but still she felt she should shoulder some of the blame. If she had handled things differently...

She pushed the thought away; it was all behind her now and she was picking up the pieces, trying to start afresh.

That's why they were currently in Max's Audi and heading to the Norfolk Broads for a week's holiday. It would be a chance for them to reconnect.

She was aware of his eyes leaving the road now as he glanced in her direction, and from the slight frown on his face, she wondered, not for the first time, if somehow he could read her thoughts.

'Everything okay, Em?'

She found a smile for him, reaching across the gearstick to link fingers with his free hand. 'I'm fine. Just a little tired.'

From the back seat, Scout whined in agreement.

'Not long now, girl. We'll be there soon,' Max told her.

'How far?' Emily asked, keen to get there too.

'Maybe another forty minutes. It's these bloody roads. I'd heard getting into Norfolk was a nightmare,' he grumbled, though it was good-naturedly.

That was Max. The easiest-going man she knew. In the time she had known him, he had rarely lost his temper and he was better at defusing situations rather than flaring them up.

This week away had been his idea. The two of them needed to spend some quality time together away from the stress of their jobs – Max worked as a firefighter and Emily as a personal assistant for a conveyancing solicitors firm – and it would also be a chance for Emily to heal from losing her dad.

Max had found the place where they were staying on Airbnb, booking it as a surprise for her. A cute little boat house, tucked away in a quiet spot just outside of a popular tourist village called Wroxham on the Norfolk Broads.

Summer had long gone, which would limit their activities somewhat, but there were still plenty of walks and cosy country-side pubs, which would benefit from the late autumnal weather. It sounded perfect and the photos of the boat house, with its big, comfy sofas and clawfoot bathtub, looked inviting.

Max was right. They did need this time alone together.

Everything was going to be okay. They still loved each other and both of them were committed to making things work.

After her third date with Max Hunter, Emily had told Francesca that he was the man she was going to marry. She still hoped that would be the case.

She just had to make sure he never ever found out about her dark secret.

2

Thanks to its secluded location, the boat house wasn't easy to find and they ended up driving into the main village of Wroxham itself, going over a cute little bridge that took them across the river dotted with boats and then through a high street lined with shops. Most of them were closed now, or in the process of shutting, to comply with Sunday trading hours, though there were still people about.

After turning round then finding the right road, they kept their eyes peeled for the turn-off that led down to the boat house, eventually finding the tree-lined lane. It was actually more of a track. Max taking it slow as the wheels hit bumps and stones, not wanting to damage his car.

It was dusk by the time they pulled into the wooded clearing outside the boat house, but even in the fading light, Emily could see that it was lovelier in real life than it had looked on the pictures Max had sent her – a tall stone structure with steps leading to a first-floor veranda and the front door, and surrounded by trees. It was the perfect spot.

The boat house was deceptively bigger on the inside than it appeared from the out, and Emily liked how the interior blended traditional and contemporary. Exposed beams and an open fireplace sitting alongside a sleek, modern kitchen and a wide floor-to-ceiling window at the back of the property, that overlooked the river at one of its widest points. In the distance on the opposite bank was what appeared to be a tiny cottage with a jetty that jutted out across the water.

The place was three storeys. The lower level comprised of twin tunnels leading out onto the water, where boats could be moored, and a storage room, while the accommodation itself was spread out across the top two floors. Downstairs was open-plan living, while a beautiful staircase with decorative iron balusters led to a mezzanine landing, where there was the one large bedroom with a bathroom leading off.

'What do you think?' Max asked, dropping their luggage on the bedroom floor and sitting down on the edge of the bed to face her.

'I think I love it.' She took hold of his outstretched hand, so he could pull her towards him. 'You picked well, Max Hunter,' she told him, smiling as she pushed him back on the bed, climbing on top of him. 'Ten out of ten.'

She pressed a kiss to his lips, though when he flipped them suddenly both over, pinning her beneath his weight, she instinctively stiffened, the smile falling from her face.

Breathe, Emily. It's just Max.

He must have picked up on her sudden tension because he eased back, smoothing her hair back off her face. 'You okay?' When she nodded, he added, 'This is going to be good for us, Em. I promise.'

'I know it will.'

She forced her body to relax as he nibbled her neck.

'I'm going to make sure you have a week to remember.'

'Is that a promise?' she asked, trying to play the part, even if her heart was no longer in the moment.

Max kissed her nose. 'Yes, it's a promise.'

Scout picked that moment to start whining from the lower floor, where they had left her with a dog chew, and Max rolled onto his back with a groan.

'Okay, girl,' he shouted to the dog. 'Give me a second.' He glanced at Emily. 'I suppose I should take her out. She was stuck in the car for longer than she's used to.'

'Give me a couple of minutes and I'll come with you.'

When she started to get up, Max shook his head. 'No, you stay here. I've got her. Why don't you settle us in? Light the fire and get things packed away. There's a bottle of fizz in the welcome hamper. Or there's red wine in one of the bags downstairs.'

The welcome hamper had been a nice touch. It had been left on the coffee table with a welcome card, filled with a few treats for them.

'Are you sure? I don't mind coming with you.'

'I'm sure. Let me walk Scout before it's dark. She needs to burn off some energy.'

He was right. The Border collie had been cooped up in the car for longer than she was used to. At home, they juggled busy jobs to ensure she wasn't left alone for long periods. It helped that Max worked shifts, so he was often at home when Emily was at work, and on the days neither of them were about, Scout went to Max's sister, who worked from home and could take plenty of breaks to spend time walking her and keeping her entertained.

'Why don't you go run that bath you've been wanting? Open the wine.' He grazed the pad of his thumb across her bottom lip. 'You chill and relax for a bit. I'll be back before you know it.'

Emily watched him head downstairs, her relief bringing with it a fresh bubble of guilt.

Max was going out of his way to look after her, to make up for how things were before, and he had no idea what she done. It was killing her keeping secrets from him, but if he found out the truth, it would destroy them.

She flopped back on the bed; her head hitting the duvet, and heaved out a breath. Somehow, she had to fix things. Make it up to him, even if he didn't know why.

She had been under so much pressure with her dad. It wasn't an excuse for what had happened, but truthfully the stress hadn't helped.

Max had said he wanted this week to be about her, but she would ensure it was for the both of them.

She heard the door open and close, the patter of Scout's excited feet on the deck outside, followed by Max's voice telling her to slow down. Then peace.

For a moment, it was eerily quiet. Emily was so used to the distant sound of traffic, but tucked away in the woods, there was nothing. A hooting owl broke the moment, then came the sound of another bird, low and mournful, cutting through silence.

She allowed her eyes to drift shut, letting the tension ebb out of her body, and didn't realise she had nodded off until the sound of a floorboard creaking below had her startling awake. It took a second to remember where she was, the antler ceiling light at first unfamiliar and a little unsettling as she stared up at it.

'Max?'

How long had she been asleep for? Was he back already?

She looked to the window and saw it was now completely dark outside.

When she received no response, she raised herself up on her elbows, listening. Had she imagined the noise?

A little unnerved, she pushed herself off the bed and wandered out onto the mezzanine landing, glancing down into the living area. The kitchen was out of sight below her, but she had a view of the rest of the large room and there was no sign of man or dog. Nothing had been disturbed.

She waited a heartbeat, but there was only silence, convincing her the noise must have been in her dream. They were set back down a tiny country lane and, from what she had seen, aside from the cottage on the opposite bank of the river, there were no other properties close by. There was no one else around. It was just Emily, Max and Scout.

Still, she glanced around the room cautiously as she descended the stairs. Just in case.

No one was in the boat house, though her attention was immediately drawn to the front door, which was wide open. Max had closed it after him, hadn't he? She thought back, certain she had heard it click shut.

She crossed the room to the door, stepping out onto the veranda. It was pitch black outside and peering over the wall at the top of the steps, she could barely make out Max's car. Anyone could be outside.

Still, she told herself she was overreacting. There was no reason why someone would go to the trouble of entering the boat house only to leave again? And nothing appeared to have been disturbed or stolen, from what she could see.

Rubbing her arms, Emily stepped back inside and closed the door. Maybe the latch hadn't caught when Max had shut it. A simple enough explanation. After a moment of hesitation, she turned the key in the lock, rationalising that it was better to be safe than sorry.

It was because of what had happened before. Deep down, she understood that. But this wasn't Leeds. She was in rural Norfolk.

She was safe here. Now the nightmare was behind her, she needed to find a way to try to move forward.

She stared out of the big picture window that overlooked the river, not liking that it was now so dark she could barely see anything. Just the half-moon and a few stars. By day, the view was so pretty, but right now it felt sinister.

The absence of curtains at the windows bothered her a little. Yes, they were looking out over the water, but the idea that while they were sitting inside anyone could be watching was a little unnerving.

Needing to warm herself up, Emily lit the fire, appreciating the burning crackle that took the edge off the silence, then stepped over the carrier bags of shopping and into the kitchen, immediately spotting the red wine and wine glass sitting on the counter.

A handwritten note beside the bottle of rioja read, 'Drink me' in capital letters, followed by a smiling face.

She remembered Max's suggestion that she have a glass of wine. He really was so thoughtful at times.

* * *

Emily had packed their things away, filled Scout's food bowl, and was sat on the sofa sipping the wine when a loud knock startled her and she jumped up, almost dropping her glass. The porch light was on and she was relieved to see Max standing the other side of the door.

'You locked me out.' Max was frowning as she let him and Scout in. 'Is everything okay?'

'You left it open. As in wide open,' she scolded, as Scout headed over to her dinner.

'No I didn't.'

'Max, I had to shut it. I thought someone had been inside at first.'

'We're tucked away out here. I doubt many people even know about this place.'

'That's not the point.'

Emily was aware she was getting irritable with him and could see from the exasperated look on his face that he was readying himself for her to turn this into a fight. Immediately, she talked herself down. She had allowed her emotions to get the better of her on too many occasions in the last few months and refused to argue over something petty. Instead she got up and went to him, linking her arms around his neck and pulling him closer for a kiss.

'Forget about it, okay. The latch probably didn't catch, but no harm was done. And thank you for the wine. It was a sweet gesture.'

She felt the tension ebb out of his shoulders, the sting of guilt reminding her that he was trying so hard to make things right again.

'You found the bottle okay then?'

Emily laughed. 'It wasn't difficult to spot. I liked your note.'

'Note?'

Max was easing back from her now and looking confused.

'The one you left on the counter with the wine. "Drink me".'

She led him into the kitchen to show him.

'I didn't write that.' He frowned at the rioja. 'And it's not the bottle I brought.'

The first flutter of fear dropped in Emily's stomach. 'It's not?'

'It must be from the owner. A welcome gift.'

'But they left us the hamper. Why would the wine not be in there?'

Max was digging through the carrier bags they had dumped on the kitchen floor. He pulled out a shiraz. 'This is my bottle.'

Emily stared at the glass she had been drinking from and for a moment thought she was going to be sick. She had looked in the kitchen when they had first arrived and hadn't seen the wine then. So if Max hadn't left it for her to find, then who had?

3

BEFORE

Emily had never had the closest relationship with her dad.

It had been the two of them for much of her childhood. Her mother and younger sister killed in a car accident in Leeds when she was just eight. They had been coming from Brownies when a driver who had been texting had ploughed into their vehicle.

While Emily had struggled to deal with the sudden loss of half of her family, her father had gone to pieces. He was barely able to hold down his job, let alone look after her, and she had been forced to grow up quickly, looking after the house and making sure they both ate. It was only thanks to Aunt Cathy, her mother's older sister, stepping in and suggesting Emily go to live with her when she went to high school that she had managed to get her life and education back on track.

Her relationship with her dad had been non-existent during most of her teenage years and her twenties. It was almost as if looking at Emily was too painful a reminder of what he had lost, and it was only in the last few years that she had, at Cathy's request, tried to mend bridges.

Her dad had moved to Scarborough after he'd eventually

pulled his life together and met someone new, though the relationship hadn't lasted, and together with Cathy, sometimes with Max too, they had tried to get together for dinner every couple of months. They usually picked a venue midway between Scarborough and the home Emily and Max shared on the outskirts of Leeds.

But then Cathy had passed away from a sudden stroke last year and as Emily dealt with her grief, heartbroken at losing the woman who had effectively stepped into the role of her mother, her dad had retreated again.

They had met up a couple of times, but then he'd stopped returning her calls. Emily had gone to his house to check on him, shocked when a neighbour told her he had been moved into a hospice. When she managed to track him down, she learnt that the cancer she hadn't even realised he'd had, which had initially started in his lungs, had now spread into his brain. He had maybe a few weeks left.

The revelation left her reeling. The hurt, anger and confusion making the diagnosis far more difficult to deal with than anything that had come before.

'I don't understand. Why wouldn't he tell me?' she said to Max that night, as they were getting ready for bed.

'You know what he's like, Em. He's never been much of a sharer.'

True, but this was different. They weren't talking about a bad day at work or buying a new car. This was about the end of her father's life. She had deserved to know.

Besides, Max had met her dad what, maybe a dozen times since they had been together? How the hell was he suddenly an expert on his behaviour?

She sidestepped the hug he tried to pull her into and headed into the bathroom to brush her teeth. His comment had annoyed her, which was ridiculous. She was being irrational and overly sensitive. Max was only trying to help and she had asked him the question.

He was already in bed, though grinning at something on his phone, when she stepped back into the room.

'Do you want me to come with you when you go back tomorrow?' he asked, not bothering to look up.

'I thought you were going to the football?'

'I am. But I don't have to go. I can come with you. If you want me to.'

If you want me to. Not, *I want to be there with you.* Max had been so supportive when Cathy had died, so why did her father's illness seem less of a big deal to him?

'No, don't worry. Go to the football. There's no point in both of us going. Besides, I'll probably be gone most of the day. We can't leave Scout alone for all that time and it's not fair to ask your sister to have her on the weekend too.'

Hearing her name, the dog's ears shot up from where she was curled up on her favourite blanket, her pink tongue lolling out of her mouth in a big grin.

Emily climbed into bed, her mood darkening when Max didn't push the subject. Today, she had spoken with her dad; tomorrow, she hoped to get some more thorough information from the staff treating him.

'Okay. Whatever you want.' Max leant across to press a kiss to her cheek. 'It's going to be okay, Em.'

It wasn't going to be okay. She had learnt that her dad was dying. How the fuck did he think it was going to be okay?

She was toying with asking him the question, wondering if perhaps she picked a fight with him, she might get this sudden burst of aggression out of her system, but the sound of a WhatsApp message pinging through demanded his attention again and their conversation appeared over. Instead, she slid down under the duvet and rolled away so she wasn't facing him.

Max's sudden burst of laughter had her shoulders tensing. 'What's funny?' she asked through clenched teeth.

'Leah. She cracks me up.'

Emily didn't react, other than to reach out to switch off her bedside light. Although she closed her eyes, her body remained tense and she knew she was too wound up to sleep.

Leah Butterworth had been friends with Max for years, long before Emily had started dating him, and the woman had never warmed to her, despite Emily's best efforts. Emily got on well with all of his other friends, so she was pretty certain it wasn't her.

Max was convinced it was all in Emily's head, but she wasn't stupid and could pick up on the vibes, and she knew that in Leah's eyes, she wasn't good enough. Luckily, their paths didn't cross very often, and when they did, Emily had given up trying to make an effort, but, right now, knowing that the woman was the source of Max's distraction was annoying.

The pinging back and forth of messages carried on for a few more minutes, then she heard Max put his phone down. The mattress dipped as he settled down beside her and as his arm snaked around her, she tried to relax. It was difficult, though, with her mind working overtime.

Was she expecting too much from him, wanting him to be more supportive? He had offered to go with her to see her dad, but somehow it wasn't enough.

But was it Max or did her dad's diagnosis have her overreacting and being overly sensitive? She wondered how he would feel if it was his own dad who was ill. Surely he would want the extra support? But then Max and his dad were much closer. His parents had separated when he was younger and his mother had an affair. Max's dad had never forgiven her and neither had Max or his siblings.

Maybe he thought that as Emily was estranged from her dad, it mattered less.

He was wrong. It really didn't.

Before long, she heard the shallow sound of his breathing and knew he was already asleep, and her throat burned with unshed tears.

She had never felt alone in their relationship before. They had always been two peas in a pod. But here he was, lying in bed beside her and the sudden pang of loneliness that hit was sharp and overwhelming.

Max and Emily. We're a team. Together forever. That's what he had said to her when they'd first moved in together, promising her that whatever they faced further down the line, it would always be the two of them, side by side, holding each other up.

So why did it feel like she was now falling and there was no one there to catch her?

4

SUNDAY

'Don't you think you're overreacting just a little bit?' Max asked, a hint of exasperation creeping into his tone.

He had been outside with the torch looking around for whoever had left the wine, even though they both knew it was a fruitless exercise. The sender had long gone.

'How is it possible to overreact, Max? Someone walked into the boat house without knocking and left it for us to find.'

'It's wine, though. Nothing sinister. It's not like they left a dead squirrel. Maybe a neighbour dropped it by as a welcome gift. I mean, they did leave a note.'

'That said "drink me",' Emily snapped. 'Don't you think that's an odd message to put with a welcome gift?'

'Well, it worked,' he teased, not taking her seriously. 'You did drink it.'

'Because I thought it was from you!' The idea that she had opened the bottle not knowing where it had come from had nausea swimming in the pit of her stomach, especially after everything that had happened. 'I wouldn't have touched it if I had realised.'

'You said it was sealed, so there's no harm done. And it's a branded label.'

Max said it as if that made everything okay. It really didn't. But then she supposed that he would have no idea why she was so freaked out, because she had kept everything that had happened this summer hidden from him.

'Don't you think that if it was a welcome gift, the person might have wanted to give it to us personally instead of sneaking into the house? The note's not even signed by anyone.' Emily hissed out a frustrated breath. 'Who did you book this place through anyway? Do you know anything about them?'

'I already told you I found it on Airbnb. The guy who owns it is called Peter and he's been nothing but friendly and helpful.'

'Does he live locally?'

Max hesitated. 'I don't know. I never asked. Why would I?'

'We're in his house! Surely you know a little bit about him.'

Scout started whining, picking up on Emily's growing agitation.

'You know how Airbnb works, Em. We've only communicated by email and, no, I didn't ask about his life history.'

Max's tone warned her his patience was wearing thin, as did the frustrated hand he shoved into his hair. And he was right. Of course she knew how Airbnb worked, which made her sound unreasonable.

The keys to the boat house had been left in a little safe box by the front door, which suggested the owner wasn't nearby and that the property was regularly rented out. The place was spotless, with fresh linen and towels, and there was the welcome hamper, but he probably employed a local service to sort everything.

'Look, I just want this week to be right, for us to spend some time together, okay? We deserve this. You deserve that, after everything you've been through, losing Cathy and then your dad.

I know we can't explain the wine, but I honestly don't think it was meant as anything other than a kind gesture. I will email Peter and I'm sure he can clear this up.' Max closed the gap between them and Emily thawed just a little. It wasn't his fault she was so worked up. And perhaps there was an innocent explanation for the wine. It was ridiculous to connect this to what had happened back home. No one knew they were here. 'I love you, Em, and we will get to the bottom of it, I promise.'

He was trying so hard to fix things for her. She reminded herself of that now. Maybe she needed to stop being so paranoid and to try to relax.

'This place is gorgeous, right? And we're here together. Just us and Scout.'

It was and she gave a little hum of agreement as she pressed her face into his shoulder, breathing in his familiar and welcoming scent as he rubbed her back.

Was she overreacting? It wasn't right that someone had snuck into the boat house, but perhaps it hadn't been with sinister intentions.

'I passed a place while I was out with Scout. It's about a twenty-minute walk away and they serve food.' Max's warm breath tickled against her ear, his tone low. 'How about we eat out tonight?'

The idea was appealing and they were on holiday after all. Emily eased back from the hug and gave him a smile of apology. 'Okay. That'd be nice.'

Max was making an effort and it was a reminder that she needed to as well.

5

The decision to go out was a good one.

Max had called ahead to reserve a table and check the place was dog-friendly, then they had wrapped up warm before heading out for a chilly walk down the dark lane.

Emily hadn't liked that bit, wishing she had persuaded Max to get a cab. Although they had the torch, it was so dark with the absence of street lights, the branches of trees tangling overhead to mostly block out the light from the moon. And the silence was almost smothering. The only noise coming from the occasional hoot or screech up in the trees, and the crunch of their footsteps against the gravelly track of the lane. Remembering the wine incident had Emily wondering if anyone was watching them, and she clung tightly to Max's hand, relieved when they eventually reached the lights of Wroxham.

Once in the restaurant, they enjoyed a relaxed evening with what she considered good pub grub. The earlier tension had lifted and Max was on good form. Chatty, amusing and attentive. His phone away and his focus solely on Emily. From some of the sizzling looks he was giving her across the table, it brought back memories of their early dates, back in the days when everything had been new and exciting and her belly had been jittery with butterflies each time she knew she was going to see him.

He had been an addiction back then. The piece in her life that she hadn't realised she was missing, and she had felt like a teenager all over again, her world suddenly full of long, heady kisses, new adventures together and, most of all, fun. No one could make her laugh like Max did, and it was fun that she now realised had been missing from their lives in the last year.

They both led busy lifestyles. Max working hard for a promotion, while Emily's job had its demands, but they had still always found time for each other. But then outside pressures had crept in – Aunt Cathy's sudden passing had left Emily shocked and bereft with grief, and she hadn't coped well with her dad's diagnosis, then what had come after had nearly destroyed her.

Date nights had gone out of the window and their sex life had become woefully neglected. Would this week help bring the excitement back?

She had been in lust and then in love with Max Hunter. And she still was. Somewhere along the line, they had lost a little of their passion, but the way his hand lightly covered hers on the table right now, the pad of his thumb drawing patterns on the soft flesh of her wrist, made her believe it could be rekindled.

This was the dream for her.

It might be a simple one, but she had the man she loved sitting across from her, the dog they both adored snoozing at their feet. The bottle of wine they had shared had relaxed her sufficiently, and she had a nice warm buzz heating her veins.

The twinge of guilt when it came, remembering that she had nearly lost all of this, was unwelcome, as was the reminder of what had happened earlier in the boat house when Max struck up conversation with the waitress while settling the bill.

She had commented on his accent, noting that the pair of them weren't from Norfolk and asking if they were visiting.

'We're staying just down the road from here,' he told her. 'Got an Airbnb by the river.'

'It's called the Stone Boat House,' Emily added. 'Do you know it?'

The waitress seemed surprised. 'I didn't realise they were letting that place out again.'

'You know the owners?'

Was it Emily's imagination or did Max seem a little annoyed that she had asked, a frown creasing his brow?

'I do. Well, I did. They used to come down and stay there regularly. I thought Peter had stopped renting it out after his wife died. He couldn't bring himself to come back here. Such a tragic accident.'

'Accident?' Emily flicked a quick glance at Max, who had fallen silent and now had a scowl on his face. 'Did it happen locally?' It was foolish and it wasn't that she believed in ghosts or anything – well, mostly she didn't – but stuff like that had always freaked her out a little.

'Yes, last summer. The poor love got into difficulties out on the water and she flipped her boat.' The waitress held the card reader out to Max as she spoke. 'She knew what she was doing, but I guess it goes to prove that you can still have an accident no matter how experienced you are.' She looked wistful for a moment. 'Such a shame. She was a lovely lady and they had worked hard to make the place nice. I heard Peter was thinking of selling it. He must have changed his mind.' Tearing the receipt from the reader, she handed it to Max. 'You two enjoy your stay. Maybe we will see you again.'

'Maybe.' Max had already pushed back his chair, seeming eager to leave as he whistled to Scout.

Emily slipped her coat on. It was warm in the pub, but she was shivering slightly, and they still had the walk back down the lane to contend with. She had planned to ask Max to call a cab, but he was already striding ahead out of the door.

Had he known about the tragedy and what had happened to the woman who died?

No, that was stupid. It was an Airbnb. Of course he knew nothing about the owners.

She thought back to the mysterious bottle of wine that had been left, immediately annoyed that her mind was trying to connect it to the tragedy. The wine had nothing to do with a poor woman who had drowned.

Still, she was distracted as she hurried after Max and Scout.

'You okay?' Max asked eventually, picking up on her silence as they crossed the road and headed away from the village. He flicked on the torch and Emily took Scout's lead, slipping her free hand into Max's. 'You're not still stressing about earlier with that wine?'

'No, I'm fine,' she lied. They had enjoyed a nice evening. She wasn't going to let her paranoia spoil it. 'I'm just full and tired. It was nice in there, wasn't it?'

She made the effort to keep her tone light and engage in conversation, keen to distract herself from the creepy walk back. It was worse heading away from the lights of the village, and it felt like the woods were swallowing them as they turned into the lane that led down to the boat house.

No one was hiding among the trees, despite her paranoia, she reminded herself. And if by some remote chance they did have company, Scout would pick up on it. She was worrying about nothing.

Eventually, they reached the boat house, the welcome glow of the front light at the top of the outdoor steps easing the knot in her stomach, though she didn't start to relax until they stepped inside, and she turned on the switch, flooding the place with light.

Her gaze darted to the kitchen counter, relieved to see there were no more gifts or notes. No one had been here while they were out. She watched Max bolt the door, relaxing further when she knew it was locked.

* * *

It was Scout's barking that woke Emily hours later and although she came to abruptly, it still took her a few moments to get her bearings.

They were in bed, Max sprawled on his back and lightly snoring, one arm tucked beneath his pillow and one leg covering Emily's. He had always been a much heavier sleeper than her and as she shifted from under him, climbing out of the bed, he remained undisturbed.

She reached for his jumper, discarded on the floor with the rest of their clothes, recalling their earlier lovemaking as she slipped it on. It smelt of him and she wrapped her arms around herself in a hug to ward off the cold. With nothing to distract them, they had spent time rediscovering one another and finding the passion that had been missing from their lives, Emily finally managing to relax and let go of the tension that had been shadowing her.

She had fallen asleep satisfied and, for the first time in a while, worry-free, her earlier stresses becoming insignificant in that moment. But Scout's initial bark was now followed by whining and she could hear the dog pacing the floor below, her nails clipping against the wooden floor, which had Emily's shoulders tensing with fear.

Scout's blanket was in the bedroom, so why had she gone downstairs? Had she heard a noise? Something was bothering her and until she found out what it was, Emily knew she wouldn't be able to fall asleep again.

She glanced back at Max, who was still dead to the world, before leaving the bedroom. Although he was out of it, knowing he was close by bolstered her confidence.

Slowly, she descended the stairs. The lower level of the house was dark with shadows, though there was enough light from the moon for her to make out the shimmering surface of the water through the big picture window.

She found Scout sat in front of the door, her ears flat and her tail tucked beneath her, the whining now having given way to a low hostile growl.

Was somebody outside?

Emily approached her cautiously, scared of what she might find. 'What's spooking you, Scout?' She kept her voice low and soothing, though couldn't quite hide the tremor.

The dog ignored her, other than to let out another whine.

It could be a squirrel or another woodland creature, Emily guessed. They were in the countryside, in the middle of nowhere.

Her mind went back to the wine and the mysterious note. Was the person who had left them outside? Perhaps she was being irrational, but standing here in the dark room with her dog unsettled and not knowing what was spooking her had her on edge.

She tried the door handle, simply to make sure it was still locked, relaxing slightly when she realised it was, then hit the porch light.

The face staring back at her had her stumbling backwards, her heart hammering into her throat as Scout went crazy, barking her head off.

Finding her voice, Emily started to scream.

6

BEFORE

'Could you move your car please? You're blocking me in.'

Emily asked the question politely, forcing a smile on her face for Rob Bristow, one of the conveyancers at the firm where she worked.

For a moment, she thought he was going to ignore her, intently studying his computer screen as if he hadn't noticed she was standing beside his desk. Just as he had ignored her when she had tried to call him, forcing her to come up to his office to ask the question.

Eventually, though, he looked up, blinking at her. 'Emily, hello. What can I do for you?'

She repeated her request. 'I need you to let me out of the car park please.'

Rob, a bald, overweight man in his forties, frowned hard as he studied her, drawing his head back, which had several chins appearing under his face. 'Are you leaving early again?' He made a point of looking at the wall clock, before telling her the time. 'It's only 5 p.m.'

'I need to go see my dad.' Emily forced the words through clenched teeth, trying not to let her smile slip.

Rob knew full well where she had to go. News spread fast in the environment she worked in and the whole office was aware of Simon Worth's diagnosis.

Her boss, James, had been good to her, regularly checking in to make sure she was looking after herself and telling her to let him know if there was anything he could do to help. He knew Emily was a hard worker and that she had been going through a rough time. First with her aunt and now with her dad. It had been his suggestion that she leave early on a few occasions and, to repay his kindness, she tried to get into work a little earlier in the mornings.

None of this was Rob's business, and although she helped out all of the conveyancers, she didn't report to him. He wasn't her boss. She just needed him to move his car. It wasn't the first time he had blocked her in and she suspected he was doing it on purpose.

'How is your dad, Emily?'

The question came from the conveyancer who shared the office with Rob, Natasha Becket, and her tone was kind. Emily appreciated her breaking the awkward silence as she waited for Rob to react.

'The staff are making him as comfortable as possible. Thank you for asking.'

'It's not an easy time. I remember when my dad was sick. Make sure you are looking after yourself too. It's easy to get run-down with the pressure.'

'I will. Thank you.'

Rob had taken the opportunity to refocus on his computer and didn't seem in a hurry to respond to Emily's initial request, so she asked again.

'Can you move your car please?'

He didn't even bother to look up this time. 'You'll have to wait until I've finished what I'm doing. We don't all have the luxury of leaving early. I'm going as quickly as I can.'

Emily bristled. His tone was light, so if challenged, he could pass off the comment as a joke. She knew how he operated, having been on the receiving end before. If she made a fuss, she would be the one acting unreasonable.

She knew exactly why he was being a dick, understanding that he now had a personal grudge against her after she had rejected his advances on a night out. Apparently, it didn't matter to Rob that she had a boyfriend. Not that she would have been interested, even if Max wasn't on the scene.

Since that night, Rob had gone out of his way to be awkward. Blocking her in so she had to ask him to move his car or phoning her with work questions just as she was about to leave.

One of the other PAs had told her to report him to James, but Emily was wary of stirring up more trouble. If he continued being difficult, though, she was going to have to say something.

Rob knew the stress she was under. What the hell was wrong with him?

She was toying with asking again, telling him she couldn't wait and needed to leave now, when Natasha spoke up.

'Rob, she needs to go. It will take you two minutes to move your car.'

Emily could see the scowl was back on his face again and that he didn't appreciate being called out by a colleague. Especially one who outranked him in terms of experience. She watched his profile as his nostrils flared before he slipped his genial mask back on and turned to face them both.

'Of course. What was I thinking? Work can wait.' He got up

and left the room and Emily mouthed a quick 'thank you' to Natasha before following.

Outside, Rob didn't acknowledge her at all. Getting in his car and reversing to let her out.

Emily put up a hand to say thank you, but got nothing back. Instead she tried to focus on seeing her dad.

In truth, she was still trying to get over her initial shock of his diagnosis and the fact he hadn't told her. Over a week had passed and she was struggling to process everything. Somehow she had to get past the hurt that had caused, given the brief time he had left.

She was still grieving for Aunt Cathy. To now have her dad dying too felt cruel and unfair.

A protective layer of numbness had settled over the routine of her life as she went through the motions of work, eat and sleep, fitting in visits to the hospice as and when she was able. For now, her focus was solely on her dad, even if he acted like he didn't want her visiting him.

Simon Worth was a proud man and didn't like to show his vulnerabilities and emotions. It had always been this way, which is why he had pushed Emily away when she was a child. Somehow, he had twisted it in his head that it was kinder to everyone if he disappeared to die like an injured animal.

Could he really not see how cruel that would be?

Max was the outlet for some of her frustration, especially the times she was tired and emotional, functioning on too much coffee and too little sleep, but his shift patterns and the time she had spent travelling back and forth to Scarborough meant they had barely seen each other over the past week, and so her feelings were mostly kept bottled. A ticking time bomb that she was desperately trying to control.

He wasn't being supportive enough. He was too busy with

work. He was more interested in having an easy life and bantering with his friends than being there for her.

Some of the time, she believed it; at other points, she understood she was being unfair and irrational, but she couldn't seem to stop herself, and leaving St Edmund's Hospice, knowing she had to make the journey home gradually became more and more difficult.

* * *

'Are you okay?'

Emily glanced up from where she sat at her father's bedside, double blinking at the unfamiliar man standing in the doorway. Concerned dark eyes were looking her up and down.

Her father was asleep, out of it on his pain meds, and she had taken the opportunity to shut her own eyes, leaning forward in her chair to rest her head in her crossed arms.

The stranger had thought she was crying, she realised, and a burst of guilt hit that she had yet to shed a tear for her father. She had been stunned, shocked, angry and frustrated, but so far she had held back on her sorrow. In part, she guessed, because she knew once the dam burst, she would fall to pieces.

'I'm fine. Thanks.' Her eyes narrowed slightly. 'Do you work here?'

He wasn't in uniform, instead dressed in a T-shirt and jeans, and she hadn't seen him on her previous visits. Emily knew she would have remembered him if she had.

He was the kind of man women noticed. His short, dark hair curling slightly around an angular face, and he had a warm, appealing smile. She put him around her own age, in his early thirties, though he was possibly a bit older.

'I'm a volunteer.' He held up a worn paperback of *Lord of the*

Flies. 'I read to the residents, keep them company... if they want me.'

Emily didn't remember her dad being much of a reader, but then their relationship had been strained, and absent even, for large periods of her life. Maybe it was something he enjoyed.

'You read to my dad?'

'I do.' The man's smile widened. 'It took us a few days to find the type of book he likes, but now we're set.' He stepped further into the room and held out his hand. 'I'm Connor Banks. You're Simon's daughter, Emily?'

She took his warm hand in her cold one. 'He's talked about me?'

'Yes, a few times. He says you've been coming to see him.'

He had? That surprised her. Her father had been annoyed when she had discovered where he was, at first asking her to leave, and she'd had to dig her heels in. That he had mentioned her at all caught her a little off guard and she wasn't quite sure how she felt about it.

'He didn't tell me,' Emily blurted the words out, not even realising she had spoken aloud until she clocked Connor's confused expression. 'He didn't tell me about any of it,' she elaborated. 'Not the cancer, not the hospice. I found out from his neighbour when I couldn't get hold of him.'

Now the poor guy looked uncomfortable, standing there awkwardly with his book, unsure quite how to react. He had signed up to help the hospice patients, not listen to people like her offload. And despite what her father had done, she didn't want Connor judging him.

Emily softened her outburst by attempting a smile. 'I'm sorry. You didn't need to know that. It's kind of you to spend time with Dad reading to him. Thank you.'

She started to get up, not relishing the drive home. Sometimes, she used the journey time as breathing space, but right now, despite the claustrophobic feeling in the house she shared with Max, she just desperately wanted to be there so she could have a shower and go to bed. She didn't even care that she hadn't had a chance to eat, figuring she would stop at McDonald's or go without.

'It's okay.' Connor still hadn't moved. 'It's a lot to deal with and not easy seeing the people we love in this situation. We're allowed to vent now and again.'

He had said 'we' and Emily looked at him curiously. He had said he was a volunteer, not a visitor.

He must have picked up on her confusion because he went on to explain. 'I lost my mum a couple of years ago.' A shadow of sadness clouded his expression and her heart squeezed.

'I'm sorry for your loss.' Emily was silent for a moment. 'So is that why you do this? Volunteer?'

He nodded. 'St Edmund's did so much for Mum before she died and I remember the volunteers who used to come and sit with her. Knowing she had their company, people to talk to, made things a little easier for me and I guess it helped with the guilt. I tried to be here as much as I could, but I still had commitments in my day-to-day life. It never felt enough.'

He got it, Emily realised, and he knew exactly how she was feeling.

She thought about him on her drive home, feeling more at peace leaving her father behind, knowing Connor was there keeping him company. He had been kind to Emily, as well as to her dad, taking the time to talk to her about how she was feeling and letting her know it was okay to vent. And he was right; the staff at St Edmund's were all great. From the receptionists to the carers and nurses she regularly spoke with.

It was late when she pulled into the cul-de-sac where she

lived. The house she rented with Max was semi-detached and on one of the newer housing estates on the outskirts of Leeds. Max's Audi was already on one side of the double drive and Emily bristled with annoyance as she parked beside him, having spotted Leah's sporty little Mazda on the kerb in front of the house. It was almost eleven. What the hell was she doing here?

Leah didn't often come over – at least she didn't when Emily was about – so why was she here now? The idea of having to be polite to the woman, with her smirky smile and sly side eye, had her mood plummeting as she climbed out of the car. She just wanted to go to bed.

She stepped inside the house, her shoulders tensing when Leah's shrill laughter filled the air. Emily forced a smile onto her face before going into the living room. It slipped slightly, though, as she spotted Leah and Max sat on the sofa together, a little too close for comfort. Neither of them had heard her. Max looking at something on his phone screen, while Leah had her hand on his arm as she cackled away. A bottle of wine with two glasses sat on the coffee table.

Emily cleared her throat and they both glanced up, but Leah was the only one who looked guilty. Her initial surprise as she shifted away from Max was quickly masked though, as her resting bitch face slipped back into position.

Max grinned at Emily, getting to his feet.

'How's your dad?' he asked, leaning down to kiss her cheek.

Did he seriously think there was nothing wrong with this whole scenario?

Her tone was clipped as she replied, 'He was asleep the whole time I was there.'

'I'm sorry, Em. Sounds like it was a wasted trip.'

He was her father and he wasn't going to be around much longer. It was hardly wasted.

Emily didn't say that; instead, she excused herself to bed, saying she was tired.

Moments later, she heard Max ushering Leah out of the door before he whistled to Scout. Emily was in bed and feigning sleep by the time he returned and, a few minutes later, she heard both of them come into the bedroom. The humph that the dog let out as she settled herself down on her blanket, then the dip of the mattress as Max slipped into bed beside her.

'You awake, Em?'

When she didn't answer, glad she was facing away from him, Max snuggled in closer so her back was against his chest, one hand lightly caressing the curve of her hip as he pressed light kisses against her neck.

She tried her best not to react, though her throat tightened at his next whispered words.

'I love you.'

Did he really? He had looked pretty cosy down in the living room with Leah. Okay, so they hadn't been doing anything when she had walked in, but it didn't mean nothing had happened.

As she considered whether to challenge him, his breathing became shallow, his hand stilling, and she realised he was falling asleep.

Her frustration built. Why was he able to forget any stresses and drift off so easily, while she lay awake staring at the wall?

In those early, heady days of their relationship, she had liked to watch him sleep. Long lashes hiding the rich blue of his eyes, his naturally sun-streaked hair in shades of caramel, coffee and sandy brown, that Emily knew many women would pay a fortune to achieve, a mess against the pillow and that generous mouth of his, with his lips slightly parted and his breathing steady. He always looked so peaceful.

Now it annoyed her and the more she thought about the

scene she had walked in on, the more sleep evaded her. It was impossible to relax.

'Why was Leah here, Max?'

When he didn't respond, already out for the count, she shifted her position, poking him hard with a well-placed elbow.

As he grunted awake, she flipped the switch on her bedside light and repeated her question. 'Why was Leah here?'

'What?' He didn't sound happy about being woken up and neither did Scout, who let out a yawning whine from beside the bed.

'You heard me. What was she doing here?'

'She asked if she could come over. What's the big deal, Emily? She's my friend.'

'Yes, your friend. Not mine. She never makes any effort where I'm concerned. Never wants to visit if I'm at home.' Emily was warming to her theme now, pushing herself up into a sitting position and glaring at him. She could see he was confused at her outburst and looking just a little bit annoyed.

'You sound jealous.'

'I'm not jealous. I'm bloody irritated. I'm your girlfriend, but she doesn't seem to be able to accept that.'

Max was propped up on one elbow now. He raked his free hand through his hair. 'She likes you fine. I don't know why you are so paranoid about her.'

'Because I haven't stopped all day. I've been at work and then in the car and then with Dad. I am dead on my feet and the last thing I needed was to walk in on you two having a fun night in.'

'It wasn't a fun night, okay? She's still upset about her aunt. They were close.'

It didn't feel like Max was there for Emily with her dad, yet he was able to comfort Leah, whose aunt had died almost a year ago.

'She didn't sound all that upset when I arrived.'

'Well she was, okay.'

'And she thought the solution was to come over here while I was out and get drunk with my boyfriend.'

'She had one glass. In case you hadn't noticed her car parked out front, she was driving.'

'Oh, I saw it all right. Doesn't she have any other friends she can go visit?' Emily snapped, perhaps a little unkindly. She couldn't help it though.

'You're being ridiculous.'

'Am I?'

'Yes, Emily, you are.'

'Well, perhaps it might be nice if I didn't have to go through this alone. If you actually gave a shit and were there for me for a change.'

The words were out before she could take them back and there was a moment of silence as Max stared at her. She could see the hurt on his face and knew her dig had stung.

The timing with her father wasn't great. Max was working hard towards a promotion and Emily knew that most nights, she would come home to find him studying. Not sitting around with Leah. And he had offered to go with her to see her dad. She had been the one who insisted he stay home.

She should apologise, take the words back. The whole situation with Leah had her riled, though, and she couldn't seem to get past what she had walked in on.

Max threw back the duvet, getting out of bed, and panic stabbed at her.

'Where are you going?'

'I'm not fighting with you, Emily. I know you're going through a hard time right now, so I'll give you that one dig.'

'Max!'

'Try and get some sleep.'

'Where are you going?'

He didn't answer and Scout, who was agitated and had been whining throughout their argument, was hot on Max's tail as he left the room.

It was another stab of hurt, but then Emily couldn't really blame the dog. It felt like she was hardly at home at the moment and when Max was on shift, Scout was spending more and more time with his sister, Charlotte.

Moments later, she heard the sound of the guest-bedroom door open, then close and for a few stunned seconds she was motionless with shock, her heart thudding.

They never fought. Okay, sometimes they bickered, but it was all silly stuff. Max leaving the toilet seat up, Emily forgetting to put the bins out if Max was on night shift. He had never gone to sleep in the spare room before.

Part of her wondered whether she should go after him, but she wasn't sure if she wanted to finish what they had started or tell him she was sorry.

Instead, she slid back down under the duvet, painfully aware that she was alone in the big bed and wanting to cry, though she knew the tears wouldn't come.

Their relationship was beginning to fracture under the strains of a difficult period. The cracks widening. And she wasn't sure if they could come back from this.

7

EARLY MONDAY MORNING

'Emily?' Max was charging down the stairs, shirtless and almost falling over himself as he tried to tug on his jeans before he reached the bottom. 'Emily? Where are you?'

He sounded worried, his eyes wide as he spotted her, and she saw him relax just a little, seeing that she was safe. Still, he crossed the room quickly, as if needing to touch her to be sure.

'You screamed. What happened?'

He must have felt the tension thrumming through her and almost certainly was aware she was shaking, because concern knotted his brow as he rubbed his hands up and down her chilled arms.

'Talk to me, Emily.'

'There's... someone... outside.'

Emily didn't realise quite how scared she was until she tried to speak, her teeth chattering, aware she was on the verge of losing it. She could see the face clearly in her mind. White, smooth, and surrounded by a hood. Just glass had separated them and if that barrier hadn't been in the way, what would have happened then?

Thank God she hadn't gone outside to investigate.

Which was what Max was doing right now, she realised, watching him cross the room, unlocking the door and flinging it open before she had a chance to protest.

She saw him reach for something. Her nerves on a knife's edge.

'Max!'

What was he doing?

He was back inside now, the door closing again, and she could see he was holding something. Her stomach churned as he showed her the mask. She had only seen the man for a split second, his smooth white face staring at her and now she realised the reason he had looked so odd was because he had been wearing a mask.

'That's what I saw?' she whispered, looking at the ghoulish rubber face.

'It was hanging up outside the door.'

'What? But someone was there. They were wearing it.'

'Are you sure?'

'I swear.'

Max nodded, heading over to the kitchen, Emily hot on his trail and Scout close behind.

'What are you doing?' she asked.

'Getting the torch.'

'You can't go back outside.'

He shook off her hand when she grabbed hold of his arm, desperate to stop him.

'No, Max. What if he's still out there?'

He wasn't paying attention, already by the door again, this time slipping his feet into his trainers. 'Wait here. And lock this after me.'

'Max. Stop!'

It was too late; he had already opened the door, Scout charging ahead of him and barking at the darkness.

'Max!'

Ignoring Emily, he disappeared outside, the door shutting on her protest.

Her heart thumped. She had her back pressed against the worktop, tense fingers holding onto the edge of the counter, almost afraid to let go. Although she was reluctant to approach the door, Max had instructed her to lock it. The man was no longer there, but she sucked in a steadying breath, quickly crossing the room and bolting it with trembling fingers, hating that Max and Scout had disappeared from sight. What if she was wrong? He could be hiding and attack them. Max might have the torch, but he hadn't taken any kind of weapon with him. And he didn't even have a top on. It was freezing outside.

And Scout might sound ferocious when she was having one of her barking fits, but she was still a youngster and soft as anything. Emily hated how vulnerable the pair of them were.

She needed to do something. She couldn't just stand here waiting for them to reappear.

Her phone. It was upstairs. She should call the police.

Realising that's what Max should have done instead of trying to play the hero, she choked down a sob, heading up the stairs to find it. She ran into the bedroom, her gaze falling on the empty bedside table, panic clawing its way up her throat. Where the hell was her phone? She was certain she had left it there.

Think, Emily.

As she frantically searched for it, she realised she was wasting precious seconds. She was so rattled, though, and couldn't think straight, which wasn't going to help any of them.

Running anxious fingers through her sleep-tousled hair, she forced herself to pause for a moment and focus.

Her phone had been with her when they had come up to bed and she had replied to a message from Francesca asking what the boat house was like. Emily remembered it beeping at her, warning it was low on battery. That was it. She had plugged it in the socket beside the bedside table on Max's side of the room to charge.

Frantically, she charged round the bed, hastily unplugging it and pulling up the keypad to call the police.

A noise downstairs had her stopping dead and fear slicing through her.

Was the intruder inside the boat house?

She had locked the door. She was certain she had.

'Emily?'

Some of that fear dissipated as she heard Max's muffled voice and, forgetting the emergency call, she rushed back down the stairs and to the door, unlocking and pulling it open and launching herself into his arms as he stepped inside. Scout was with him and she barked as she danced around them, no longer agitated, which suggested they were definitely alone.

Max was icy cold and Emily hugged him to her, still mad with him for going outside, but for now just relieved he was okay.

'Did you see him?' she demanded, easing back so she could look at his face.

He shook his head. 'No one is outside, Emily.'

Did he not believe her? 'He was there. I know what I saw!' Emily's hackles were rising. 'And Scout saw him too. Her barking woke me up. She knew someone was outside.'

'Take it easy. I never said I doubted you. Someone had to have left the mask. But whoever it was has gone.' Easing out of her embrace, Max went back to the kitchen, picking up the mask from the counter. 'Are you sure you definitely saw someone wearing it? It was hanging right in front of the door.'

'Of course I'm sure.

'It was probably someone playing a prank.'

'It wasn't a prank. Someone was wearing that mask!'

Was it her imagination or did Max seem sceptical?

'I know what I saw, Max. I'm not making it up!'

She was getting agitated and, after locking the door again, Max led her to the sofa, pulling her down beside him. Emily glanced at the coffee table where he set the mask down, and he cupped her chin with his hand, guiding her attention back to him.

'I know you're not making it up,' he told her, taking hold of both of her hands. 'Talk me through everything. You said you heard Scout barking.'

'I did. She woke me up.' Emily told him about how the dog had initially been barking and whining, but how she had started growling at the door. 'I knew something was spooking her, but I thought it was probably a squirrel or a rabbit. That's when I turned the porch light on and saw him. He was just standing there, staring back.'

'And you're sure it was only one person out there?'

'Yes!' Emily's eyes widened. 'You think he wasn't alone?'

That was a worrying development she hadn't even considered. The idea of one masked man outside was scary enough, but if he had friends with him...

'I found empty beer cans near the woods. That suggests to me it was teenagers fooling around and maybe daring each other to pull a prank.'

'Teenagers? It's the middle of the night.'

'It's just gone 2 a.m. Not that late.'

'Max, it wasn't teenagers. I know what I saw.' Emily was exasperated.

'You saw a mask. And yes, I get that it scared you. I imagine that was the intention.'

Emily wasn't having it. 'I want to call the police.'

'And tell them what? That someone hung a mask up outside the house? I think they have better things to do.'

'Someone *was* on the doorstep.'

And they could still be outside watching. Anyone could look through the big picture window and see what they were doing. It was unnerving not having blinds or curtains.

'You can't prove it, though. Anyone could have left it there and you know it's Halloween in two days. Masks are being sold everywhere.' Max was sounding frustrated now. 'No harm was done. No one tried to break in, and whoever left it there has probably long gone. The door is locked. Scout will soon alert us if anyone comes back. Can we just go back to bed now, please?'

'I don't like it here. I want to go home.'

'Emily. You're overreacting over something that could be perfectly innocent.'

'But what if it's not? We're out here in the middle of nowhere.'

When she pouted, Max shook his head, 'Look, if anything else happens, we'll call the police. Okay?'

It wasn't okay, but it was a compromise, she supposed. And Max was right. No crime had been committed. The man had just stood there on the doorstep, but he hadn't broken in.

Could it really have been kids messing around? She supposed he had a point about it nearly being Halloween.

'You promise?' she asked.

'You have my word.' Max offered her a smile. 'It's freezing out there. Can we please go back to bed?'

Emily nodded. 'I'm not going to be able to get back to sleep, knowing he could still be out there,' she grumbled, letting Max lead the way. Scout barging past them on the stairs.

Max squeezed her hand as he glanced back at her. 'I'll distract you,' he winked.

Emily make a little 'hmm' noise in response, but as soon as his back was turned, she gave the front door a last glance.

It was locked, she reminded herself, stepping onto the landing and following Max into the bedroom. Scout would alert them if the intruder returned.

Was she overreacting? First finding the mysterious note and wine, the open door suggesting a stranger had been in the boat house, and now a masked face at the door. No wonder her nerves were fraught. But were the two things connected?

She wanted to be like Max, to relax and assume everything was going to be okay, but it wasn't that easy. He had no idea what she had gone through and she knew she was going to be fretting about both things till at least the morning.

This break was supposed to be an escape from everything. Against the pretty backdrop of the woods and river, it was a fresh chance for them to fully reconnect and for Emily to relax for a few days, and when Max had shown her pictures of the boat house, she had considered the secluded location as a plus. Now she wasn't so sure.

8

BEFORE

The next time Emily saw Connor Banks, he was on his hands and knees on the floor of her father's room, retrieving something from under the bed, and guilt swamped her when she realised that the first thing she had noticed when entering the room was the way his jeans fit snugly over his bum, rather than the distressed expression on her dad's face.

What the hell was she thinking? This wasn't the place or the time. Her father was dying, becoming frailer and more confused with each visit, and besides, she had a boyfriend. Since meeting Max, Emily had seldom looked at other men. In past relationships, her eye had often wandered, but finally it seemed she had met the right one.

Her dad spotted her first, quietly saying her name, and annoyed at the kick of lust in her gut, she quickly crossed the room, taking hold of his hand. 'What's happened? What's wrong?' He was getting weaker by the day and while it was awful to watch, he was no longer viewing her through hostile eyes.

Connor was on his feet now and Emily spotted the crumpled photograph in his hand.

'What's that?' she asked as he handed it back to her father.

'He usually keeps it in his wallet,' Connor told her as her dad stared at the picture, his eyes damp. 'But today he had it out. He was trying to show me when he dropped it.'

Emily moved closer, sitting on the edge of the bed so she could look at the photograph. It was one she hadn't seen before, though she recognised herself as a child, along with her sister, Megan, and their mother, and her gut twisted, realising it couldn't have been taken long before the accident.

So her father had held on to this picture, treating it like treasure, but he had abandoned his one remaining daughter. Emily's stomach twisted with hurt.

Would he have felt any different if she had died along with her mother and Megan? She suspected not.

'You didn't know that he had that photo, did you?' Connor spoke quietly after her father had fallen asleep.

Was she that transparent? He must have picked up on her shock.

'No,' she admitted. 'I didn't.'

This time when he offered to talk, Emily took him up on the offer. She had arrived earlier than usual, so had time to spare, and they went to the breakroom, where he poured her a cup of coffee.

There was nothing to feel guilty about. She regularly spoke with the staff who worked here. It was no different just because Connor was a volunteer. She struggled to talk to Max about her visits to the hospice, unwilling, for whatever reason, to share how she felt. Francesca was her only outlet, but she had her hands full with a new-born and Emily didn't like to burden her too much.

Yes, Connor might be attractive, but it was not like anything was going to happen. He was just being friendly and right now, she could really use a friend. Especially one who understood exactly what she was going through.

'Has he talked about the accident with you and told you what happened?' she asked, warming her hands around the mug Connor handed her.

'He has, though it was difficult for him. He misses your mum and sister a great deal, and I think he has regrets about not being there for you more when you were growing up.'

'He does?' Emily looked up, finding herself caught in the steady gaze of dark-brown eyes.

Connor nodded. 'Being in here and knowing the end is near, it's given him a lot of time to reflect. I think if he could do things over, he would do them differently.'

His words surprised Emily, particularly given her dad's annoyance when she had first showed up. He had softened in recent days, though, so perhaps Connor was right.

She studied him now. He had such a kind face and was really quite attractive. Dark hair that, although worn short, curled slightly at the root, and dimples that cracked his cheeks when he smiled. When he held her gaze, she was aware of her heart hammering a little faster and she looked down at the table, again flushed with guilt. It didn't stop her discreetly looking at his left hand. No ring, she noted. But surely there was a girlfriend at home waiting for him. Men who looked like Connor tended to be taken.

Where Max was lean and sinewy, Connor was stockier. Wider chest and arms, though they were hard with muscle, and she suspected he worked hard to maintain his build.

Gym, work, volunteering. Did he really have time for a girlfriend?

'Penny for them?'

Emily had fallen quiet, distracted by the man in front of her, and heat crept up her neck as she realised he thought she was lost in memories about her dad.

Seriously, Emily. Where do you get off?

Her train of thought was not appropriate and completely disrespectful to a man who had shown her nothing but kindness.

Still, before she left the hospice, his hand covered hers in a sign of solidarity and comfort, and heat spread through her.

Connor was sweet and safe and compassionate, but Emily couldn't help but think she was playing a dangerous game. Especially when she agreed to take his phone number. It was just for if she needed to talk, but it was hard not to read more into it.

She tried to justify everything on the drive home. There was nothing she had to feel guilty about. They had only been talking about her father, nothing more.

Her phone rang, breaking her train of thought, and she saw on the dashboard that it was Francesca. Her thumb hit answer on the steering wheel.

'Hi, is everything all right?' Her friend didn't usually call this late.

'I'm fine. Adam is out and Harry's asleep. I hoped I would catching you driving home. How's your dad?'

'Sick.' Emily let out a humourless laugh. She didn't have to pretend around Francesca. They had been friends for years and knew each other too well to cover things up.

'Oh, Em. It must be so tough to see him like that. And so soon after Cathy. I wish I could be there with you.'

Emily would like that too, but they both knew it wasn't possible. Harry was still a baby and needed his mum. He had to come first.

'Is James still being good about letting you leave the office early?'

'Yes, he's been great. Everyone at work has... well, except that arsehole, Rob.'

He was still being difficult with the car park and Emily had actually taken the decision to use the nearby pay and display, simply so she didn't have to fight with him most days.

'And what about Max? Has he been to see Simon yet?'

The last time they had spoken, Emily had told Francesca that she had felt Max wasn't being as supportive as he could, and Francesca had insisted Emily should have it out with him. The conversation had never happened, though, because the pair of them barely saw anything of each other. Hell, they hadn't had sex for several weeks. Their relationship felt like it was on autopilot.

'He's busy with work, Fran.'

'No excuse. He should find the time. What about Miss Skanky Pants?'

That brought a smile to Emily's lips. Francesca had never been one to hold back her thoughts on Leah.

'Still on the scene. Still skanky.'

Francesca laughed at Emily's comment before her tone grew serious. 'I know she's Max's friend – God knows why – but he needs to be prioritising you right now. You need someone to lean on, Em. Even if it's only to talk to.'

'I know, and I kind of do.'

'Really, who?'

Emily hesitated before answering. She had only met Connor twice and it almost felt wrong mentioning him. 'There's a volunteer at the hospice. Connor. He's been spending time with Dad, reading to him and talking with him. He's been offering support to me too... I mean, we've been talking.'

'You have? That's good, Em.' Francesca fell silent for a moment. 'Does Max know you've been talking to this Connor?'

There hadn't been any accusation in her tone, but Emily couldn't help herself going on the defensive. 'No, there's no need. He's busy with work and you said I need someone to talk to. Connor understands me. He lost his mum.'

'Relax. I wasn't judging. It's good that you're talking to someone.'

'I know. I'm sorry.'

It was because Connor was attractive. If he wasn't, there would be any guilt attached.

Emily drew in a breath, ordering herself to relax, and switched subject, asking after Harry and Adam, and the pair of them talked for the last twenty minutes of her journey, finally saying goodnight as she pulled into the close where she lived with Max.

The first thing she spotted was that the driveway was empty. Max must have gone out somewhere. Was he with Leah?

She immediately shook the thought away, telling herself not to be ridiculous.

Inside the house, she whistled to Scout, but there was no response, then moments later, she found Max's note on the kitchen worktop, and understood why no one was home. He had gone into work to cover a late shift due to sickness and had dropped Scout off with his sister, saying he would collect her on his way back, so Emily didn't have to turn out again.

Immediately, she regretted doubting him. Picking up someone's shift who was sick was typical of Max. He never let anyone down. And he had left her dinner in the oven. A pasta bake he had made that just needed heating.

Emily's heart swelled, then was pricked with fresh guilt. Although nothing had happened between her and Connor, she still felt like she had betrayed her boyfriend.

Max was a good man and didn't deserve to have a partner who was lusting after someone else.

* * *

Emily was warming the food in the oven when the doorbell rang. Glancing at the clock, she frowned, wondering who it could be so late in the evening. Possibly Max's dad or one of his siblings, though generally they called first.

Unless something was wrong.

Oh God. What if something had happened to Max? Sometimes it was easy to forget that the job he did was often dangerous.

Panic took over and she charged to the door, her fumbling fingers turning the lock and pulling it open, then surprise silencing her when she saw Leah standing on the front step.

What the hell was she doing here? She never stopped by if Max wasn't at home.

'Emily?' Leah sounded shocked herself, her eyes widening and for once seeming a little unsure of herself. 'How come you're home?'

'I live here.' Emily fought to keep the sarcasm out of her voice as realisation hit.

It was because Max's Audi was parked on the driveway. He had insisted Emily take it to Scarborough after the brake pad light came on in her Polo. As he was supposed to be on a rest day, he had taken hers into the garage to be fixed. So Leah had clearly stopped by hoping to find him home alone? That would explain why she was wearing a low-cut top, her breasts straining against the fabric, and had a face full of make-up.

Emily's temper bristled. 'What do you want, Leah?'

Max had always insisted there was nothing going on between them, but the woman had guilt written all over her face and she smelt like she had fallen in a vat of perfume. She hadn't expected to find Emily at home.

'Is, um, Max here?' she asked, shuffling and looking uncomfortable as she asked the question. It made a change to see her wrong-footed.

'He's working.' Emily didn't bother to elaborate that he had stepped in to take the extra shift. Instead, she stared pointedly at Leah. 'Can I pass on a message or would you like to come in?'

She didn't want Leah in the house, but was confident in asking, knowing her offer wouldn't be taken up.

She was right.

'Um, no, it's okay. I was in the area, so thought I'd just stop by. Tell him I'll catch up with him later.'

Leah couldn't wait to get out of there, already dashing back down the driveway to her car before Emily even had time to answer.

As she watched the woman drive away, Emily realised that the impromptu visit had unsettled her. Was anything going on between Max and Leah other than friendship?

As she closed and locked the door, going back into the kitchen, she wondered whether she should ask Max outright.

That probably wouldn't go down well. Max's friendship with Leah predated Emily and it was one she always felt she couldn't interfere with.

Did Max have it in him to cheat, though? He had stopped speaking to his mother after it was discovered she had been having an affair behind his dad's back. Adultery was something he had strong views on. It would be rather hypocritical of him to cheat on his own girlfriend.

Still, Emily stewed over it while she ate before the ping of a WhatsApp message distracted her. Glancing at the screen, she saw Connor's name flash up and the little fizz of excitement she felt was quickly quashed down by guilt.

Why though? She was doing nothing wrong.

She read his message.

I enjoyed talking to you earlier. Happy to chat again if it helps.

It was all innocent enough. He was only helping her to deal with her dad's illness. She was doing nothing wrong.

Still, she hesitated before replying, wondering if it had been a mistake to give Connor her number.

Eventually, she tapped out a message. Brief, but friendly. Nothing that she should feel guilty about.

Thank you for the coffee. I enjoyed talking to you too.

9

MONDAY

It was Max's idea to go for a walk the next morning. He was keen to explore more of the local area and Emily was just happy to get out of the boat house. As it turned out, both the exercise and being out in the open, seeing how pretty their location was, helped shift her focus away from the disturbing events of the previous day and night.

She had been tired from the travelling and unfamiliar with her surroundings. Given what had happened in the summer, was it any wonder she had responded the way she did?

In daylight, she was more willing to consider the possibility that she had overreacted, at least to the wine and the note. The masked man at the door still scared her and she wished Max hadn't talked her out of calling the police, even if perhaps he was right and it had just been teenagers trying to spook them.

Tomorrow was Halloween and that meant the trick or treaters would be out in force. Even though the boat house was off the beaten track, would they become targets again?

There had been no more incidents or disturbances through the night, and although Emily had lain awake for a while, listening for every creak and groan of the house, sleep had eventually come.

Max had left her to lie in this morning while he nipped into Wroxham for groceries, and now she was up and out, it was with a clearer head and a more positive mindset. She was determined to treat today as a fresh start.

It really was a lovely place. She had never been to the county before, though she had heard of the Norfolk Broads, and it surprised her just how peaceful and isolated it was. Although they were only a few miles from the city of Norwich, the surrounding countryside made it feel like that they were further away, especially as their route took them away from the village, through the woods and then along the banks of the river.

In the summer, Emily imagined it was much busier, but with winter just a few weeks away, there weren't that many people about. They only encountered the occasional jogger or fellow dog walker, much to Scout's delight.

There were not many properties either and the farms and thatched cottages they passed were spread few and far between. It was a slower pace of life to what she was used to, the air brisk and the colours of nature a mix of bold greens with the golds and burnt oranges of autumn creeping in, and you could be forgiven for thinking you had time travelled back to an earlier century. Max joked that it reminded him a little of Middle Earth, and Emily smiled, realising as she looked around her that he wasn't wrong.

They followed a route that took them through Wroxham and across the quirky bridge, stopping off for a pub lunch along the way. Their return path took them back along the riverbank and, glancing across the water, Emily realised they were almost directly opposite the boat house.

She grabbed hold of Max's hand to slow him down. 'Hey, look. It's us,' she said, pointing.

'Oh yeah. I thought that jetty up ahead looked familiar.'

Emily followed him off the trail to the cottage she had seen across the water on the afternoon they had arrived. She had assumed it was inhabited, but up close, she could see that no one lived there. The glass panes in the windows were cracked and dirty with years of neglect and the front door was hanging off its hinges.

She stepped down from the path onto the jetty, where an old rowing boat was moored, pulling her phone out as she walked to the end, realising it was the perfect spot to take pictures of the boat house.

'If the weather was warmer, I reckon we could swim across,' she said to Max, glancing round when he didn't answer and realising he wasn't there. 'Max?'

Emily wandered back to the abandoned cottage, wondering if he had gone inside. She hesitated by the loose door, screwing her nose up at the stale smell of urine and neglect. 'Max? Are you in here?'

'Yeah, I'm in the bedroom. Come check this place out.'

His voice carried through from the back of the house, as Scout came bounding into the hallway to meet her.

Careful to watch where she was walking, for fear there could be broken glass or nails, Emily stepped over the threshold.

Someone had lived here once. There was furniture in some of the rooms, though it was all in a bad state. Fragments of moth-eaten curtains hung at the windows and the doors were missing on most of the kitchen units. In the back bedroom, where she found Max, the mattress of the double bed was torn and filthy and the dresser wonkily sitting on three legs, with two of its drawers missing.

'I wonder what happened to the owner,' she mused. Truthfully, she found the house a little unsettling. It was quite creepy.

Max stepped over rubble as he headed back into the hallway. 'Maybe they died but had no one to leave it to. It's crazy places like this exist. The plot alone must be worth a fortune.' He glanced into the bathroom, wrinkling his nose as he backed away. 'Don't go in there.'

Emily had no intention to. She had already wandered into the second bedroom. This one was in slightly better condition. The curtains drawn, blocking out the light, and the brass bedstead in better nick, though it was missing its mattress.

Spotting a rucksack on the floor beside the bed, she wandered over. It looked newer than anything else in the cottage, which had her curiosity piqued.

'What are you looking at?' Max asked, coming up behind her.

'Someone's been in here recently. Look.'

The rucksack contained bottles of water and packs of cereal bars. Lifting them out, Emily realised there were clothes packed in the bottom. A navy hoodie, socks and underwear. Whoever it belonged to also had a rolled-up sleeping bag.

'Do you think whoever this belongs to is homeless?' Emily whispered, now feeling like she was intruding. She shouldn't be going through someone's things.

'Maybe,' Max agreed. 'Or perhaps they are just passing through. Either way, I don't think they're doing any harm. We should just leave them be.'

Emily went to put the contents back in the rucksack, spotting another item in the bottom of the bag. As she pulled it out, her heart started hammering as she realised what she was holding.

A mask. Identical to the one that she had seen the man wearing last night.

She looked at Max now, her mouth suddenly dry. 'It's him.'

She watched his eyes narrow, saw he was considering the possibility.

'The mask is in the boat house,' he said eventually. 'I left it on the coffee table.'

'Yes, but what are the chances?'

'Well, it is Halloween tomorrow. And you know there is going to be more than one person with the same mask.'

'Why the hell does a homeless person need a mask, Max?'

'You're assuming whoever's stuff this is, is homeless. Like I said, they could be passing through.'

'Well, if they are, it still doesn't explain why they need a mask.' Emily was aware she was sounding irrational and she took a deep breath to try to calm herself down. 'This cottage overlooks the boat house,' she reasoned. 'It's all a little coincidental, don't you think?'

'So what is it you expect me to do?' Max asked, his tone exasperated.

'I don't expect you to do anything. I want to call the police.'

'You know we can't do that. No crime has been committed and they're not going to come out because we've been going through someone's things. We're the ones trespassing right now.'

'What if they're stalking us?'

Max had the nerve to roll his eyes at her comment, which had temper spiking her fear.

'You still don't believe I saw anyone outside last night, do you? You think I just saw the mask.'

'I never said I didn't believe you.'

'It's written all over your face, Max. You think I am overreacting. Go on, admit it.'

The flash of annoyance in his eyes told her she was pushing his buttons, though he didn't deny the accusation.

'Look, I know you saw something last night. I just want you to consider the possibility that it might not have been what you thought it was. Okay?' When she didn't answer, he took it as a green light to continue. 'You've had a lot going on this year and I know how difficult it has been for you losing your dad and so soon after Cathy died. It's why I brought you here. To try to give you a break away from everything. I get you thought you saw someone on the doorstep, but the mask was hanging up. Whoever left it there obviously intended to scare someone, and it worked, but I really don't think anyone was out there wearing it waiting for you to come to the door.'

'I know what I saw.' Emily snapped. She was struggling to hold her temper.

'I know you do, but don't you think it's possible it could just have been kids who hung it up for a joke? They were probably long gone when you woke up and saw it.'

She didn't believe that, but was fed up fighting. 'Let's just go back.'

Ignoring Max when he tried to catch hold of her hand, she instead strode out of the bedroom and back down the hall, whistling to Scout, and was pleased when she was out of the cottage. The place had already been creepy, but the discovery of the mask made it all the more sinister. The dog was in her element with all the new smells, and she tore herself away reluctantly.

The walk back wasn't quite as pleasant, the tension of their disagreement hanging over them and the afternoon air having turned cooler.

Back at the boat house, Emily headed up the outside steps to the front door, staring down into the woods while she waited for Max to unlock the door.

Ignoring her sulking, he went straight to the kitchen to put on the kettle, while she made a beeline for the sofas. She looked at the coffee table, shouting to Max, 'Where did you say you left that mask?'

He didn't hear her at first over the sound of running water.

'What did you say?'

'I asked, where is the mask?'

She heard the clunk of the kettle being put down, then the sound of his footsteps. 'I told you, it's here on the...' He trailed off, staring along with Emily at the empty coffee table. 'Did you move it?'

'You know I didn't touch it' she huffed, meeting his now surprised stare. 'So tell me, Max. Where the hell is it?'

10

Someone had been in the boat house again. Emily was certain of it.

It wasn't just the missing mask. Other things weren't quite right. Especially upstairs.

The lid was loose on her face cream and her toothbrush was wet, as if recently used. But, most disturbing of all, the zipper to the compartment of her suitcase – that she hadn't bothered to unpack – and which contained her underwear, was open. She knew it had been closed.

'I want to go home, Max. This is getting beyond a joke.'

'You're being ridiculous.'

Max was still burying his head in the sand, despite having no answer as to why the mask had disappeared, and he was turning the downstairs of the boat house upside down on a mission to find it.

'Am I really?' The fight that Emily had hoped to avoid was now brewing and she couldn't help but resent him for not believing her. She knew she was right. Someone had been inside the boat house while they were out. 'So how did they get in?'

Max's blue eyes were heated with temper, probably because he thought she was being unappreciative of his efforts in arranging this week away and that she was trying to spoil everything. 'The door was locked, Emily, and I have the key. Nothing is broken, no windows have been forced open and we don't know that someone took the mask.'

'Are you definitely sure you did lock the door?'

He laughed harshly. 'Of course I'm bloody sure. You watched me do it.'

Had she? She could remember standing outside and waiting for him – and yes he was right, she was pretty certain she had watched him lock the door. In fact, now she thought about it more clearly, she was sure of it. So why had she struggled to remember that detail when she was so certain of everything else that had been happening?

Max was hunting round the back of the sofa now, the one that sat in front of the coffee table, and she watched him dip down to retrieve something from the floor.

'Ha, I knew it would be here somewhere.' He held up the mask for Emily to see. A look of triumph on his face. 'See. I told you no one had broken in.'

Emily's stomach was heavy with resignation, aware it was another strike against her.

'How did it end up behind the sofa?' she asked, stubbornly continuing to argue her case.

'I have no idea. One of us must have accidentally knocked it off the coffee table. Or perhaps Scout took it.'

The collie's ears pricked up at the mention of her name.

It was a stretch, but Emily guessed it was possible.

Did Max have a point? Was she linking dots that weren't actually there?'

She had experienced so much stress relating to her dad and

then, of course, there had been everything else that had come after.

She no longer seemed to have a grip on what was real and what wasn't, and that scared her.

Suddenly, it was all too overwhelming and the hot tears that pricked at her eyes before burning down her cheeks took her by surprise, as they did Max.

Neither of them were sulkers, preferring to tackle things head on, and given how laid-back Max usually was, any fights between them tended to be brief, as neither of them held on to anger.

'Emily, it's okay.' He gathered her to him as if she was a broken bird, and in that moment, Emily wondered if she was. Although she wasn't aware of any mental illness in her family history, the thought that there might be something wrong with her scared her. Was her mind really convincing her of things that simply weren't there?

The man at the door of the boat house. He had looked so real, but was Max right? Had it simply been a mask? And she was convinced that things had been tampered with inside the boat house. But was she imagining it?

'I'm sorry,' Max whispered against her ear, and while his words soothed, Emily couldn't help but think about the fact he still didn't believe her, and that perhaps he was right not to. 'If it will make you feel better, I'll call the police.'

'No. Don't call them.' Emily eased back from his embrace, wiping her eyes dry.

'Are you sure?'

'You're right. There's nothing they can do.'

She left it at that, not adding that she was starting to question her own sanity. Kissing Max lightly on the lips, she told him she was going upstairs for a bath.

Tossing the complimentary salts that the owner had left into the clawfoot tub, she watched the water run. Her head was a jumble and she needed this little while to herself, though she gave Max a grateful smile when he came upstairs, Scout on his heels, to bring her a glass of wine.

'It's the bottle I brought,' he told her, before she could ask the question.

Emily watched him go back down. Scout remained, seeming to want to keep her company as she settled on the floor.

Stepping out of her clothes, Emily climbed into the tub, taking a moment to appreciate the lightly scented warm water as it immersed her.

Downstairs, she heard the faint clatter of cupboard doors opening and shutting, of pans and utensils being moved about. Max loved being in the kitchen and did most of the cooking in their house.

She took a few sips of the wine, setting the glass back down on the little table beside the tub, then sank back, closing her eyes.

It was the appearance of the mystery bottle, along with the note, that had started it. It must have shaken her more than she had realised.

Or perhaps the man at the door last night had been real. Scout had been disturbed and Max had found the mask.

But could there have been an innocent explanation. Had it simply been teenagers fooling around? The more she considered the possibility, the more certain she became.

That just left today that couldn't be explained. The discovery of the mask in the backpack in the cottage. Though perhaps that too was a coincidence.

Emily allowed her mind to wander back to her troubles in the summer. Her frazzled brain seeking a way to connect them to what was happening now. But that was just stupid. It was behind her and she had to move past everything.

Besides, the things that were happening now, whether real or imaginary, were very different.

It was foolish to believe that someone wanted to scare her or perhaps hurt her.

Wasn't it?

11

BEFORE

Emily brought the drinks over to the table. A pint for Connor and a Coke for herself as she was driving.

Her dad had been in the hospice just over two weeks now and this was the third time she had ended her visit by going for a drink with Connor in the pub around the corner, after he had urged her to take some time for herself.

She still felt guilty. The trips to Scarborough were to see her father and she was reluctant to be away from him, given how precious little time they had left together. She had resisted going to the pub the first time Connor had suggested a drink, but he kept pushing, and eventually she relented.

She was doing nothing wrong. It was just an innocent drink with the man who was helping to make her father's last days more comfortable. And she had to admit that even though she only ever stopped for one drink, it was good to get away from the hospice. The staff were lovely and they tried to make the place as welcoming as possible, but despite how clean it was, a sweet, cloying and sickly scent seemed to linger in the air that overrode the bleach and the air fresheners, and clung to Emily's clothes, even after she had left.

That first night, she had stayed for just thirty minutes in the pub with Connor, but tonight they had already been here an hour and she was reluctant to leave.

She needed this. It was like therapy, having someone to talk to. Someone who understood what she was going through and just how difficult it was for her. No one could begrudge her that. Her dad was becoming weaker and sleeping more, so he didn't know she was slipping away a little earlier. If things changed, if he became more lucid, then, of course, she would knock this time away from him on the head. It was unlikely to happen. She knew that. The hospice staff had warned her that the end was approaching, and Emily knew things were going to get steadily worse, not better.

Max didn't understand and he didn't seem to care. Connor was the only one keeping her sane right now and she couldn't do this without him.

They spoke about everything. About Emily's childhood and her relationship with her father. About her job and the challenges and rewards that came with it. And about her friendship with Francesca, and how Emily doted on Francesca's little boy, Harry.

'Do you want kids one day?'

The question took Emily by surprise and she spent a moment considering her answer.

'I guess so.'

Truthfully, it was something she had never discussed with Max, which perhaps was foolish, given how serious they were about each other. That said, they had never discussed marriage either. She realised that despite being together for over two and a half years, she had no idea if he wanted either.

'I suppose it depends on whether you meet the right man,' Connor said now, and Emily smiled, her conscience pricking.

'Yeah, I suppose it does.'

She still hadn't told him about Max.

It wasn't as if she had lied to Connor. He had never asked if she had a boyfriend and the opportunity to mention that she did had simply never come up.

To be fair, she had never asked about his personal life either. He could have a wife, maybe kids too. The lack of wedding ring meant nothing.

Of course they had talked about some stuff relating to him. It wasn't all about Emily. She knew that he was thirty-eight, so slightly older than she had first thought, and that he had grown up in Scarborough. He had his own house here, and he had told her that he had been in the Army for a while, but was now self-employed as a cyber consultant. Like Emily, both of his parents were dead and he was an only child.

'Kids are important to me,' he told her now. 'I'm the last of the Banks bloodline and at the moment, if I die, all memory of my family dies too. I really want to have kids to continue that.' He wrinkled up his nose. 'Sounds stupid, doesn't it?'

No, it really didn't, but talking about children and relationships was dangerous ground, and given that Emily hadn't mentioned Max at all, she felt she now couldn't bring him up without making things a little awkward. She also didn't want to lie, and her response was pushing her in that direction.

She swiftly changed the subject, asking Connor about his day, relieved when he obliged, telling her an amusing anecdote about an awkward client he was dealing with who had received his comeuppance. He told the story well, with the right delivery and accompanying expressions, and had Emily bursting into laughter.

It wasn't until she wiped at her eyes, her cheeks aching, that she realised it was the first time she had laughed in a while.

'Why don't you stay in Scarborough tonight?' Connor suggested quietly when she said that to him. 'You look exhausted most of the time and you have so much on your plate. It's no wonder you haven't had time to laugh.'

'I can't.' It wasn't just Max, though he was a factor. He was off work sick with a stomach bug and she already felt bad about leaving him to come see her dad. 'I have work in the morning.'

'Can you take a few days off? I'm sure they will understand if you take some compassionate leave. Self-care is important, Emily. You need to look after yourself. If you don't want to stay at your dad's place, you are welcome to stay with me.' When her eyes widened, he blushed, quickly adding, 'I have a spare room.'

He wanted her to stay with him?

Even if she took Max and her job out of the equation, she still wasn't comfortable about spending the night at Connor's house. And although she had a key for her dad's place, if she stayed there, it would mean getting up at stupid o'clock to get back to Leeds in time for work. She didn't want to let her boss down. Not after he had been so good to her. And she also didn't want to give Rob Bristow anything else he could twist and use against her.

'I'm sorry, it's just not that easy.'

After they had finished their drinks, Connor walked her back to the hospice car park, frowning when she clicked her fob at the Audi.

'New wheels?'

It wasn't the first time Emily had brought Max's car to Scarborough, but last time Connor hadn't seen it. She hadn't given it much consideration this morning when Max had suggested she take the Audi. As he wasn't in work and wouldn't be going anywhere, he reasoned that it was newer and more reliable for the journey, even though her Polo had recently been repaired.

'Um, no. This isn't mine.'

Connor's brows were raised in question, so she couldn't not elaborate.

'I, um, borrowed it.'

'A friend lent you this?'

It wasn't an assumption. He knew she had no other family than her dad.

Put on the spot, she nodded.

'Very nice.'

Connor looked like he was about to say something else, so she quickly opened the driver's door and got inside the car.

'Right. I'd better get on my way. Thanks for the chat.'

He started to speak, but she was already closing the door, annoyed she hadn't considered that he would see Max's car as they headed back from the pub. Connor was going to figure out something was up if she kept acting like this, which in turn had her questioning herself just why was she so reluctant to tell him about Max.

Because you fancy him, a little voice niggled in her head.

She ignored it. Connor was good-looking. Just because she could admit that didn't mean she was attracted to him. Max was her boyfriend and, okay, their relationship wasn't in a great place at the moment, but it didn't excuse her lying to Connor about his existence.

It was a problem she was going to have to figure out a solution to before she saw Connor again, and right now, she couldn't see that she had any other choice but to come clean. Even if it did make her look bad that she had kept it from him.

She couldn't avoid him, just as she couldn't stay away from

her dad. She needed Connor's support right now, but would he still be willing to give it when he knew the truth?

Although he hadn't made a move on her, she had seen the way he sometimes looked at her, and she suspected he wanted to.

But, regardless of that, why should she feel guilty about their friendship? Nothing had happened between them and she would make sure nothing ever did. Max was friends with Leah, so why shouldn't Emily be allowed to hang out with Connor?

She just needed to start being honest with him about Max. Hopefully, he would take the news okay.

12

TUESDAY

While Max took Scout for an early-morning walk, Emily put together a picnic. Their plan for the day was to head into Wroxham and hire a boat so they could explore the broads. Although it was still cold, the weather was dry and the sun out. Not bad for the last day of October and they intended to make the most of it. Especially given that the previous night had passed without incident.

Max had cooked, making a curry, and after they had eaten, they had curled up on the sofa together and watched a movie. Emily had still been a little rattled from finding the mask in the backpack at the cottage and she appreciated him letting her pick a romcom when she knew he would have preferred a thriller. It had been a pleasant evening, the film making her laugh and keeping her mind off things, and she managed to sleep the whole night through.

If anyone had been outside the boat house during the night, she hadn't known about it.

So far, she felt she had dampened their week away and Max had made such an effort. Today, she was determined she was going to put things behind her, try to shake off her mood and enjoy herself. She didn't want this to be a wasted trip.

* * *

There wasn't much traffic on the river and, probably because they were out of season, they had been given a choice of boat, though from what Emily could see, there wasn't that much difference between them. The vessel was only covered at the front, leaving the back open to the elements, which would probably be lovely on a warm day, but not so much at this time of year. Still, she gamely sat on the rear seat with Scout while Max steered, wrapped up warm in her jacket and scarf, as she enjoyed the views.

Wroxham was a busy little hub, even out of season, with several shops and touristy outlets, and she expected it probably got very busy in the summer months. As the boat headed away from the centre, the banks were dotted with riverside properties, some set back with beautifully manicured lawns, while others were close to the water's edge, many of them with boats moored up. There were single- and double-storey houses, cosy cottages with thatched roofs, and sleek, modern builds with glass balcony walls. Emily suspected that many of the properties were second homes or holiday rentals, much like the boat house. They passed a few people in gardens, some of whom waved, but she wondered how many places were even occupied.

As they headed further out in the countryside, the houses became fewer and further between, the mouth of the river widening, and the banks covered in high bushes and trees, and their only company were the ducks and swans and other wildlife that lived on this stretch of the broad. The motor purred as the boat cut a path through the water, the pace slow and peaceful, and despite the cool temperature, she realised she could stay out here all day.

'Look, there's our place,' Max shouted over the engine. And Emily glanced over at the boat house, nestled in its own secluded spot. From the water, it looked imposing, standing high above them, even though it was small and cosy inside. It was because the accommodation was built over the double arch where boats could be stored, making it seem bigger than it was.

Emily looked into the dark mouths of the tunnels as they passed. A black space where the water flowed in and a walkway that led back to the storage room. With the absence of any boats, it looked a little creepy. She recalled the waitress at the restaurant saying the wife of the owner had died in an accident on the water. Had her boat been destroyed?

On the other side of the river was the abandoned cottage with its jetty. Emily wondered if the person who owned the rucksack was inside. Had they realised someone had been going through their things?

As both the boat house and the cottage disappeared from sight, she focused on the route ahead and over the next couple of hours, they took turns at the wheel and enjoyed soup, sandwiches and coffee, while conversation between them was relaxed and easy.

This was her and Max at their best. Happy and enjoying each other's company, and for a while, Emily was able to forget everything that had come before and the terrible secret she was keeping.

They moored the boat at a pub later in the afternoon, stopping for a drink and to allow Scout to stretch her legs. The dog was in her element, loving all the new sights and smells, and as they journeyed back, her tongue was hanging out and she had the biggest grin on her pretty, black and white face as she watched a family of ducks bobbing by on the water.

When Emily spotted the boat house again as they approached Wroxham, her heart sank a little. In the dusky light, the dark arches of water beneath the property were like something from a scary movie and the vantage point of the water showed just how isolated it was.

It was hard not to think back to the unsettling events that had happened since they had arrived.

She told herself off for being a wimp. Once the lights were on and the fire lit, it would be cosy and welcoming again. So what if it sat on top of a creepy mouth of water?

As she stared at the floor-to-ceiling window that looked out over the water, she remembered how she had worried about being exposed, and she realised that from the jetty of the abandoned cottage, you would be able to see everything. It was a little unsettling.

A beam of light from inside the house startled her and she double blinked. It wasn't the sun, which had already set, and as the boat moved closer, she could see it was still there, bouncing around the dark room.

Was someone using a torch?

'Max!' He didn't hear her above the engine and she had to raise her voice to get his attention. 'Max! Look. Do you see that?'

Her heart was thumping as she pointed to the window. Part of her scared the light would disappear and he would accuse her of making it up again.

She saw his eyes narrow as he slowed the boat, his face deepening into a frown.

'What the hell? Someone's in the bloody house.'

Emily was scared, but it didn't stop the rush of relief that he had seen it too. At least she was no longer alone with her fears.

'What are we going to do?'

'We're going to go and find out what the hell is going on. That's what we're going to do.'

'Is that a good idea? Maybe we should just call the police.'

'Whoever it is will be long gone by the time they arrive.'

Max was already guiding the boat towards the two dark tunnels and Emily realised she didn't have a choice but to go with him.

'What if they have a weapon?' she tried to reason. 'We have no idea who it is or what they want.'

'Maybe you should wait here while I go check it out,' Max suggested, pulling the boat into the left tunnel and killing the engine before tying off the rope.

'Down here, alone?' Emily practically squeaked out the words.

'Scout can stay with you.'

Love her as she did, the dog's presence wouldn't give Emily any added reassurance. Scout was smart, agile and wily, but she was also soft as anything. She certainly wasn't a guard dog.

'That doesn't make me feel any better. I'm coming with you.'

'Okay, well come on.' He reached a hand down to help her up out of the boat.

Emily glanced around the tunnels. It was just as creepy on the inside as it was from out on the river. Shadows bounced off the stone walls and the water looked almost black as it gently lapped against the wooden walkway that led to the storage room and back outside.

It was the first time she had been down here, but Max had been for a nose around after they first arrived and told her the storage room was mostly full of junk. It was also where the electric circuit board was housed and the water tank.

The door was locked, but that meant nothing. The main

house was locked up too, yet someone was inside. She had seen enough scary films over the years and that was why she had no intention of staying down in the tunnels alone. Anyone could be lurking around down here.

Besides, it wasn't a good idea letting Max confront whoever was in the house by himself. That's why it was better Emily and Scout were going with him. Safety in numbers.

Despite the absence of any other boats, there were a couple of discarded oars, and Max picked one up, which told Emily he was at least taking the threat seriously.

She let him take the lead, one hand clutching Scout's lead, the other tugging onto the back of Max's coat as they followed the walkway out past the storage room and round to the steps that led up to the house.

There were no vehicles present, which suggested whoever was in the house had approached on foot.

Scout let out an agitated whine as they climbed the steps and Emily hushed her.

She was no doubt picking up on their apprehension. Hardly surprising. Emily couldn't stop trembling, her nerves already shot to pieces, and while Max might be taking charge, she could feel tension bouncing off of him too.

Neither of them knew what to expect, but it still took them both by surprise when they found the front door locked.

'How did they get in?' Emily whispered, hating the panic in her tone.

She had expected to find the lock had been busted open. But it all looked fine.

'Shush.' Max quietly unlocked the door, opening it and stepping inside, Emily and Scout staying close behind him. No one was in the lower part of the house, which suggested whoever it was had gone upstairs. Scout hadn't barked, though, or tried to pull ahead, which Emily found a little strange.

'Wait here. I'll go check it out,' Max instructed. His tone little more than a whisper.

Ignoring him, Emily stuck close. They had no idea who was upstairs or what they were dealing with. There was no way she was leaving him to investigate alone.

All of her nerve endings were on edge as they stepped into the bedroom, finding it empty, but that still left the bathroom.

She held her breath as Max nudged the door open with the oar, her grip tightening on his coat. The door swung wide and although the light was off, they could be see no one was hiding in there.

'Where are they?' she whispered to Max.

'I don't know.' His tone was grim as he pulled away from her, moving quicker now as he flipped on light switches, looking under the bed and opening cupboard doors. By the time he had finished thoroughly checking everywhere, they were both certain it was just the two of them, and Scout, in the house.

'I don't like this, Max,' Emily complained when he double-checked the door was locked before eventually putting down the oar. Yesterday had passed without incident, lulling her into a false sense of security. She should have realised it was too good to be true. 'Can we please call the police?'

This time, Max nodded, and when he spoke, his tone was resigned. 'Yeah, I think we should do that.'

13

BEFORE

Connor wasn't at the hospice when Emily next visited. Nothing unusual with that. He did have a job and a life away from the place. This was only a volunteering role.

Still, it surprised her when there was still no sign of him during her next two visits. He hadn't mentioned anything about going away and he did tend to spend a fair amount of time at the hospice. Was he avoiding her?

Of course it was possible he was spending time with another patient, but Emily didn't think so, as she hadn't spotted his car.

Although she had his phone number, she didn't feel it appropriate to ask him where he was. They had WhatsApped just a couple of times, but both occasions had been instigated by Connor and conversation had been casual.

He hadn't been active on Facebook when she checked. Not that he posted much anyway.

He had sent her a friend request that first night she had joined him in the pub and Emily had panicked for a moment before accepting, feeling as if she was doing something wrong.

Max wasn't on there; he hated social media. But a few of his mates were and they were connected to Emily.

She had reminded herself that Connor was just a friend by circumstance, quashing down the feeling of relief that her account didn't reveal her relationship status. She didn't upload many photos on Facebook, so there were none of just her and Max together, but deep down, she knew she was treading a dangerous path, keeping him a secret.

And it bothered her that she had chosen to do so. She wasn't ashamed of Max, but things weren't great with them right now. And after Leah had shown up at the house that night, Emily couldn't help being a little wary. Was Max up to something behind her back?

He wasn't being cagey with his phone, still happily leaving it lying around if he wasn't in the room, and Emily had considered on more than one occasion checking his messages. She hadn't – yet, aware it would be a huge betrayal. Still, the temptation was there.

It had been obvious to Emily from the first time they'd met that Leah had feelings for Max. Was this just a case of her trying to capitalise on Emily not being around? Perhaps it was all innocent on Max's side. He had always been blinkered where Leah was concerned and unable to see what she was really like.

As for Connor, Emily would be a liar if she said she wasn't attracted to him, but was it that she simply craved being wanted, her confidence needing a boost, or did her feelings extend further?

She was so confused and the emotions of dealing with her dad weren't helping.

When she did see Connor, she needed to come clean. After she had nearly been caught out with the Audi, she had resolved to tell him about Max, even if the idea did fill her with dread. So, while his absence at the hospice both confused and disappointed her, a part of her wondered it was perhaps for the best that she hadn't seen him.

She could already imagine his dark eyes filling with disappointment. Wondering why, despite having countless opportunities, she had decided to keep the fact she had a boyfriend a secret from him.

Maybe he had put two and two together with Max's car and realised Emily had lied to him, and hadn't borrowed it from a friend. Or maybe her dad had said something to him. He had met Max before. Was it possible that during one of his more lucid moments, he had said something?

The thought heated her cheeks as she sat by his bedside now.

Connor had spent a lot of time with her dad. Why was it only occurring to her now that he might have told him she had a boyfriend?

She was a fool and should have been honest from the start.

She toyed with mentioning something to her dad now, but although he was awake, he seemed lost in a world of his own and she didn't want to plague him with her own worries when he was so ill. Emily had tried to keep a conversation going, but it was mostly one-sided and becoming hard work, her dad struggling, and for the last half-hour, they mostly sat in companionable silence. She knew things were becoming more uncomfortable for him, especially talking, and it was another harsh reminder that their time together was limited.

She glanced at the copy of *Lord of the Flies* that Connor had brought in, picking it up and looking at where the page had been bookmarked.

'Would you like me to read to you?' she offered.

When there was no reply, she decided to go ahead anyway, keeping her tone low, and glancing up between sentences to try to gauge if she should carry on. After about ten minutes, her father's eyes started to close and when his breathing seemed to settle, she put the book to one side, cupping her hands over the bridge of her nose and rubbing at her tired eyes.

'Are you okay, Emily?'

She looked up to see Jeff Caldwell, one of her father's nurses, watching her with a sympathetic smile. He was always kind to her and her favourite member of the team.

She nodded. 'Yes, thank you, I'm fine. I'm just tired.'

He came into the room. 'Your dad's asleep now. Why don't you head on home and get some rest too?' he suggested, fussing with the bed, then taking the crumpled photo Emily's dad kept with him, the one of their family before tragedy struck, and placing it on the bedside cabinet. Since the day it had fallen on the floor, her dad had stopped hiding it, seeming to want to keep it close.

Maybe Emily should call by his house and see if there were any more photos she could bring in for him. Perhaps it would comfort him to have more reminders of his family around him as the end approached. The nights were drawing out and if she left now, she could go tonight before heading home.

Deciding she would, she said goodnight to Jeff, kissed her dad on the cheek, then headed out to her car.

Her father lived about a ten-minute drive away, but the bonus was it was on her route back to Leeds, and a short while later, she pulled up outside his modest, semi-detached house.

Emily fished in her pocket for his key as she headed up the front path and unlocked the door. She pushed it open, reaching inside to flick on the light switch before entering. Although dusk was only just starting to settle, the hallway was dark and gloomy with shadows and she was grateful in this moment that her dad had insisted on keeping the utility services switched on.

It had been a difficult conversation Emily had broached after her first visit to the house. Simon Worth wouldn't be coming home, so was it wasteful to keep the gas, electric and water running? He was insistent, though, that he wanted to keep paying the bills. Maybe it was that last little bit of control he had over his life.

The place didn't have a huge amount of personality. Beige walls and a neat, but dated, kitchen. It was functional, but that was it. Just a simple space with the bare necessities. No pictures on the walls and no cushions on the sofas. Her dad had needed somewhere to exist and this house was his shell.

So was she wasting her time looking for photos? Would he really have kept any?

No. He had held on to the one he had carried in his wallet. Surely there must be others.

Despite having the best intentions, Emily still felt guilty as she hunted through the drawers and cupboards of the sideboard in his lounge. It was still his house until he died and although it would fall on her to clear everything out when that happened, she hadn't been a part of his life, or indeed this house, for long enough to feel she had the right to go through his things.

Still, she pushed that to one side when she came across a photo album buried under old magazines and boxes of leads. Dusting it off, she opened the black leather cover, her heart catching when she spotted that the first photograph was of her parents on their wedding day. Her mother looking beautiful in an elegant white satin dress, and both of her parents smiling happily at the camera.

Emily barely recognised her dad. His face was lit up, his grin telling the whole world how lucky he thought he was. She couldn't remember seeing him smile like this in all the years since her mother and Megan had died.

Pushing aside the boxes and magazines, she made herself

more comfortable on the floor, resting back against the cabinet, the heavy album balanced on her knees as she carefully turned the pages. Each picture was a treasure that she didn't know existed. The only family photographs she had were ones that Aunt Cathy had taken. She had never seen these ones before.

There were pictures of her as a baby and then of Megan, of the two of them together, or posing in some shots with their parents, while other photos appeared natural, caught in the moment. Her mother barefoot and her hair pulled back in a messy ponytail, the smile of surprise as she realised at the last second her picture was being taken.

And then there were the celebrations. Birthdays where both Emily and Megan were either blowing out candles or opening presents and Christmas, with both of them sat in front of the tree.

Cathy was in many of the photos too, smiling and laughing with Emily's mum. Happier times before the accident and before everything changed.

Going through the album evoked so many memories and the pain of the loss Emily had suffered was stronger than it had been in a long time.

When she finally closed the album, she realised it was already dark outside. She hadn't meant to spend so much time here and quickly loaded the boxes and magazines back into the cupboard, before scooping up the album.

She supposed she should do a walk-through of the house before leaving, just to check everything was secure. The last time she had been here had been a fleeting visit and she hadn't had the chance to.

As it was dark outside, she flipped on lights as she went, heading upstairs first to check the two bedrooms and bathroom. Nothing was out of place that she could tell and she went back downstairs, going through into the kitchen and the little utility room that led off it.

And that was where she found the open window. Well, not wide open, but it was definitely ajar.

Had someone been inside the house? The window was just big enough that a small person could climb through.

Was this something to be concerned about or had it always been this way?

She toyed with ringing the police, but was this really enough cause to call them out?

Nothing appeared to have been disturbed in the house or stolen, from what she could see.

Perhaps it was best to gently raise some questions with her dad tomorrow.

She didn't need to worry him with her suspicions. Just casually ask if it was possible he might have left it open before he left the house.

Deciding that was the best option, Emily closed the window, making sure the catch caught, before turning off the lights and letting herself out of the house.

With her father in the hospice and his home standing empty, it might be a good idea for her to keep a closer eye on things going forward. It was probably nothing to worry about. But, still, it was better to be safe than sorry.

14

TUESDAY

Calling the police proved to be a waste of time, because there was simply no evidence that any crime had been committed. The door and all of the windows were locked and there was no sign that anyone had tampered with them. Plus, nothing had been disturbed, as least not obviously. There wasn't anything broken and, as far as Emily and Max were aware, nothing had been stolen. Nor had they come across anyone inside the boat house.

Given the remote location and the fact there were no cameras up, there was no evidence to work with, and, as the young police constable who came out to see them was quick to point out, neither Max nor Emily had seen anyone. All they had to go on was a light flashing inside the house, which could have been caused by a number of things.

Emily didn't believe that and she was relieved Max didn't either. Usually easy-going, she could tell his temper was bubbling, and he was getting snappy with the officer, which wasn't going to get them anywhere. They needed to keep the police onside and not have them think they were a pair of irrational tourists, which, to be honest, she was starting to feel they were becoming, even though she knew they were right. Someone had been inside the boat house, and not only today.

'What about the man in the mask?' she asked as the constable finished the cup of tea she had made him. She had already shown him the mask Max had found hanging up outside the door, in the hope it might act as evidence.

To his credit, Max had kept his mouth shut about his doubts over what exactly it was she had seen, though he still played the incident down more than Emily would have liked.

'Again, there's very little we can do' the PC told her. 'Whoever it belongs to didn't try to break in, so no crime was committed. As your boyfriend initially suspected, Miss Worth, we have Halloween coming up and the shops are full of masks. It was probably just kids fooling around.'

They should have called the police at the time and Emily was kicking herself for letting Max persuade her not to. Reporting it now made it appear like they were clutching at straws and that it hadn't been quite such a big deal as she was making out. Still, she pressed on, telling the officer about the supposed welcome gift of wine and the note that had been left with it.

It was all irrelevant, as the PC didn't seem interested, suspecting, as Max had, that the gift was most likely from the Airbnb owner to welcome them. It was most likely it had been there when they had first arrived and they had simply missed it.

Before he left, he told them he would leave the file open, and they were welcome to call up if anything else happened, though Emily didn't miss the slightly patronising tone to his voice. He didn't believe them.

Max saw the constable out, closing and locking the door after him, before turning to Emily with a shrug. 'Well, that was a complete waste of time.'

Emily still had hold of her mug, trying to warm her hands.

Ever since they had arrived back, she couldn't seem to get rid of the chill going through her.

'Do you think he is right? That maybe it wasn't a torch?'

Max's laugh was harsh and had her eyes widening. 'That's ironic, don't you think? You're the one who's been convinced someone is messing with us and finally you get me on board, now you're doubting yourself? Come on, Emily. Really?'

His comment had her back stiffening. 'Well, is it any doubt I keep questioning everything? You made me feel like I was going mad.'

'I did and I'm sorry.' He crossed to the sofa where she was sitting and took the mug from her, setting it down before catching hold of both of her hands and warming them between his larger ones. 'I saw the torchlight, though, and it wasn't a trick of light... Someone *was* in the boat house, Emily.'

While she was grateful to at last have him on her side, his words did little to comfort her. 'But how did they get in?'

'I don't know. But I promise we will figure it out.'

After the visit from the police, Max wanted to leave Emily to wait in the boat house while he returned the boat to Wroxham, but she really didn't like the idea of being left there alone, plus it was already dark. In the end, he called the boat company and explained the situation, agreeing to pay extra if they could keep it overnight. His car was still in the pay and display car park. Emily knew they would likely face a ticket for running over the time there too. She really didn't want to be here alone, though. Especially as she was certain it wasn't the first time the intruder had been inside.

'Did you ever hear back from the owner?' she asked Max now. 'If someone has been breaking into their property, they deserve to know.'

'No, nothing. I'll get in touch again.'

'Is there a number on the website you can call?'

'I'll have a look.'

Emily already had her phone out. 'Here, I can do it.'

'Don't worry about it, now. Leave it with me to sort.'

'But I'm on the site.'

'I said I will do it!' Max snapped out the words and she paused her search to stare at him, her eyes widening.

'Sorry!' Emily kept her tone cool. 'I was trying to help.'

Max scrubbed his hands over his face, his shoulders sagging. 'I'm sorry, Em. I'm irritated by that bloody constable. I shouldn't take it out on you.' He took her phone from her, placing it down on the coffee table. 'Let me try to contact the owner again. I'm the one who's dealt with everything. Leave it with me to sort, okay?'

Emily must have still looked a little huffy because he leaned forward to kiss her nose and then her mouth, eventually teasing a smile out of her.

'Look, we were having a nice day before all of this. Why don't we order in a takeaway? We can get a Deliveroo and have a chilled night, and I'll make sure everywhere is locked up tight before we go to bed.'

'What do you fancy?' Emily asked, relenting. He was right. Everything had been perfect until they had seen someone in the house. They had checked everywhere thoroughly though and no one was here, except them. Whoever had been in the house was probably long gone.

'I don't mind. You decide.'

'Let me have a think while I go upstairs and get changed.'

'Okay.' Max kissed her again, this time deeper and more passionately. 'We can either watch another movie or have an early night. Whatever you fancy,' he added with a cheeky wink.

Emily eased herself out of his embrace. 'Let me have a think about that too,' she told him with a grin and a wink back.

With Max in the house with her, she at least felt safe enough to relax. She knew there was no one upstairs, the windows locked and everywhere thoroughly searched. Still, she drew the blinds in the bedroom, afraid of who may be looking in from the outside, before changing into a pair of pyjama bottoms and a hoodie top. After washing her face, she went back into the bedroom and pulled out her vanity case from her luggage, wanting her moisturiser.

The crudely written words on the mirror inside the lid of the case had her gasping.

I know what you did, Emily.

'Is everything okay up there?'

Hearing Max's voice, she quickly put the lid back down. She must have been louder than she realised.

'Yes. I'm fine. Just be a minute.'

When she didn't hear his footsteps on the stairs, she opened the case again, looking at the words. They were written in red. Blood she thought at first, before realising it was her lipstick. The lid off and the wax broken.

She had used the vanity case several times since arriving in Norfolk, so she knew the writing hadn't been there before leaving home.

Did that mean whoever had left the message had followed them?

Realising it was possible had her stomach twisting in knots.

What the hell was happening?

Her mind went back to everything that had happened in the summer. Was this somehow connected?

She had honestly believed it was over. The idea that her

nightmare could be about to resurface had nausea burning her gut.

And Max. She had kept everything from him, knowing the truth would tear them apart. There was no way he could find out now. He would never forgive her.

Maybe she had it wrong and paranoia had her overreacting. Deep down though, she struggled to believe that was true.

Think, Emily.

The wine, the mask, the tampering of her stuff. She had assumed they were being taunted by someone who lived locally. But this... it was personal.

Knowing that she couldn't risk Max seeing the message, that it would invite too many questions, she took the vanity case into the bathroom, every part of her shaking as she dampened a wad of toilet paper and scrubbed at the lipstick. But while it was easy to erase the wax written words, she knew the thoughts and fears racing through her mind would linger.

This changed everything.

If this was to do with what had happened back home, then this time, she was all on her own. And that scared the hell out of her.

15

BEFORE

It was Friday evening. Or what Emily and Max had come to know as date night. On the Fridays when Max wasn't working, they would set time aside for one another, either going out to a restaurant or the cinema, or staying home, but making the effort to cook nice food and drink fancy wine.

But because of the situation with her dad, nothing had even been mentioned about doing anything tonight. It was a foregone conclusion that Emily would be by his bedside, as she was most other nights. In fairness to Max, he had offered to go with her, but there was nothing he could do other than sit there with her, and truthfully, she was worried about an awkward encounter between him and Connor.

Max didn't seem too bothered when she turned his offer down and Emily suspected it had been a token gesture anyway. He didn't really want to go and knowing that stung more than she cared to admit.

As it turned out, she need not have worried about him running into Connor because Connor wasn't there again anyway.

This was the fourth visit she hadn't seen him and Emily's fingers were itching to send him a message. She didn't, though she couldn't resist asking Jeff, when she saw him on her way to her father's room, if he knew where Connor was.

If the nurse was suspicious of Emily's reasons for asking, he didn't show it.

'Knowing Connor, he's probably wrapped up with work. He doesn't come in that often. Maybe once or twice a week.'

That was odd. 'But he's always here,' Emily pointed out. 'I usually see him every night.'

'He has been here more the last two weeks,' Jeff agreed. 'I think that's because he has a soft spot.' He winked and Emily's face heated.

'What?' She didn't mean to snap out the word but couldn't help it.

Jeff's eyes widened in confusion. 'He has a soft spot,' he repeated, this time hesitantly. 'For your dad. I think that's been why he's been here more. Did you need me to pass on a message to him?'

'No.' Now Emily was mortified. She had jumped to conclusions, snapping at Jeff unnecessarily. 'I was just curious. But thank you.' She hurried off towards her father's room, pushing away thoughts of Connor. He wasn't the reason she was here.

She had the photo album with her and hoped her dad wouldn't be mad at her for taking it. He was asleep for the first part of her visit, so she waited patiently by his bed, caught up in the past as she studied his gaunt face, trying to commit every line of it to memory, aware she wouldn't have that chance for much longer. There was so much time that had been lost between them and it saddened her that it was too late to change things.

When he did eventually wake, she showed him the album,

her heart squeezing when his face lit up, and they spent time together going through the photos. It was the closest Emily had felt to her dad in a long time.

She stayed far later than intended, this visit having been both satisfying and bittersweet. She felt that she had finally reconnected with her father, but knowing their time together was almost over, and seeing him so weak, made it all the harder.

It was gone ten when she eventually left the hospice and she had to dash through puddles to reach her car thanks to a sudden, sharp downpour. Climbing inside the car, she ran fingers through her wet hair, not looking forward to the drive back to Leeds in damp clothes, especially in these conditions and while she was so tired.

She wanted to go back via her dad's house too and make sure everything was as she had left it. Although she had managed to broach the subject of the utility-room window, her dad hadn't been much help. Since the cancer had spread into his brain, he became easily confused, so she hadn't pushed it.

Ten minutes later, she was pulling up outside his house, relieved to see that everything seemed to be in order.

She turned off the engine, and sat for a moment listening to the sound of the rain pelting the roof of the car as she looked at the dark building, knowing that she really needed to go inside and check to be certain.

Reluctantly, she made another dash to the house, almost losing her footing on the wet driveway, jamming her father's key in the lock, eager to be in and out as soon as possible.

The house was quiet, other than the pattering rain against the windows, and she turned all the lights on as she walked through the downstairs rooms, banishing the darkness and heading straight for the utility room. She let out a sigh of relief when she saw the window was still locked. Her dad must have left it open.

Still, as she was here she would check the whole house again, just to be on the safe side.

Back in the hallway, she glanced up the dark stairs. As her hand went to the light switch, she heard a very distinct creak and froze.

Was someone up there?

Emily paused, waiting. It could just be the house. Floorboards sometimes made random noises.

Several seconds passed and certain that's what it was, she flicked on the light and ascended the stairs. Everywhere was locked up and she had only checked the house last night. Of course no one was here. She was just being jittery.

But then she saw it. The plant pot smashed on the landing. Soil everywhere.

It hadn't fallen off the windowsill by itself.

She froze midway up the stairs, for a moment too terrified to move.

If there was an unwelcome visitor, they were going to know she was in the house.

Then came the thump, sounding like something – or someone – stepping heavily on the floor, and Emily nearly fell down the stairs in her eagerness to get out of the house. Perhaps she was being a wimp, but she was here alone and no one knew where she was.

Once in the safety of her car, some of her bravado returned. She should call the police, she supposed, but would they really consider it to be an emergency? Besides, how foolish would she look if they showed up and it turned out to be a false alarm?

Unsure what to do, she rang Max. He sounded sleepy and she heard the TV playing in the background, guessed he was on the sofa. 'What time will you be home?' he asked.

'I'm still in Scarborough.'

'Why?' He sounded more alert all of a sudden and she knew she now had his full attention. Cutting straight to the point, she told him her concerns.

'Don't you dare go back in the house, Emily. Phone the police.'

She had suspected that might be his reaction and she bit down on her frustration. It wasn't his fault; he was seventy miles away and she had known he wouldn't be able to help her.

'What if it's nothing though?'

'It doesn't matter. It's better to be safe than sorry.'

Emily wasn't convinced, but she told him she would and promised him she wouldn't go back inside, at least not alone.

'Call me back when you've spoken to them,' Max ordered.

Agreeing, she ended the call, her finger hovering over the keypad, unsure what to do. Despite Max's instruction, she still wasn't certain that calling the police was the right option. It was a broken plant pot and a creaking floorboard. She didn't want to waste their time.

If only she knew someone local who could help her.

She could knock on a neighbour's door, she supposed. But it was late at night and she didn't know any of them well enough to feel comfortable doing so.

Or try to get hold of Connor.

That last idea crept to the forefront of her mind, as she tried to pretend she hadn't already been thinking it over.

She had his number. Would he answer?

Not allowing herself time to consider the question, she switched to her contact list, pulling up his name and pressing call.

Nerves jittered in her belly, fully aware that this was a convenient excuse to get in touch with him. Really she should be calling the police like Max had told her to do, but the phone was ringing now.

He answered after half a dozen rings.

'Emily?'

He sounded pleasantly surprised to hear from her.

'I'm sorry to be calling you and so late.'

'Honestly, you're fine. I was just in the gym.'

'You're out. I'm sorry. I shouldn't have disturbed you.' This had been a bad idea. It was a Friday night. Of course he was going to have plans.

'No, I meant my home gym. I converted my basement. You're fine,' he repeated. 'It's good to hear from you. What's up?'

Relieved by his response, she told him about her dad's house and he seemed as concerned as Max. He didn't suggest calling the police, though. 'Are you there now? Can you give me the address?'

As soon as she did, he told her to sit tight and wait in her car.

'I'm on my way.'

Emily did as told, unsure whether the nerves fluttering in her belly were from fear that someone could be inside the house or at the idea of seeing Connor again.

She turned on her engine, switching on the heater and warming her cold hands as she waited, telling herself she hadn't done anything wrong by calling him instead of the police. They had become friends, but that was it. Nothing had happened between them and nothing was going to. And she had no need to feel guilty about anything. Max was friends with Leah after all.

Within a few minutes, a car turned into the road, headlights sweeping across the wet tarmac, and slowing as it approached, before pulling to a halt in front of her. Recognising Connor, Emily switched off her engine again and got out to meet him. He was already out of his car and rushing over to her, his dark hair instantly slick again his head and a worried expression on his face.

'Are you okay?' His deep voice was gravelly with concern.

Even though she nodded, she must have looked dejected, as his arms came around her and she found herself leaning into him. It was just for comfort, she told herself. There was nothing more to it. Still, she was aware of everything. How his large hands were rubbing her back, the unfamiliar scent of him, and how warm he was, despite the rain. He felt different to Max. Still muscly, but there was more bulk to his build. He was so solid.

'You're dripping wet. We both are. Let's get inside and I'll check the house out for you.'

'Thank you.' Emily eased away from his embrace and led the way back to the front door, unlocking it again. Although she was still a little nervous, her confidence was bolstered having Connor with her.

'You heard the noise upstairs, right?' he whispered.

She nodded. 'Yes.'

'Wait down here, okay?'

Emily grabbed at his sleeve. 'I should come with you.'

He looked like he was about to say no, but then he relented. 'Okay, but stay close.'

She intended to.

Creeping up the dark staircase had her stomach twisting in knots, unsure what they were going to find, but very much aware this was horror movie territory.

Stepping over the plant pot, Connor went into the bathroom, pulling the light cord. It was empty, though Emily immediately spotted the soil marks in the sink.

What was going on?

The spare room was empty too, and nothing out of place, though Connor insisted on checking the wardrobe and under the bed. He was down on his hands and knees when an ominous growl came from the other bedroom.

Emily's eyes widened as she looked at him.

This time there was no mistaking the noise. And it wasn't creaks and groans of the house.

16

The shape moved as Connor stepped into the main bedroom and flipped the switch, while Emily clung to his free arm, and she saw green eyes staring at her. They weren't human though. Instead they belonged to the black cat on her dad's bed.

A cat? She had been freaked out by a fluffy little feline with a pink collar around her neck.

Now it all made sense. The cat had come in through the utility-room window and Emily must have accidentally locked her in the house last night. Poor thing.

'I think we've found your intruder,' Connor announced, and she could hear the smile in his voice, though to give him credit, he didn't tease her.

How could a cat have scared her so badly? She thought back to the loud thump she had heard. It must have been jumping down off something.

Although the cat looked comfortable, she couldn't stay, and no doubt she had an owner worried and wondering where she was. Luckily, she seemed friendly enough and after picking her up and depositing her outside, Emily turned to Connor.

'Do you want a coffee?' she asked, figuring it was the least she could do to repay him. She should really call Max back, as she had promised, but she couldn't do that while Connor was here. 'There's no milk, though, so we'll have to drink it black.'

'Black is fine with me.'

He followed her through to the kitchen and leant back against the counter, folding his arms. A big, strong, commanding presence in the small room.

'I was thinking someone probably should keep an eye on your dad's house as it's empty. Next time it might not be a cat.'

Unsure quite where his train of thought was going, Emily looked up at him.

'Let me help you, okay? I live locally, so I can stop by a couple of times a day, make sure everything is okay.'

'I can't expect you to do that.'

'Honestly, I don't mind. You have enough on your plate with everything that's going on with your dad. You really don't need all this extra hassle. Let me deal with it for you.'

It would be easier, she knew, and she did need to keep an eye on things going forward.

'Thank you,' she said gratefully. 'I really appreciate it. It's not easy keeping an eye on the house while Dad's away.'

Away? She cursed her poor choice of word. Simon Worth wasn't on holiday or a work trip. He was dying and would never return to this house. The reality of that suddenly hit hard and Emily turned her attention to the drinks she was making, so Connor didn't see her eyes filling up. She bit down on her bottom lip hard to try to stop the tears.

'I can't imagine it is. That's why I want...' Connor trailed off. When he next spoke, his voice was filled with concern. 'Emily, are you okay?'

She nodded as a comforting warm hand touched her shoulder, squeezing gently, and that was the moment the floodgates opened.

She wasn't a huge crier and had so far held her emotions in check when it came to her dad. At first, she was embarrassed, showing her raw emotion in front of a man she had only known for a couple of weeks, but then Connor was holding her again and it felt so good to sink against him and let him take some of her burden. He was going to help her. He was being there for her when Max wasn't.

She turned her face into his shoulder, liking how the stubble around his throat tickled against her cheek and how he was rubbing slow, comforting circles on her back.

He turned slightly too, his head dipping so their cheeks grazed, their mouths perfectly positioned for when his lips touched hers. And for a moment, Emily was lost as the gentleness heated into possession, locked in his embrace, the kiss that had started tender now growing in intensity as he claimed first her mouth, then her jawline and down to her neck. Their bodies were entwined and she felt him harden against her. It was the shock of that prod against her stomach that brought her to her senses. The alert from her brain finally sounding loud and clear in her head that this was wrong. She had a boyfriend.

'STOP!'

Connor was so caught up in the moment, his hands already roaming over her arse and then under her jacket, that for a moment, he didn't register her instruction.

When he finally seemed to come to his senses, he eased back, surprise on his face. 'Wow. That was hot.'

'That was wrong. We can't do this.'

'Why? I like you. You like me. I think it's safe to say we have chemistry.'

He reached for her again and Emily flinched away, this time putting distance between them.

Connor's face clouded in confusion. 'I don't understand. What's wrong?'

It was the moment of truth and she couldn't look at him, the words sticking in her throat before she managed to speak them.

'I, um... I have a boyfriend.'

'What?'

She chanced at look at him, saw his confusion turn to shock and then bitter disappointment as her confession sank in.

'But I don't understand. This, us, I thought we liked each other.'

He looked so hurt that Emily's tears started falling again. 'We do – I do. I'm so sorry. I never meant to lead you on. I should never have called you here tonight.'

For a moment, she thought he was going to agree. The frown of anger darkening his cheeks. She could see he was still struggling to take in the news. But then his expression softened. 'You needed my help.' He was silent for a moment, looking thoughtful. 'What's his name?'

Emily's throat was dry. Guilt not only for leading on Connor, but also for betraying the man waiting at home for her. 'Max.'

'Do you love him?'

She nodded.

He looked utterly cut up by that. 'And is he good to you?'

This time, there was more of a hesitation. Her mind going to Leah. Was there anything going on between her and Max? Still, it was none of Connor's business.

'Yes, he is.'

Connor's smile was tight. 'Well, I guess that's all I can ask for. You deserve someone to love you and treat you well, Emily.'

His words were laced with bitterness and she wasn't sure how to answer, so she simply nodded again, feeling really shitty about how this had all played out.

'I don't expect you to keep an eye on the house.' Not after this, she had been tempted to add, but instead she trailed off.

There was a quick flash of anger in Connor's dark eyes. 'I promised I would, and I will.'

'Honestly, it's not a problem. I will figure something out.'

'I said I would do it!'

He snapped the words and Emily's eyes widened.

'I'm sorry,' he apologised. 'I didn't mean to shout at you. Look, why don't you go get some rest. I can sleep on the sofa if you want, so you're not here alone.'

Emily shook her head. She couldn't stay here, especially not with Connor. Not after what had happened. 'I need to go.'

She saw his face fall again, another knife of guilt cutting into her.

'But you're exhausted.'

'I'll be okay. I really do need to get home.'

God, would he just stop looking at her with those doleful eyes! She couldn't handle it and needed space to get her head straight.

'I'm so, so sorry, Connor.'

'I told you it's fine.'

Leaving the untouched coffee, she backed away from him, heading out of the kitchen and across the hall to the front door. Grateful when he followed. 'It's not okay. And I really am sorry.' She stood stiffly as he stepped out of the house, a look of reluctance on his face like he wanted to say something else, to have the moment linger, but wasn't sure what, and as she locked up, she tried not to focus on how she had just used him and led him on, or how she had betrayed Max.

* * *

Emily's skull was pounding with a headache all the way back to Leeds, the rain making the drive difficult, and her eyes were sore with tiredness and from her earlier crying bout.

By the time she reached home, she was exhausted, unlocking the door and surprised to find Max asleep on the sofa. Scout was on the floor beside him and, spotting Emily, she got up, found her favourite stuffed toy, and brought it over, her tail wagging furiously.

Emily crouched down to hug her, whispering against her soft fur and telling her how much she loved her, before going to switch off the TV.

'You're home.'

Max's voice was groggy with sleep and he sat up yawning as she turned to face him.

'I thought you'd be in bed.'

'I wanted to wait up and make sure you got home safely. You never phoned me back and you didn't pick up when I tried to call you.'

Had he tried to call her? Emily's phone had been on silent in her bag on the journey home, and the radio on to help keep her awake. 'I'm sorry, I must have been distracted.'

'Was everything okay at your dad's? What did the police say?'

She sat down, snuggling up against him. 'Everything's fine,' she told him, going on to explain about the cat, but conveniently leaving out Connor.

'And what about your dad?' Max smoothed a hand over her hair. 'How was he tonight?'

'It was a good visit. I showed him some photos I found in the house. He's getting more confused, though, and he looks so weak.' She buried her face into Max's shoulder, breathing in his familiar smell. While it was comforting and safe, she couldn't shake the guilt that crept in.

'I'm sorry, Em. I know it's not easy for you.'

It wasn't, but she would find a way to deal with it, the same as she had with Aunt Cathy and, before that, her mum and Megan.

She let her eyes close, wanting to focus on memories of happier times, but instead of her family and Max, all she could see was Connor's face looking back at her.

17

WEDNESDAY

Emily's first realisation when she woke up was that someone was downstairs. Remembering there had been an intruder in the boat house had her eyes blinking open, and she reached for Max, only to find his side of the bed empty.

Her heart thumped in panic for a moment, but then she heard him below, talking to Scout as he fastened her lead to her collar.

Was he going to return the boat without her? She had told him last night that she wanted to go too, so why hadn't he woken her?

She almost fell out of bed, rushing onto the mezzanine landing.

'I thought we agreed we would go together?' she shouted down, noticing that he already had his coat on.

Both man and dog looked up at her.

'You were asleep and I didn't want to disturb you. I figured I could be gone and back before you even woke up.'

He sounded so reasonable, as if she was panicking over nothing, but, although their evening had passed without further incident, despite her worries over it being Halloween, the idea of being left alone in the boat house scared her. Surely he could understand that?

'I don't want to stay here by myself.'

'I'll be an hour tops. Back before you know it.'

'Max! You promised.'

A flicker of irritation clouded his face. 'Okay, fine. Though I do think you're overreacting.'

'Someone was in this house.' How could he have changed his tune so quickly?

'And they are long gone. Don't you think that if they meant us harm, they would have come back overnight?'

'No. Whoever it is has been lingering around ever since we first got here.'

Emily knew a part of Max still believed it had been kids that first night who had scared her, and while it was perhaps safer for her that he thought that, it was still frustrating. He had no idea why she was so frightened, and she couldn't tell him.

For a moment, he looked like he was going to argue the point, but then he decided against it. 'Look, just go get dressed, okay? We need to get this boat back.'

Emily nodded, dashing back into the bedroom.

She was ready in minutes, foregoing her shower and quickly throwing on jeans and a jumper, leaving her face freshly scrubbed as she tied back her messy bob.

Max was waiting near the door, impatient to leave, following Scout outside before Emily had even reached the bottom step and she hurried after them, aware of the tension in his shoulders.

'You're in a bad mood.'

'No I'm not. I'm fine,' he insisted. Though he didn't speak again as she followed him round to the door that led into the tunnels.

'Are you fucking kidding me?' he snapped, stepping inside.

'What?'

Emily was still a few steps behind him, but as she closed the distance, stepping through the door and peering into the tunnels, she understood why Max was upset.

The boat was gone.

'Oh shit. Where the hell is it?'

Max turned and looked at her grimly, his face dark in the shadows. 'If I knew the answer to that, we wouldn't be standing here right now.'

'Okay. There's no need to get tetchy with me. It's not my fault.'

'I know, I know. I'm sorry.' He rubbed a hand over his jaw.

The boat hadn't come adrift. She remembered it been securely tied.

That left only one possibility and Emily knew Max was considering it too, even if he didn't want to admit it.

'I saw you tie the knot.'

She phrased it as a fact, not a question, but he took the hump anyway.

'Of course you bloody saw me. I'm not stupid.'

'I never said you were. I meant there's no way it came loose by itself.'

'So where the fuck is it?'

Max start pacing, more agitated than she had seen him in a long while. Generally, he was the more laid-back of the two of them. Very little fazed him and he was often the one to calm Emily down if she was overreacting. This time, she realised, it was up to her to take the lead.

'Someone must have untied it.'

'Seriously? You're starting that shit again? It's not the time, Emily.'

She bristled, but tried to shake off the insult. He was just lashing out. Right now, she needed to keep her head. 'Either you didn't tie it properly or someone untied it. This isn't rocket science, Max.'

When he didn't respond, continuing to pace and the scowl on his face refusing to budge, she pushed past him.

'Where are you going?' he demanded.

'We're missing a boat. I'm off to find it,' she snapped back.

It was possible that whoever had taken it may still have the boat and be long gone, but Emily didn't think so. For starters, they wouldn't have a key. She had no idea how easy it was to hotwire a boat, but even so, would they really have gone to the trouble?

No. Given everything that had been happening, she suspected it had been untied simply to inconvenience them, and if her hunch was right, it would be somewhere close by.

She heard Max huff and wasn't sure if he was going to follow, but then came the sound of footsteps and Scout's panting as she strained at her lead trying to catch up with Emily.

'The river is huge,' Max grumbled. 'Even if it was let loose, it could be anywhere.'

Emily ignored him, focused on her task and relieved when she spotted the boat just a few minutes later, caught up in reeds on the opposite bank.

'There.' She pointed. 'Though I don't know how we're going to get to it.'

'Here. Take Scout.' Max handed over the dog's lead, bending down to unlace his trainers.

'What are you doing? You can't go in the river. Max, it's November, and you don't know how deep it is.'

Was he crazy?

'We don't exactly have a choice, do we?'

She watched him as he kicked off the trainers, then peeled off his socks, balling them up inside, before shrugging off his jacket, his expression having gone from scowling to focused, and she realised he was going to do this regardless of what she said. 'Here, take these,' he instructed, handing everything to her.

'What about the house keys?'

'They're in my jacket pocket.' He held up another key. 'I've just got the key for the boat.'

'Be careful of the reeds,' she warned, watching him slide down the bank into the water. It only came to just above his knees, but it could be much deeper in the middle.

Scout whined as Max waded out towards the boat, tugging on her lead, then barking at Emily when she was told to sit. She didn't understand why she couldn't go in the water with Max, her whimpering becoming pitiful as she watched Max moving further away. Emily didn't need to be dealing with a wet dog as well as a grumpy boyfriend, though, and kept her grip on the lead tight.

'Are you okay?' she called when Max was about halfway.

Although the water was a little deeper, it still hadn't fully covered his thighs.

'Yeah,' he shouted back, though didn't turn round. 'It's bloody freezing though.'

She could have told him that it would be.

Eventually, he reached the boat, clambering over the side.

From her position on the bank, the vessel didn't look damaged, but, still, she was relieved when the engine started.

'I'll meet you and Scout back at the boat house,' he shouted across the water, starting the engine and easing the boat back, away from the reeds.

Emily did as instructed, keeping hold of his things, along with Scout's lead as she headed back in the direction from which they'd come.

Max was already mooring the boat when her and Scout arrived back at the house and, noticing he was shivering, she was quick to pass him his jacket.

'Wait here. I'm just going to nip upstairs and change,' he told her.

Emily didn't like that idea one bit. 'I'll come with you.'

'No, Em. I'm not risking the boat disappearing again. You need to stay down here and keep an eye on it.'

Although she understood his point about leaving the boat unguarded, she really didn't want to wait in the tunnels alone. It gave her the creeps. Her nerves had already been on edge, but the message left on her vanity case mirror had scared her senseless.

Max must have realised how unhappy she was about it because he added, 'Wait on the riverbank if you want. I'll only be five minutes. I just need to get out of these wet clothes.'

Emily handed him his trainers, following him out of the tunnels and watching as he disappeared round to the steps leading up to the house. Doing as he asked, she made her way down the bank to where the tunnels led out onto the river. Here she at least had a good view of the boat.

After yesterday and spotting someone in the boat house, she had hoped Max would say they could leave. He still didn't seem to think there was any threat, though.

If only she could tell him why she was so nervous. But she had hidden the truth from him for all this time. If he found out now, it would only make things worse.

Maybe she was wrong and this wasn't connected to before. She kept clinging to that hope.

She was thinking back to the crude lipstick words, when Scout started growling ominously, and instantly, all of Emily's nerve endings were on edge.

Hearing a cough, she realised she wasn't alone.

18

Emily was aware of footsteps before she heard the sound of a voice. She looked around frantically and spotted a man in a navy hoodie. He stood on the other side of the tunnels, a large Alsatian type of dog with him off the lead, which had Scout going nuts, even though the Alsatian took no notice, too busy sniffing the path.

At first, she thought he was alone and had been talking to his dog, but then she saw him turn to someone who was just out of sight, muttering something to them. Unsure who he was or what he wanted, she tightened her grip on Scout's lead, grateful that the water separated them.

'Is this a dead end?' he asked, the question directed at Emily, even though it was pretty bloody obvious the only way he could continue on the path would be to wade across.

She nodded, still wary. He could be harmless, but she hadn't seen anyone else down by the boat house path since they had arrived. Well, apart from the masked man.

'We'll have to go back on ourselves.' That comment was directed to the person who was out of sight and this time, Emily picked up the Scottish lilt in his voice. Perhaps he was just another visitor to the area. He looked a similar age to her and Max, and he had a backpack with him.

A curse came from whoever he was with. A female voice, and she didn't sound happy.

Emily relaxed just a little bit. It really did sound like they were a couple out and about with their dog.

'If you go up past the house into the woods and cross the clearing, it will take you to a lane,' she told them. 'On the other side of that, you can pick up the path again.'

'Okay. Thanks.'

The man lingered. His girlfriend, wife, whoever, still out of sight.

'So, do you live here?'

It was an innocent enough question under normal circumstances, but given everything that had been happening since they arrived, Emily's belly was suddenly jittery with nerves again.

'Um... we've rented it for a week.'

'I see.'

The man continued to study her, though said nothing else.

'Are you visiting the area?' Emily asked, partly to cover the awkward silence, but also because she was curious.

'Yeah.' He didn't elaborate and she didn't push.

'Come on then!' It was the girl's voice again, sounding impatient, and finally it seemed to get the man moving.

'Okay.' The man glanced briefly at Emily again and rolled his eyes, as if they had just shared a secret joke about his girlfriend. 'Well. Have fun.'

'Bye.'

He had just turned to walk away when Max returned.

'Who was that?'

'Another couple staying in the area,' Emily told him.

Now Max was back and she was no longer alone, she felt slightly foolish for her reaction. Everything was making her too jumpy.

'I thought I heard Scout barking,' he commented, taking her leash and heading back up the bank and round to the door that led to the tunnels.

'They had a dog.'

'That would explain it.'

He climbed into the boat, Scout jumping in after him, then held out a hand to help Emily. Now that they had the boat back, she had hoped his mood would have improved, but, if anything, he seemed in more of a grump, and as they headed out onto the river, back towards Wroxham, he retreated into himself, seeming lost in his thoughts. When Emily attempted to strike up conversation, she received monosyllabic answers, and after a while, she gave up and they rode the rest of the way in silence.

Max wasn't a sulker, which suggested something was playing on his mind. He didn't look like he was in the mood to share though, so she didn't broach it, and the only time they spoke again was as they approached the boatyard, Max telling her that as there was no damage to the boat, it was perhaps wise not to mention anything about what had happened overnight to the owner.

Emily agreed and, in their first stroke of good luck for the day, knowing the circumstances why they had been unable to return it the previous day, the man took pity on them, waiving any additional charge.

Unfortunately, the pay and display car park wasn't so lenient. Admittedly, they didn't know the circumstances and snatching up the fine from under the windscreen wiper, Max grumbled that he was going to contest it.

As he wandered round to the driver's door, the scowl on his face deepened.

'What the fuck!'

'What's wrong now?'

When he didn't reply, instead dropping down on his haunches, Emily wandered round the vehicle.

She stopped short. 'Oh my God.'

The word 'BITCH' had been scratched into the black paintwork.

Emily's gut tightened, her lungs suddenly feeling like they weren't getting enough air.

Okay, so it was just one word, but it was very clear who the intended target was.

'Max, your car. I'm sorry.'

Perhaps sorry was the wrong thing to say, as it suggested she was guilty or that she knew what was going on.

She went to touch his shoulder, but he shook her away, so she stood quietly, waiting for him to react. Not sure if he was going to be mad at her or start demanding answers. Ones that she couldn't give him.

The seconds ticked by as he looked over the damage, then, without saying a word, he calmly got up and slowly wandered around the car park. Emily assumed he was looking for cameras, and although she didn't move from her spot, from where she was standing, she couldn't see any. Her eyes were on Max as he eventually returned to the car, but he ignored her as he let Scout onto the back seat, before getting in himself.

He shut the door, starting the engine, and she hesitated, nervously clenching and unclenching her fists. She hadn't expected this silent response and it unnerved her a little.

The window wound down a fraction, but he still didn't look at her. 'Are you getting in?'

She didn't wait to be asked again, rushing round to the passenger side and climbing in the car. She snuck a glance at Max as she buckled her seat belt. His jaw was clenched and he didn't look happy at all.

Not sure there was anything she could say to him at this point that would make things better, she stayed quiet, and they drove back to the boat house in uncomfortable silence. Whoever had scratched the word into the paintwork had to be the same person who had written on her vanity case mirror, and she was pretty certain she knew who it was. The fact that they had followed her to Norfolk, trying to get a clear message across, scared her senseless.

Back inside the boat house, she went straight upstairs and locked herself in the bathroom, convinced she was going to be sick. Splashing cold water on her face, she willed the feeling to pass.

This was supposed to be a fresh start. *Her* fresh start. A chance to try to put everything behind her and find a way to move forward.

She had been so convinced she had dealt with the threats, but it seemed she had that wrong.

Max couldn't find out what had happened in Scarborough and unless her tormentor revealed themselves, she wasn't sure what the way forward was.

Last time, they had made their motive clear, but this felt more like a punishment.

If only she could tell Max the truth. Maybe they could figure it out together.

She would give anything to be able to do that. To relieve herself of this burden she carried. But she also knew it wasn't possible.

This would destroy them. He would never forgive her, and she couldn't bear the thought of losing him.

Emily could hear him talking to someone and she unlocked the bathroom door, easing it open. The open-plan set-up meant she was able to hear almost every word of his conversation, even though he was talking quietly, and she quickly realised he was on the phone to someone about getting his car fixed.

She pictured the crude word that had been carved into the bodywork, hating that it was because of her that he had been targeted.

Knowing she couldn't stay hidden upstairs all day, Emily made her way down to the kitchen, careful to keep out of Max's way as he paced. She made tea. Two cups. Leaving Max's on the counter and taking hers over to the sofa. And as she curled up there, Scout wandering over and settled herself at Emily's feet. Both of them watched Max as he spoke into the phone, Emily too unsettled to focus on anything.

Eventually, he ended the call, glancing briefly in her direction.

'I made you a cup of tea,' she said quietly, warming her own mug between her cold hands.

Max nodded, though made no attempt to get it.

Instead, he came over to the sofas, taking a seat on the one opposite Emily. When she glanced up at him, she realised he had a piece of paper in his hand. He unfolded it and laid it on the coffee table, the written words facing her so she could read them.

You have no idea what your girlfriend is capable of. Has she told you what she did yet?

The accusation was clear and Emily's stomach roiled. She was aware of the heavy silence in the room and the weight of Max's stare challenging her to look at him again.

Her heart thumped uncomfortably when she did, spotting the heat of anger in his blue eyes, though, when he spoke, his tone was calm.

'I think it's time you told me exactly what the hell is going on.'

19

'Where did you get this?' Emily whispered the words. She was still holding the mug of tea, and although her mouth was dry with fear, she couldn't bring herself to take a sip. Her hand was shaking so badly, she didn't trust herself not to spill it everywhere.

'It was lying on the doormat when I came downstairs this morning. The envelope had my name on it.'

'Why didn't you tell me earlier?'

There was a hint of accusation in her tone and she saw Max's eyes narrow in annoyance.

Instead of answering her question, he repeated the one he had asked her. 'What's going on, Emily?'

Was this the only note he had received?

And if not, how much did he know?

This explained why he had been in such a bad mood all day.

Max was still waiting for her answer, and she was aware he was watching her carefully.

What the hell was she supposed to say to him?

She looked down at her lap, clenching and unclenching her

hands, knowing that if she was going to lie to him, she couldn't do it while looking at him.

'I don't know,' she said carefully, unable to hide the tremor in her voice. She was going to have to try to feel her way forward, and she had no idea how this conversation was going to play out.

'You don't know?' Max laughed harshly. 'Come on. I'm not stupid. Everything that has been happening. The wine, the mask, the boat and my car. It's because of you, isn't it?' Even though he was angry, he managed to keep his tone even.

The silence stretched as she tried to think how to respond. Eventually she nodded. 'I think so.'

'Why?' he demanded.

The why she couldn't tell him, but perhaps she could give him a version of the truth.

'For a while back home, I was being followed. I thought it had stopped. I swear I had no idea it was connected.'

'What do you mean, you were being followed?' he sounded annoyed. 'By whom?'

'I don't know who he was,' she lied, knowing she was on dangerous ground.

'So it was a he? Did he threaten you? What did he want?'

'I don't know, Max. But he was everywhere I went.' And it had terrified her. Much as it was doing now. The idea that her nightmare wasn't over had her nerves in shreds.

'You said, "for a while". So had it stopped?'

Emily nodded.

'So why would he be here, in Norfolk?'

'I don't know. I might be wrong. It could be unconnected.'

'You really believe that?'

Honestly, she didn't know what to believe.

She was aware of Max hesitating, and wondered if he was going to call her out on it, but then he asked another question and this time she could hear the hurt in his voice. It nearly broke her.

'Why didn't you tell me?'

How was she supposed to answer that? It certainly couldn't be with the truth, yet by lying, she was going to hurt him further. If only Francesca was here and could help her figure out the best way forward. She could really do with her best friend right now, but instead she was all alone, and she realised she had to give Max an explanation.

Tears pricked at the back of her eyes as she answered him, trying to keep the emotion out of her voice. 'I was scared.'

Her reply had knocked him, she could tell by the silence as he processed those three words, and there was no way she dared look at him.

'Scared of what?' he demanded eventually. 'Of me? Of my reaction? To you being followed? Are you mad?' The heat of anger was coming through now, and she could hear his frustration as he tried to rein it in. 'Have I ever given you any reason to be afraid of me?' he pushed.

'No, of course not.'

'So why the fuck would you be scared?'

'I don't know, Max. Maybe because of how you are acting right now? Distrustful, blaming me like I have done something wrong.'

Emily was on the defensive now. She had to be.

'Well, have you?' He stabbed his finger at the paper. 'This suggests you have.'

'Someone leaves you an anonymous note and you automatically take their side over mine.'

'I'm not taking anyone's side, but what am I supposed to think? It's obvious that whoever wrote it seems to know a hell of a lot more about you than I do.'

Ouch. Emily looked at him now and could see he was still seething.

'That's not fair.'

'No, it's not fair, Emily. I'm your boyfriend. If you were being harassed by someone, I deserved to know. Don't you trust me?'

'Of course I do.'

'So why did you keep me in the dark?'

When she didn't answer, because, after all, he was right, Max shook his head.

'I need to go out and get some air.' He got up from the sofa, whistling to Scout, who was quick to follow. 'Come on, girl.'

His words had Emily's eyes widening. 'Max, wait.'

He paused, arching a brow at her as he waited for her to speak.

'I don't want to be here alone.'

'Well, I'm sorry. I need to clear my head.'

Without waiting, he clipped on Scout's lead, opened the door and let himself out of the boat house.

Emily put her now cool mug of tea down on the table, her hands still shaking as she rubbed at her cold arms and tried to process what had just happened. Was this nightmare ever going to be over?

20

BEFORE

Simon Worth passed away on the first Saturday in June, just ten minutes before Emily arrived at the hospice.

She would have been there sooner, but she had stopped to buy him flowers, figuring they would cheer up his room and help mask the unpleasant odours, and she had walked into the lobby, a smile on her face for the receptionist, knowing immediately from the girl's expression that there was bad news.

Spotting her from down the corridor, Jeff was quick to approach, offering her his quiet sympathies before taking her to her dad's room so she could say her last goodbye.

Her dad was still in bed and looked more peaceful than Emily had seen him in weeks, but the moment felt surreal and she struggled to move through the doorway, the colourful bouquet now limp in her hand.

'If this is too difficult...' Jeff began.

'No, I want to do this.'

'I can stay with you if it's easier,' he suggested kindly.

'I'll be okay. I just need a moment. But thank you.'

He went to walk away.

'Jeff?'

'Yes.'

Emily held out the flowers. 'He doesn't need these and they're too pretty to waste. Can you...' She trailed off, finding it difficult to talk through the ball of threatening tears that was growing in her throat.

'I'll take care of them for you,' he said gently, taking the bouquet from her and giving her arm an affectionate squeeze.

She nodded her thanks.

And then he was gone and Emily was alone, summoning all of her strength to go and say goodbye, walking stiffly to the bed and taking her father's still warm hand in hers.

He was pale and so horribly still. Had he known when he was taking his last breath? Did he wonder where his daughter was, or had he been glad to die alone?

Stop.

These questions were too overwhelming for her to think about right now.

A polite cough had her looking up.

'Do you need some more time?' Jeff asked from the doorway.

Emily shook her head, a numbness taking over as he gently explained the next procedure and how the team would now perform post-mortem care.

'You are welcome to stay,' he told her.

She appreciated the offer, but right now she just needed to be alone. The hospice had the details for the funeral directors.

With a final kiss to her father's forehead, she left his bedside for the last time, heading back into the corridor and hoping not to have to face anyone, especially Connor. Luckily, there was no sign of him. He hadn't been at the hospice, at least not that she had seen, since their ill-fated kiss over a week ago, and for that she was both grateful and guilt-ridden. Her dad had liked him, though. And an upsetting thought struck. Had she deprived him of Connor's company in his last days? She really hoped that wasn't the case, but the idea lingered as she left the hospice, getting into her car for the drive home. She was still numb with shock. Even though she had been expecting the end, having watched her father slowly fade away in front of eyes, it had still caught her off guard, and despite having Max waiting at home, the loneliness was overwhelming.

All of her blood relatives were gone. Her mum and sister, Aunt Cathy, and now her dad, and she was struggling to process that.

She hadn't called ahead to tell Max what had happened or that she was on her way back early, but she wished she had when she turned into their road and saw Leah's car parked in her space on the drive.

Cheeky cow!

This was all Emily needed in this moment: having to deal with Miss Smirky Face.

Max was going to have to ask her to leave.

Emily parked on the road, hearing barking from the direction of the garden as she got out of the car. Scout must be outside. She let herself into the house, expecting to find Max and Leah sat on the sofa, but they weren't in the living room, so she assumed that they were outside with the dog. Briefly, she considered sneaking upstairs so she didn't have to tell Max what had happened while Leah looked on.

As she kicked off her boots and hung up her bag, she heard Leah laugh, the sound carrying through from the kitchen.

It was tempting to hide away, but Emily wouldn't do that; it was her house after all. Instead, she would ask to have a word with Max privately. Hopefully the annoying woman would get the hint.

Steadying herself, she crossed the living room, the sight through the open kitchen door stopping her dead.

Max had his back to the counter, his hands on Leah's arms. Her rear was facing Emily, but she could see from the woman's position, on tiptoe, her breasts mashed against Max's chest, that they were kissing.

Her eyes widened, a strangled sob escaping from deep inside her. At which point, Max broke the kiss, a look of horror on his face as he realised she was standing there.

'Emily.'

He shoved Leah out of the way and was stepping towards her.

Emily couldn't deal with this, not right now, not in the aftermath of her dad dying. As Max reached for her, she pushed hard at him, and he momentarily lost his balance.

She didn't wait for him to recover, refusing to look at him or Leah, their faces a blur, as she turned on her heel, pausing only to grab her bag, keys and boots before fleeing the house.

Max was charging after her as she got into her car, starting the engine. She locked the doors, ignoring him as he ducked down to her level, trying to get her attention through the driver's side window.

'It wasn't what it looked like, Emily.'

Lies. She had seen him and Leah together with her own eyes. How dare he try to pretend it hadn't happened? And after everything he spouted about adulterers.

Desperate to get away from him, she floored the accelerator, refusing to look in the rear-view mirror at what she was leaving behind.

At first, she drove around blindly, unsure where to go, before she found herself heading towards Francesca's.

By the time she arrived, the tears had started and she was struggling to see clearly to drive. She didn't even stop to put her boots on, getting out of the car and ignoring the wet chill of the puddle that she stumbled through in her socked feet, just eager to get to the door.

By the third ring of the doorbell, it was clear no one was home. Francesca's car was parked on the driveway, but it was possible they had gone out in in her husband Adam's van.

It was then that she remembered. They had gone to visit Adam's family for the weekend. She had been so caught up in her own drama, she had forgotten.

Wiping tears away, Emily made her way back to her car, hugging the steering wheel as she rested her head, unsure what to do next. Although she got on well with her work colleagues, she didn't feel close enough with any of them to share this burden, and that just left the women who were the girlfriends of Max's close circle of mates. Although they all got along well, she knew she couldn't go to them. Not about this.

Beside her on the passenger seat, her bag started vibrating. That would be Max trying to reach her, no doubt hoping to worm his way back in with his lies.

Angrily, she shoved the bag on the floor.

Eventually, she started driving again, at first aimlessly around Leeds, but then with purpose as she headed east out of the city.

There was only one place left to go.

Back to Scarborough and her dad's house.

Emily's head was pounding by the time she arrived, her eyes tired and gritty from crying and wanting nothing more than to go to sleep, simply so she could escape this nightmare.

The wave of grief as she stepped through the front door, realising that her dad had existed in this space, that it had been his home for years, but that he was no longer here, was overwhelming. Emily had known he would never come home from the hospice, but, still, the finality of it hit her.

She filled the kettle and as it boiled, thought about all of the steps she would have to go through over the coming days. Registering his death, organising the funeral. She didn't even know who she was supposed to invite. Would there be anyone there apart from her? Come Monday, she would have to call into work too and let James know she needed compassionate leave.

Her phone started vibrating again and she fished it out of her bag, saw she had dozens of missed calls and messages from Max. She was also down to 22 per cent charge and worryingly had no cable with her.

In fact, she had nothing with her at all, she realised. Just the things she was wearing and her handbag. Although the shops would be open for another couple of hours, she couldn't think about buying new clothes today or even essentials like milk. She just wanted to rest and forget everything for a while.

Switching her phone off, partly to conserve the battery, but also to stop the incessant buzzing, she decided she needed something stronger to drink than coffee and was grateful when she found a bottle of whisky in the lounge cabinet.

Pouring a generous measure, Emily carried it with her upstairs.

She headed into the spare room, unable to bring herself to go into her dad's room. Not on the day he had died.

The bed in the spare room was made up, but she noticed as she crawled on top of the duvet that there was a general mustiness to the linen, suggesting it hadn't been used or changed in a long while. Had her dad even used this room? She couldn't imagine he ever invited people to stay over.

Emily closed her eyes, willing sleep to take over, but everything that had happened was playing on loop, a slideshow in her head that she couldn't escape. Seeing her dad in the hospice bed this morning, knowing that she had missed her chance to say goodbye. Connor's face when she had told him she had a boyfriend. And that lying, cheating piece of shit who she had given her heart to, in their kitchen, holding onto Leah as he stuck his tongue down her throat.

Emily had felt awful about the kiss she had shared with Connor, but it had been a mistake. A terrible mistake. Max kissing Leah was different. They had clearly been having an affair behind her back for a while. Not only had Max cheated on her; he had humiliated her too, making her look a fool. And he had done it while knowing she was going through the worst possible time of her life.

Anger and grief welled together as Emily struggled to relax, tossing and turning on the unfamiliar bed, growing frustrated when she couldn't switch off.

The ring of the doorbell that finally paused the slideshow had her bolting upright, her eyes wide open, and she glanced at the alarm clock on the bedside table.

It was just gone 7 p.m.

Was it Max? Had he followed her here?

She rubbed at her eyes as she waited a beat, wishing like hell she hadn't parked her Polo outside. He was going to know she was in the house.

When the second ring came, she was torn whether to answer.

What if it was someone else? It could be important, relating to her dad's passing, or perhaps a neighbour needing to speak with her. Besides, knowing Max's style, he would have been calling to her through the letterbox by now.

Still, she didn't want to be wrong and regret opening the door. She couldn't face him. Not until her head was clearer.

She needed to know who it was, though.

Getting off the bed, Emily crossed the landing to her father's room, careful to remain hidden in the shadows of the room as she peered out of the window. It was still light outside and the rain had cleared, leaving a pleasant summer evening.

Although she couldn't see whoever was on the doorstep, there was no sign of Max's car outside. She wasn't up for visitors, but it could be important.

Another ring, this time followed by an urgent-sounding knock had her making her mind up, and before Emily could over-think her decision, she headed downstairs, certain from the bulky build she could see through the opaque glass that the caller was male.

She rubbed her fingers over her eyes, hoping it didn't look too obvious she had been crying, before opening the door. Stupid really, she supposed, as whoever it was probably knew about her dad and it was only natural she would be upset. But even so. Her grief was private.

Her mouth fell open when she saw who was waiting on the doorstep.

Definitely not Max and not a stranger.

Emily stared at Connor, both surprised and a little shocked to see him.

'What are you doing here?' Her tone perhaps wasn't as friendly as it should be, but she really hadn't expected to see him again after their last awkward encounter.

'I've just come from the hospice. I'm so sorry about your dad, Emily.'

She sniffed, but managed not to cry. 'Thanks. I guess it shouldn't be such a shock. I knew it was going to happen.'

'That doesn't make it any easier, though. I remember.'

Of course he did. He had been in this position, going through the exact same thing with his mum.

Her expression softened a little. 'I don't know how to feel. Everything is numb.'

'That's normal. Your world has stopped, but everyone else's is still going, right?'

Emily nodded. He had summed it up perfectly. That was exactly how it felt.

'How did you know I was here?' she asked after a moment.

'I didn't.' Connor shuffled his feet, his head dipping as he studied his shoes. When he glanced back up at her, she noticed he seemed a little uncomfortable. 'I promised I would keep an eye on your dad's house for you. I was stopping by and saw your car. Can I come in?' When Emily's eyes widened, he quickly added, 'Just for a minute.'

She didn't want company, but it felt wrong to say no, especially after the time he had spent with her dad, and the fact he had been going out of his way to keep an eye on the house, even after she had rejected him.

'Okay,' she relented, opening the door wider so he could step inside.

Connor stepped through into the lounge but didn't attempt to sit. He turned to face Emily as she closed the door and joined him, and they both stood there awkwardly for a moment as though now he was in the house, neither of them was sure what to say.

It was the elephant in the room, the encounter that should never have happened, and Emily hoped to hell he didn't mention it. What with everything else that had happened today, she didn't have the strength to deal with that too.

'How come you came here?'

The question caught Emily off guard and her mouth flapped open and closed, the words not coming.

She must have looked a little shocked too because his dark eyes softened with fresh sympathy. 'I'm sorry. It's not my place to ask. I just thought you would have wanted to be home with...' He trailed off, seeming unable to say Max's name. His eyes suddenly widened and he looked around. 'Is he here, with you?'

Emily shook her head, managing the word, 'No,' before the floodgates opened again.

Realising he had upset her, Connor took a step towards her, looking like he was about to console her.

It was a terrible idea and she moved away from him, holding up her hand to stop him.

'I'm sorry, but I can't have you here right now,' she managed through her tears. 'I need you to go.'

Rather than looking offended, Connor seemed concerned. 'I can't leave you like this, Emily. If you don't want me here, fine. But at least let me call someone for you.'

'There is no one!'

Emily didn't mean to snap out the words, but her emotions were getting the better of her.

'What do you mean, there is no one? What about your boyfriend?'

He spoke the last word as if it left a nasty taste in his mouth.

When she didn't answer, his eyes narrowed. 'Emily, what's going on? Talk to me please. You're scaring me.'

'Max and I are over.' It was out there now and she couldn't take it back. 'I caught him... I found him with someone else.'

The scene she had walked in on started playing again in her head and for a moment, her tears were choking her so hard, she was struggling to breathe. She didn't want Connor's help and tried to push him away when he caught hold of her, but he was too strong and, exhausted from trying to fight him, she eventually collapsed against him.

He was stroking her hair and whispering to her that it was going to be okay, and although she didn't want to lead him on, right now she needed someone to lean on.

When the worst of her crying bout was over, he finally eased his grip and started to draw away. And, damn it, Emily really didn't want him to let go.

It was wrong, but while he had been holding her, she had at least felt like she wasn't going through everything on her own. But she didn't want him to mistake her grief for something else.

'I'm sorry I cried all over you,' she managed.

'It's okay. You needed to.' Connor ran an affectionate hand down her arm before breaking contact completely.

'Well, thank you.'

He was already backing towards the hallway, but then he hesitated.

'I really don't think you should be here alone.'

'I'll be okay.' She shouldn't have unloaded on him like this. Right now, it was best for her to be by herself. She needed time to process everything.

He studied her for a moment. 'No, I'm not happy with this. You shouldn't be here in this house by yourself where everything reminds you of your dad. It's too soon and you have so much to process.'

When she simply looked at him, unsure where he expected her to go, he told her his proposal.

'I'm going to take you back to mine.'

That was a terrible idea, worse than being here alone, and Emily immediately protested.

'No, I'm fine here. I can't go back to your place.'

'Why not?'

'Because... because it doesn't feel right.'

She didn't add that it was wrong after what had happened between them. They both knew exactly what she was talking about.

She might not have said it, but apparently Connor was ready to address their kiss.

'This isn't about anything other than friendship, Emily. Forget last week. It shouldn't have happened. You need a friend right now and I am here for you. I have a spare room you can use and it's yours for as long as you want it.' His tone dropped a notch, and he sounded so sincere. 'I understand what you're going through. I can help. I want to help.'

Emily was torn. Her instincts still told her this was wrong, that Connor wasn't the right person to lean on, but he had promised her his offer had no strings, and she really could use a friend right now.

She managed a watery smile. 'Okay.'

21

Connor's house was only a short drive from where Emily's dad had lived, but she was surprised when he told her he had come on foot.

'I thought you said you came straight from the hospice?' she questioned as they got into her car.

'I did. I nipped home first, though. After I heard about your dad, I wanted some fresh air, so I decided to walk across the park.'

'Are you sure this is okay? I don't want to be a nuisance and interrupt any plans you have.'.

'You're not. I don't have any plans.' He gave Emily an easy smile, as he directed her where to turn as they approached a set of traffic lights. 'Make a left here.'

She took the turn, heading into a road that narrowed into a lane, the houses spread further apart and set back down driveways.

'You see that park,' Connor pointed to the green space that stretched for some distance on the other side of the road. 'Your dad's place is the other side of that. Maybe tomorrow, I can take you for a walk over there. Help clear your head. All the bluebells are out at the moment and it's very pretty. I think you'd like it.'

'That would be nice,' she agreed, saying nothing when he reached across and placed his hand over hers on the gearstick. It was warm and comforting.

'Slow down,' he instructed after a few moments. 'Turn in here, just past the post box.'

Emily did as told, pulling onto a gravel driveway surrounded by a high hedgerow.

She double blinked at the house – a generous mock-Tudor build that was nothing like what she had been expecting. Somehow, she had Connor pegged for something smaller and closer to the town centre. A terrace house or maybe even a flat. This house looked too big for just one person.

'You live here?'

'I inherited it after my mum died.'

'It's huge.'

'Wait until you see inside.'

She followed Connor into the house, the polished wooden floors and high-gloss, white kitchen with its opulent low-hanging lights above a huge centre table distracting her briefly from everything that was going on. The place certainly had a sleek look about it, and although she wasn't an expert, the fittings and furniture looked expensive.

He insisted on giving her a tour, showing her the marble fireplace and leather sofas in the lounge, the mantle filled with photos of an older, attractive woman who Emily guessed was Connor's mum. He was in a couple of the photos with her, but there was no sign of a father figure anywhere. He had never said much about his dad, other than he had passed away, and Emily wondered if the pair of them had been estranged.

'Your parents had a lovely home,' she commented, subtly fishing.

She watched his expression instantly tighten.

'I said it was my mum's house,' he said stiffly. 'My dad didn't live here.'

She had said the wrong thing, she realised. 'I'm sorry,' she murmured, wanting to fill the silence.

'It's okay,' Connor told her after a moment. 'Come on.' His tone was suddenly all business like. Keen to move on. 'Let me show you the rest of the house.'

Emily followed him into a large conservatory that overlooked a low-maintenance garden, mostly patioed and filled with planters, though the majority of them were empty. Upstairs, there were four bedrooms, though only two were used to sleep in. One room was set up as an office with a big, oak desk, on which stood two large monitor screens and a MacBook, while his mum, he told her, had converted the smallest bedroom into a walk-in closet with a bank of mirrored wardrobes.

Although he didn't take her into his room, Emily caught a glimpse of a large bed with an imposing leather headboard as they crossed the wide landing to the room she would be staying in.

This one was simple and understated, with plain walls and white bedding, though the attached bathroom had an enormous, walk-in shower.

'This place is amazing.'

He shrugged, his earlier brusqueness having softened. 'My mum liked nice things. I haven't liked to change it much since she died.'

Emily could see that. The house certainly had a feminine touch, with floral feature walls and the kind of accessories more likely to be purchased by a woman. Patterned cushions, pretty vases and decorative mirrors. The only room that seemed to suit Connor was the basement, which he had converted into a home gym.

'Do you have bags in the car?' Connor asked as she stood there clenching her hands together, still a little uncomfortable with being here. The whole day had a surreal feel about it and she really hadn't expected it to end up here. Her dad had just died and she should be at home, but Max had made that impossible.

'I didn't bring any.' She forced a smile. 'I kind of fled after I caught them.'

Connor's eyes widened. 'That happened today?'

Emily nodded. 'I think they were expecting me to be away for longer, but obviously there was no need for me to stay after...' She trailed off, not needing to explain the reason why she had gone home early.

'Oh, Emily. No wonder you're devastated.'

He looked so upset on her behalf, his eyes filled with compassion, and his reaction helped her relax a little.

Perhaps coming here was the right thing to do after all. Cooped up in her dad's house with all of his memories wasn't the best idea, not just after he had died.

'Let me find you some spare clothes. I know they will be too big, but I have a couple of jumpers and some joggers that should be comfortable.'

'Thank you,' she told him appreciatively, following him back to the closet room.

He slid open a door and she saw it was mostly filled with dresses, shoes and handbags. He obviously still had all of his mum's things. Had he found it too painful to pack them up?

One small section was filled with Connor-type clothes and he carefully picked out a few items.

'Here you go,' he said, handing her a pair of grey joggers, an army-green T-shirt and a navy sweatshirt. 'Do you want some socks too?'

'Please.' Even though her socks had dried from where she had earlier stepped in the puddle, it would be good to have something clean to put on her feet.

She kept her own jeans and T-shirt on for now, just changing the socks. They were a little big for her, but at least they were warm. The T-shirt would be good for sleeping in, she decided, a little uncomfortable at the idea of being naked in his house.

'I think, all things considered, you deserve a drink after the day you've had,' Connor told her, leading the way back downstairs.

'That would be nice. Thanks.' Just the one to help her relax a bit and hopefully turn the slideshow off in her head for a little while. She had drank the whisky back at her dad's, and although that was a while ago, she was in an unfamiliar house and would rather keep her faculties about her.

'And are you hungry? I have leftover Chinese I can heat up. Or we can order a takeaway if you prefer.'

Truthfully, despite not eating since breakfast, Emily had no appetite. She supposed she should try to eat something, though.

'I'm happy with the leftover Chinese.'

She followed him into the kitchen, noting as he reached into cupboards and drawers that he didn't like clutter. The gloss worktop was bare apart from a coffee machine, its surface gleaming. It was a world away from her tiny, oak kitchen back in Leeds. There, everything was a bit of a mishmash. She had plants on the windowsill and her Emma Bridgewater storage jars on display. And there were the colourful magnetic letters Max had stuck on the fridge that he often used to leave her messages. Sometimes they were boring like 'need milk', but other times he used them to tell her he loved her.

The thought of the stupid magnets had her eyes filling again and Emily bit into her lip, willing them to stop. She didn't want to spend all evening in tears.

'Are you okay, Emily?' Connor was looking at her in concern.

She nodded, trying to think of something else to say, anything they could talk about that didn't involve Max or her dad.

'It's okay, I get it,' Connor told her, his voice soft. 'It's the little moments. They sneak up on you.' When she nodded again, he refocused on getting her a drink. 'Is red wine all right? I know you said you like white, but I don't have any in the fridge.'

'Red's fine. Thank you.'

He plucked a bottle from a wine rack built into the units, a Malbec she had never tried before. 'Is this okay?'

When she nodded again, he used a fancy-looking corkscrew to open it before taking two glasses from a wall cabinet, filling them halfway and handing her one.

'Let's raise a toast to your dad, shall we?'

Emily nodded. If there was any comfort to be had, it was knowing her dad was no longer in any pain.

'To Simon. I wish I'd had the opportunity to get to know you better,' Connor said. 'I liked you a lot. And thank you for the chance to meet your beautiful daughter.'

Emily blushed, a little uncomfortable with the comment.

She realised he was watching her and waiting for her to say something in toast too. Feeling a little self-conscious, she raised her glass again. 'I'm going to miss you, Dad. I love you.'

She took a large gulp of the wine, wanting the alcohol to hurry up and relax her.

'Right, food. Why don't you take your glass through to the living room. I'll put some music on.'

'Okay.'

As Emily made her way down the hall, a chilled R&B tune piped out of a speaker.

More than one speaker, she realised, walking into the lounge, the volume low, but now surrounding her.

She took a seat on one of the sofas, sinking back into the soft leather, and again was reminded of the stark contrast between this house and her own home. Which made her thoughts turn once more to Max.

Was he driving around looking for her? And what about Scout? Did she wonder where Emily had gone?

She had finished the wine by the time Connor brought the food through and, although she had wanted to stick to the one drink, didn't protest when he insisted on topping up her glass. After the hell of a day she had experienced, she deserved to relax a little.

While they ate, Connor kept the conversation light and for that, Emily was grateful.

She had little appetite and picked at her noodles, surprised with how quickly her second glass of wine was disappearing. Between them, they had already gone through a bottle.

'I'll go get some more wine,' he told her, getting up.

'No, it's okay. I shouldn't really drink any more.'

'Emily, I think of all the days, this is one where you deserve to switch off a little.' Connor's tone was firm and her willpower was waning. 'I won't let you get drunk, I promise.'

She nodded. 'Okay.'

Her thoughts returned to Max while she waited for the second bottle. Would he consider that she had come to Scarborough? Even if he did drive here looking for her, he wasn't going to find her at her dad's house. He had no idea she was here. No one did.

But that was okay. She trusted Connor. They were friends.

And it was good that Max couldn't find her. She couldn't face dealing with him. At least not tonight.

Remembering her phone needed charging, she asked Connor if he had one she could borrow when he returned to the room.

'You've got an iPhone, right?'

'Yes.'

He nodded, topping up her glass with the new bottle. She noticed it was much fuller this time. 'Not a problem.' He sat down on the sofa beside her, apparently not in any rush to get it. 'I'll go fetch it in a bit.'

Emily sipped at her drink, spotting that he had barely topped up his own glass. She ordered herself to relax. Her world had fallen apart today and she deserved a night off. Connor knew that and he was probably being the sensible sober one, so he could keep an eye on her.

She rolled her shoulders, trying to ease the tension in them.

'Here, let me help you.'

When he inched closer, placing his hands on her shoulders, her eyes widened.

'Relax, Emily. You're full of knots. Let me help you. Here, turn around.'

At first, she hesitated, but then he slowly kneaded his warm fingers, catching one of the spots where she was aching most and it felt so good she yielded, letting him guide her so her back was facing him.

It felt wrong, but also so good as he worked magic on her shoulders. Usually, it was Max who gave her a massage, working out the tension when she'd had a bad day at work, and she couldn't help feeling guilty, even though she owed Max nothing.

She sipped at her wine, not realising she had almost finished the drink. They were wide glasses and it was deceiving how much they could hold. Glancing at the bottle on the table, she was shocked it was nearly empty. It was hardly surprising she could feel the warm buzz of the alcohol now heating her up inside. She needed to slow down, aware that pleasantly tipsy could soon turn to drunk.

'You're so beautiful, Emily. I hope you know that.'

When she didn't respond because she wasn't quite sure what to say, Connor leant in close and whispered in her ear. 'Max doesn't deserve you.'

No, he didn't, and her eyes filled with the reminder.

'You need someone who is going to take care of you and put you first.'

He was nuzzling against her neck now and she couldn't help but ease back against him.

'Relax, baby.'

His hands moved from her shoulders and under her arms, fingers skimming down her sides and she felt him moving closer so she was nestled against him. Hands now on her hips, he adjusted her position, twisting her slightly so he could see her face, his mouth closing over hers and kissing her greedily.

For a moment, Emily let it happen. Maybe she needed this. A night of meaningless sex with a good-looking man. She had never done the whole one-night stand thing. Perhaps it was time she gave it a go. But as Connor deepened the kiss, his tongue snaking into her mouth, and his hand slipping inside her top, rationality kicked in.

This was wrong. They were just friends and she didn't want or need this now. Her head wasn't in the right place and she couldn't trust her emotions after everything she had been through today.

She pulled away sharply, the last of the wine sloshing in the glass she was still holding and wobbling unsteadily as she got to her feet.

This was a bad idea; she should go.

'Connor. I can't do this.'

'Why not?' He was on his feet now too and she could see the hurt in his eyes. 'I love you, Emily.'

What?

'No you don't. You can't. We've only known each other for a few weeks.'

Now anger flashed across his face. 'I knew the moment I saw you. When I walked into your dad's room at the hospice.'

He was being ridiculous. It was the wine talking.

Except, he sounded perfectly sober. Emily was the one slurring her words.

'You can't go back to him. Not after what he's done. I can treat you better.'

'I'm not going to go back to Max. But this... we're just friends, Connor. I need you to be my friend. Especially tonight.'

He looked sulky and upset, and she realised she had made a terrible mistake in leading him on.

'I should go.'

'No.' His tone was insistent. 'You can't be alone tonight.'

'I have to. I'm so sorry. I should never have come here. I didn't mean to give you the wrong idea.'

'Don't be sorry. I want you here. Emily, please don't go.' He was pleading with her now, begging her to stay. 'I'm sorry. I thought this was what you wanted.' He held his hands up. 'Please stay. I promise, just as friends.'

It wasn't a good idea, but to get back to her dad's, she would need to call a cab. She was too drunk to drive. And she was so tired.

'Look, I made a mistake. I crossed a line and I shouldn't have. Please stay.'

He looked so contrite and Emily believed him. This was her fault. She had been the one giving him mixed signals. He had only reacted to them. It would be easier if she stayed, though. It wasn't as if they would be sleeping in the same room, and now she had set out boundaries. Made it clear what their relationship was.

'Okay,' she relented, watching his face light up again.

'You won't regret it.'

He picked up the wine bottle, went to tip the rest in her glass.

'No, I don't think I should drink any more.' She stifled a yawn. 'In fact, I should probably try to get some sleep.'

'Come on. I don't want to end the night on a bad note. Have one more drink with me before you go to bed. It doesn't have to be wine. I have spirits if you prefer. In fact, how about a cocktail? I make a wicked porn star martini.'

Emily wavered. She really was tired, but he was right; she didn't want the night to end awkwardly either. 'Okay, but just the one and can you go easy on the alcohol, please? This wine has really gone to my head.'

'Okay, I promise.' He grinned, heading for the door. 'Sit back down, relax and I'll be back in five minutes.'

Emily did as he asked, resting her head back and closing her eyes.

She must have drifted off because when she opened them again, he was back in the room and handing her the drink.

She really didn't want it. Eager now just to go to bed, but he had gone to the effort of making it and it looked amazing.

Connor held up her glass and toasted her. 'To us and to friendship,' he said, sounding far too sober. Why wasn't the alcohol affecting him?

She took a sip, at first finding the passionfruit refreshing, but after she had managed half the glass, it started to become sickly and she could taste the strength of the alcohol.

What happened to making her a weak cocktail?

He was chatting away about something and she found she was struggling to focus on his words. She needed to quickly finish the drink so she could go to bed.

She downed the rest of it and went to get up, but the room was spinning fast and she almost dropped the glass as she attempted to put it on the coffee table.

'Steady up. Are you okay, Emily?' Connor sounded concerned as he caught her, easing her back on the sofa.

'I need to go to bed.'

She tried to get up a second time, finding the simple task too difficult. Was she really that drunk?

'Here, I'll help you.'

No, that wasn't a good idea. After what had happened earlier, she didn't want to give him the wrong idea again.

She started to protest, but he had his arm around her and the floor seemed so far away. She wasn't sure if she could make it up the stairs without his assistance.

He was helping her towards the living-room door now and she couldn't feel her feet. It was like she was dreaming the moment and wasn't really in the room, her anxiety spiralling out of control. Why was the alcohol making her feel so bad? Yes, she had drank a fair bit, but it wasn't the first time.

She had no recollection of getting up the stairs, but suddenly she was in bed, the ceiling spinning above her. She didn't like this. Where was Connor?

As though conjuring him up, his face came into focus.

'Don't leave me. Please.'

'I'm right here, Emily.'

He was undressing her, she realised. Peeling off the socks she had borrowed and unbuttoning her jeans.

'What are you...' She couldn't finish the sentence. Could barely remember what it was she wanted to say.

Connor leaned in close, pressing his lips to hers. 'Shh. You're going to enjoy this, I promise. You just lay there and let me take care of...'

Emily didn't hear the rest of the sentence. The darkness pulling her under.

22

When she first awoke, Emily couldn't figure out where the hell she was.

Her limbs were heavy and her head thumped when she tried to open her eyes. The room was dark, so it must still be the middle of the night.

Gradually, everything came back to her. Her dad dying, seeing Max kissing Leah, Connor taking her home, and she winced at the fresh stab of pain those memories brought.

The last thing she remembered was Connor helping her to bed. She had drank too much wine and then he had made her the cocktail. That's right. A porn star martini. The drink that had tipped her over the edge. She had been just the wrong side of tipsy on the wine, but the cocktail must have been strong because she had vague memories of the room spinning and then of being in bed as he helped her undress.

Shit, not properly undress though. Just down to her underwear, right?

She reached beneath the duvet, expecting – no, hoping – to

find she still had her bra and knickers on, maybe her T-shirt too, and letting out a tiny whimper when she realised she was naked.

He had taken off all of her clothes.

Why would he do that? She had made it clear she just wanted to be friends.

But he had kissed her again.

Her memory was patchy of getting up the stairs and into bed, but then it was a complete blank. Had she changed her mind at some point?

No, she was pretty sure she'd blacked out after he'd kissed her.

Her head was thumping as she tried to sit up, panicked about what had happened and the fact she couldn't remember, and she had to wait a moment for the feeling of nausea to pass. She had never been drunk like this before and losing complete control had been scary.

As Emily glanced round the dark room, it occurred to her that she wasn't in the guest bedroom. She was in Connor's bed. And as if to remind her he was there, he rolled onto his back beside her and let out a snore.

Why had he put her in his bed?

This wasn't right.

Her senses were gradually coming back and she realised her breasts were tender. And was that stickiness between her legs?

Had they had sex?

How could that happen and she not realise?

Her heart was drumming now, wondering what the hell had happened in the missing blank period of her mind.

She hadn't consented to this... had she?

You're going to enjoy this.

He had said that to her. One of the last things she remembered before blacking out.

Oh God. How had she let this happen? She had promised herself she wouldn't have much to drink, but Connor had insisted on continually topping up her glass.

And he had promised her. He had said he would look after her. That he wouldn't let her get drunk. He had lied. But then he had also promised that she could stay here as a friend, that nothing would happen between them.

How could they have had sex and she not remember?

She hadn't wanted this. Why the hell hadn't she stopped drinking?

It made her sick to her stomach that he had betrayed her trust, but also a nagging little voice kept chirping away in her head.

You fancied him.

You led him on.

You could have stopped drinking.

Was she also partly to blame?

It was all too much to deal with and she just wanted now to get out of the house. She couldn't stay. Not after this.

She was careful as she climbed out of bed, having to steady herself as her vision blurred and her legs wobbled, and also conscious that she didn't want to wake him.

Everything was fuzzy as she staggered around, gathering what she could find of her clothes. Her knickers were balled up on the floor along with her bra, and her jeans and T-shirt flung over a chair. She snagged everything up, then crossed the landing to the guest bedroom to get dressed.

Now she was up, she knew she had definitely had sex. She was sticky and a little sore and there were love bites on her breasts.

How the hell could she not remember any of it?

She had been really drunk before, but never to the extent that she couldn't remember having intercourse.

Intimacy had fallen by the wayside in her relationship with Max. It was something they had always made such an effort with, but lately with everything going on with Emily's dad, neither of them had bothered with sex. Perhaps it should have struck her as odd that Max had lost interest. Maybe then she would have seen the signs with Leah, and not ended up in this situation.

Damn it. She never wanted to have sex with Connor. Why would he have thought this was okay?

As soon as she was dressed, Emily found her boots and handbag, making sure her phone was inside, then crept back out onto the landing, glancing briefly into Connor's room to check he wasn't awake. He was still snoring away, and relieved she didn't have to face having a conversation with him, she snuck downstairs and let herself out of the front door.

She was still a little wobbly on her feet and suspected she might still be over the limit to drive, but she would have to take a chance. She couldn't stay here for a minute longer.

Luckily, she remembered the way back to her dad's, breathing a sigh of relief when she pulled up outside his house. His street was quiet and empty, all of the residents asleep, but although the place was dark with no light on to welcome her, she was glad to be back there.

She let herself inside, bolting the door and going upstairs to shower, scrubbing at her skin, desperate to feel clean again. It was all too much for her to process and exhausted both physically and mentally, she sank to the floor of the bath, hugging her knees to her as she sat under the hot spray. Feeling broken, she started to sob.

Her father was dead. Her boyfriend had cheated on her. And she had just had sex – though she couldn't remember any of it –

with a man she had thought was her friend. Who she had thought she could trust. Never had she felt so low or vulnerable.

How would Connor react when he realised she was gone? Would he track her down? Her car was outside, so he would know she was here.

She couldn't see him. Not after what had happened. The idea of coming face to face with him made her nauseous.

Perhaps she wasn't blameless, and yes, the last few hours were a blank, but what he had done was wrong, taking advantage of her on the night of her father's death.

The front door was locked. She was so tired and still a little disorientated, but she sure she had locked it after coming inside. He wouldn't be able to get into the house. Would he?

23

Emily lost track of time. After she had eventually crawled out of the shower and dressed, she had gone downstairs, sitting on her dad's sofa, the television on, but struggling to focus on the shows playing as she tried to make sense of the last twenty-four hours.

She still hadn't switched on her phone, aware the battery was low, so had no idea if Max was still trying to reach her.

And why couldn't she remember having sex with Connor? She must have had such a bad reaction to the wine. She didn't often get drunk, but she had never blacked out like this. She was so mad at him. He knew she wanted to keep their relationship platonic. How dare he do this to her? He had abused her trust.

When the doorbell rang, she pulled the blankets she had cocooned herself in tightly around her.

It was going to be Connor, she knew it, and she couldn't face him. Couldn't stand the idea of even looking at him. He needed to go away.

She stayed where she was, waiting for him to give up and leave. Willing him to stop pressing the bloody bell. He had to understand he couldn't talk his way back from this. He had betrayed her in the worst possible way, and she refused to open the door to him.

A few moments later, she heard the letterbox open.

'Emily? I know you're in there.'

Max?

She didn't want to see him either, but her anger at Max was different. She was so mad at how he had let her down. How he wasn't the man she had believed him to be.

'Go away!' she yelled back.

'Not until we talk.'

'I have nothing to say to you. Leave me alone.'

'I've been to the hospice, Em. I know about your dad.' There was a pause. 'I'm not going anywhere. I'll wait here all day if I have to.'

Stubborn bloody man. She didn't want to see him. Not after what he had done.

He wasn't Connor, though, and she wasn't afraid of Max. Just angry. That's why she eventually got off the sofa, fed up with his constant ringing of the bell, ready to give him a piece of her mind.

Pulling open the door, she wasn't prepared for the way her heart hitched. She hadn't realised it was raining and he was soaked through. His hair plastered to his head.

Still, she wasn't going to feel sorry for him. Not after what he had done.

'Emily. I'm so sorry.'

'Go home, Max. I'm not interested.'

'I'm not going anywhere until you hear me out.'

She was already trying to slam the door shut in his face, annoyed when he pushed back, forcing it open again, then followed her into the house when she turned to get away from him. He was alone, which had her wondering where Scout was. Though she didn't ask.

'Go away! I don't want to see you.'

'Emily. Don't do this.'

'I have nothing to say to you. Leave me alone.'

She fought hard to make him go, but he was digging his heels in, and eventually, worn down from fighting with him, she collapsed back onto the sofa, wrapping herself back up in her blanket fort and, childish as it was, literally burying her head inside the cocoon so she didn't have to look at him.

She hoped that might make him leave and was hopeful he had when she heard the front door shut, but, then moments later, she felt the sofa dip beside her and heard his intake of breath before he spoke.

'I know you're not going to believe me, but nothing is going on with Leah.'

Liar!

Emily muttered the word internally, determined not to give him an audience.

'She kissed me, Em. I swear it caught me off guard.'

When he didn't get any reaction, Max continued.

'I'm not blameless. I've guessed for a while she likes me and I'm not going to lie, it stroked my ego. I know that makes me sound like a real prize dickhead, because I have you and I love you to bits. Okay, had you. But I didn't think through the consequences and I'm really sorry.'

So that was it? Max had shifted responsibility onto Leah, who, in fairness, was just as guilty. Did he really expect Emily to believe his bullshit?

'I shouldn't have encouraged her, but I swear I had no idea she was going to try to take it further. I thought it was just a flirtation thing. Stupid, I know. One moment we were talking, the next she was kissing me. I tried to push her away.'

Emily recalled the scene she had walked in on. Max with his back to the counter, Leah leaning into him. She remembered how he had hold of Leah's arms and had assumed it was to steady her as she reached up on tiptoe for the kiss. Was it possible she had got that detail wrong? Had Max been trying to push her away?

No!

She mentally kicked herself for being drawn in. That one little detail did not absolve him of guilt.

'I'm not interested in Leah, Em. Not like that. I never have been. Regardless of what happens next with you and me, I've already told her I can't see her again. She wasn't happy about it, but you're too important to me. I'm so sorry I screwed up and that I hurt you. I will do anything to fix it if you let me.'

He tapped at the duvet and Emily flinched.

'I know you're listening and I get that you're mad. I also get that the timing is really shitty too after what happened yesterday. I'm really sorry about your dad and that I haven't been there for you as much as I should. I've been a selfish prick and I should know better.'

He fell silent, though remained seated beside her. Damn him.

It was so bloody hot under this duvet and what air there was to breathe was musty. It was getting uncomfortable.

Still, she remained where she was as she tried to process everything he had said, wondering if there was any truth in it.

She had never been cheated on before and had been one of those girls who had defiantly claimed they would never put up with being treated that way.

It wasn't so black and white, she realised, when you were in the relationship.

The times she had shared with Max had been mostly good

and, despite what she may or may not have witnessed yesterday, she knew he loved her. These last few weeks with her dad had been so difficult, but she had to shoulder some responsibility and knew that she had pushed him away.

And what about Connor and last night? He might have abused her trust and she might not remember anything about what he had done to her, but she had kissed him and led him on a little. If Max knew what had happened, would he still want her back?

The strong, determined woman inside her didn't want to forgive his indiscretions, but she was desperately lonely and vulnerable right now, and she needed someone to lean on.

Her head broke through the duvet cocoon and she angled a wary look in his direction.

'Where's Scout?' she demanded, changing the subject to buy herself time. 'Have you left her home alone?'

'No. She's with my dad.'

When she fell silent again, he added, 'I love you, Emily.'

He looked earnest and worried, the stress lines around his red-rimmed eyes and bags underneath them suggesting he had been upset and likely hadn't slept.

'I hate you.'

The words were harsh, but she spoke them without conviction.

Max nodded, his expression solemn. 'I know you do. But if you give me another chance, I promise I will spend the rest of my life trying to make it up to you.'

* * *

In the first few days after leaving Scarborough, Emily tried to pick up the pieces of her life, wondering how she was supposed to move on.

There were moments where she worried if she had made a huge mistake in taking Max back. If he was lying and it hadn't been all Leah's fault, he was going to believe he could cheat again in the future and get away with it. She didn't want to be that gullible girl who continually fell for her boyfriend's lies.

And she heard nothing from Connor, which both surprised and relieved her. She didn't want to see him ever again and wished she could just forget he existed.

She was still trying to process everything that had happened at his house, and while she was mad at him for how he had taken advantage of her, she was also annoyed with herself. She hadn't told anyone about that night because she was too ashamed that she had been tricked, believing that he would look after her.

She had gone through a huge range of emotions in the aftermath, having moments where she felt vulnerable, weak and worthless, blaming herself for being such a fool and trusting him, then becoming angry and enraged, hating him for what he had done.

Plus, on top of that, she was dealing with the loss of her dad.

Max put her tears and her withdrawn behaviour, as well as her reluctance to get intimate, down to grief, and for the latter, she was grateful. It was something she was going to have to deal with and overcome, but right now it was too soon. She felt violated and used. She also didn't want him seeing her naked until the bite marks on her breasts had healed.

He hadn't spoken to his mum in years after her affair behind his dad's back. How would he react if he knew about the night at Connor's house?

Max was insistent that nothing else had ever happened with

Leah and that the one kiss had been instigated by her, completely catching him off guard. Meanwhile, Emily had kissed Connor twice and then had sex with him. Even though it hadn't been consensual and she remembered nothing about it, she had still gone to his house willingly and had been foolish enough to trust him, letting him get her drunk.

Would Max forgive her if he knew the truth?

She decided he could never find out.

24

WEDNESDAY

Emily's heart was racing.

Realising they might have been followed to Norfolk had a chill slithering down her spine, taking her right back to that night at Connor's house.

As the months had crept by, she had started to believe the nightmare was over, but now everything was escalating again and she knew that if she didn't tell Max about Connor, he might find out the truth another way.

He was already annoyed with her and she understood he was frustrated by the lack of answers she was giving him. But mostly he seemed hurt that she hadn't confided in him.

It made her even more fearful for when he did find out what had happened. She had kept him in the dark because she was scared he would blame her, but had she made a terrible mistake? Because, right now, she couldn't see a way forward where he didn't discover the truth, and knowing she had hidden everything from him, as well as learning what Connor had done, was going to be so much worse.

She knew how angry he was already because he had left her alone in a place he knew she feared.

Emily had locked the door after him, but as the hours ticked by, apprehension began to gnaw at her gut.

He was coming back, right? All of his things were here. He wouldn't just leave her.

She hadn't seen him grab his car keys or heard the engine, but she went to the window to check anyway, relieved when she spotted his Audi was still parked outside.

By the time dusk settled, her belly was skittish with nerves. She was jumping at every little sound, but also sick with worry about Max.

She switched the porch light on for him, but where was he? Fight or no fight, he should still be back by now. She had tried to call him a handful of times, but it had gone straight to voicemail, suggesting that he had switched his phone off.

What if he was hurt or worse?

She contemplated calling the police again, but knew if she did that the truth really would come out. Instead, she waited, figuring she would give him until it was completely dark, hoping she wouldn't be forced down that route.

Making a cup of tea, because it was something to do, not because she particularly fancied it, she took her mug over to the sofas, looking out of the window across the river. There was a low mist clinging to the surface of the water and there was just enough light left that she could see it swirling around the jetty on the opposite bank. It made the abandoned cottage behind it look spookier than normal.

She hated that the cottage overlooked the boat house and could see right into their window, especially remembering the backpack they had found with the mask.

What if whoever it belonged to was watching her across the water right now?

A little unnerved by her train of thought, she switched the living-room and kitchen lights off, leaving just a table lamp on. Although it made the boat house much darker, the lamp still gave off a comforting, warm glow.

Going back over to the window, she now had a clearer view across the water and could just about make out the windows of the cottage. There were no lights on inside and she doubted there had been any electricity in the place for a good few years.

As she stood watching, she realised there was a figure standing in the doorway. At first, she hadn't noticed them because they were dressed in dark colours and had been standing still, but now she could see they were stepping out onto the jetty and moving closer towards her.

Was it possible it was Connor? Had he been watching her in the boat house before she turned the lights out?

She was processing that unwanted piece of information when the person turned and walked back towards the cottage.

Emily glanced at her watch and saw it was almost 5 p.m.

She decided she would give Max thirty more minutes. If he wasn't back by then, she was going to call the police.

25

BEFORE

It was one week to the day when Connor made contact again. A warm Saturday just ten days before her dad's funeral. Max had been up first, out on one of his early-morning walks with Scout and by the time Emily surfaced, he was back in the kitchen, cooking breakfast. As she ambled down the stairs, still in her dressing gown, making her way into the kitchen, he turned and smiled at her.

'You hungry?'

'A little,' she replied.

She had been struggling to eat in the aftermath of everything that had happened, picking at the food Max had put in front of her, insisting she needed to keep up her strength. Gradually, though, her appetite was returning.

She sat down at the table, sipping at the coffee he made her and opening a WhatsApp message on her phone from Francesca, asking how she was and saying she would stop by on Sunday afternoon.

As Emily typed a reply, half listening to Max as he mentioned the band Stereophonics, who were coming to Leeds later in the year, her phone buzzed with another incoming message.

Max's words became a whir of sound in her head as she realised who the new message was from.

Connor.

It was just two words and she didn't need to open the message to read them.

You okay?

Everything inside of her went cold and she was glad she was sitting down.

Why was he messaging her? Hadn't he already done enough damage?

She had half expected him to turn up at her dad's house in Scarborough the morning after and she had been scared every time she heard a noise.

Even after Max had shown up, she had been on tenterhooks in case Connor made an appearance, grateful when he didn't, and with each passing day, she had grown a little more hopeful that he was out of her life for good.

'So what do you think?' Max asked, his attention on the two plates he was loading up with food.

'Huh?'

'Shall I try to get us tickets?'

'Um, okay.'

She read the two words from Connor again. Did he really expect her to reply? He was acting as if nothing had happened. Did he have no idea what he had put her through?

The idea of having any kind of contact with him made her feel sick.

Max set the plate of scrambled eggs on toast down in front of her and despite the smell that was wafting up into her nostrils, Emily wondered how the hell she was going to eat it. Her appetite had completely vanished and she was aware of panic bubbling in her gut. Her skin was hot and clammy and as she forced the eggs into her mouth, she thought for a moment that she was going to throw them back up.

At least Max didn't seem to notice that he was almost single-handedly keeping the conversation going. Emily managing the occasional 'hmm' or 'yes', even though she could barely focus on what he was saying.

He wanted to go out for the day, take Scout up to the Yorkshire Dales, but she feigned a headache.

'Getting out of the house for some fresh air might help,' he gently pointed out.

'Or it might not,' she reasoned back. 'Why don't you and Scout just go.' She found a weak smile for him. 'I'll stay here and try to get some sleep. It might help shift it.'

Max seemed disappointed, though eventually agreed. He had been so good with her this past week, and patient too given how withdrawn she had been.

Finally alone, Emily curled up on the sofa and stewed over the message.

How could two words manage to upset her so badly?

Connor needed to stay away from her, but she couldn't bring herself to open the message and reply to him. She didn't want any kind of contact with him at all.

Eventually, she dozed off, but she hadn't been asleep long when her phone vibrating loudly on the coffee table woke her up.

She reached for it, her stomach knotting as she realised it was another message from him. Pulling down the top of her screen, she was again able to read the text without opening it.

Why are you ignoring me? I know you were on WhatsApp earlier when I messaged you. I could see the time you were active.

Shit.

When she didn't respond, this time scared to even open the app, the messages continued.

You never said goodbye.
Have I done something to upset you? Xx

Was he kidding? He knew exactly what he had done. She wasn't going to spell it out for him. He needed to leave her alone.

Emily, please talk to me.

That was it. She was blocking him. How dare he contact her like this, pretending nothing was wrong? She opened her settings and selected his number, blocking him first on WhatsApp and then on her phone. That was it. He was gone. Something she should have done as soon as she had received the first message. Wanting to wipe all trace of him, she went back into the message trail and deleted it.

Knowing he couldn't contact her gave her back a little bit of control, and although she was still jumpy, she was already trying to put the messages behind her by the time Max and Scout returned.

'Do you fancy eating out tonight?' he asked, hanging up Scout's lead before filling her dish with fresh biscuits.

He was determined to try to get her out and about, convinced that it wasn't healthy for her sitting around indoors.

Emily felt it was still too soon, though. What had happened at Connor's house had preoccupied her and she still hadn't really had a chance to process her dad's death. She was going back to work on Monday having had a week of compassionate leave, and that would be enough social interaction for her at the moment.

She agreed to compromise, though. If they stayed in tonight, she would go out somewhere with him and Scout in the morning. And she made more of an effort that night, helping Max with the cooking and trying to hold up her end of the conversation as they ate, doing her best to push Connor's messages to the back of her mind. He was blocked and could no longer contact her. It was time to try and put what had happened behind her and find a way to move on.

* * *

The following morning, they went out on a hike. Max was right; the fresh air did help, and Scout was in her element, sniffing at everything and working off some of her energy. It almost felt like they were back to how things had been in the early part of their relationship and for an hour or two, Emily's mood was lifted. She started to believe that with time and work, they could find a way forward and put Leah and Connor behind them.

On the way back to the car, they stopped at a little café for tea and cake. As Emily took Scout and found a table, sitting down to wait while Max queued at the counter, she reached for her phone, frowning when she realised she had a slew of text messages from a number she didn't recognise. Opening the message trail up, her eyes widened in horror.

I can't believe you blocked me.
Why are you doing this to me, Emily?
It's because of him, isn't it? I saw you with him at your dad's house.

After you snuck off, I came to find you. You promised you wouldn't take him back.
Does he know about us?

'You okay?'

Emily jumped, not realising Max was on his way over to the table, carrying a tray.

'You look white as a sheet.'

'I'm fine,' she lied, hurriedly slipping her phone back into her bag. She had actually been quite hungry after the long walk, but her appetite vanished. How was she going to manage to eat the generous slice of red velvet cake Max had placed down before her?

Still, she picked up her fork and gamely attempted, the cream cheese frosting, which she would normally enjoy, only making her feel sick. She had blocked Connor and thought she was rid of him. Why was he doing this to her?

She was quiet on the ride back, but Max didn't seem suspicious, and when he referenced the upcoming funeral, seeking to reassure her that he would be there with her, helping her to get through it, she realised he thought that was what she was worrying about.

Once home, he disappeared outside to wash the cars and Emily went upstairs to the sanctuary of their bedroom, sitting on the bed and steadying herself before she opened the message trail again.

She didn't want to have any contact with Connor, but it was clear he wasn't going to leave her alone, and she didn't like how his messages had turned a little aggressive in tone.

The *after you snuck off* comment rankled her. How dare he say that? Especially after what he had done to her.

One message. She would keep it to the point.

Although she took her time, wanting to find the right words that would convince him to leave her alone, she kept her message brief.

I don't want to see you again. Not after what you did to me. Please leave me alone.

She pressed send, hoping he would read it and take the hint.

Unfortunately, it was wishful thinking and a message pinged back within seconds.

What I did to you? What are you on about? I enjoyed our night together. I thought you did too.

Was he insane?

Despite her intention to only send the one message, he had riled her.

How could I enjoy it? I was passed out. I told you I only wanted to be friends. You took advantage of me and abused my trust.

Connor's next message pinged through.

Don't lie. You wanted it as badly as I did.

No, she hadn't. Why would he say that? Had he lost his mind?

Leave me alone! I never want to hear from you again.

Emily stared at her phone screen, waiting to see if he replied again. Several minutes ticked by and she wondered if he had finally got the hint.

A little of the tension eased out of her shoulders, though his messages still had her nerves on edge.

She was about to block his new number when her phone pinged again.

This time, she could see there was an attachment.

She read his words first.

I wonder if I should send Max this.

Dread knotted in her belly and she had to steady herself before opening the attached file.

It was a picture and when she realised what it was, her hand went to her mouth in shock.

The image was a selfie taken by Connor. In his bed with his arm around Emily, both of them naked. Her eyes were shut and she knew it was because she had been unconscious. But to anyone else viewing the photo, they would think she was just asleep.

Nausea returned, clawing its way up her throat, and for a moment, she thought she was going to be sick.

He wouldn't send it to Max. He was bluffing. For starters, he didn't even have Max's number.

Unless he had gone through Emily's phone. She had it set to unlock with touch recognition and it would have been easy enough to get her fingerprint while she was out of it.

She stared at the picture, realising how damaging it looked.

Connor had her backed into a corner and she had no idea how to react.

26

The doorbell rang and Emily almost jumped out of her skin.

Max had shouted up the stairs to say he was heading over to return some cables he had borrowed from his brother and he would be back soon. He had taken Scout with him, and alone in the house, her sole focus on the photo she had been sent, Emily for one awful moment thought it was going to be Connor.

It didn't matter that she had never given him her address. She was sure he wouldn't find it that difficult to track her down.

At first, she didn't dare move, but then, when the bell rang again, she pulled herself up from the bed and peered out of the window.

Francesca's car was parked on the driveway and her friend stepped back at that moment, glancing up at the window, her eyes meeting Emily's.

'Are you going to let me in?' she shouted.

Emily nodded, quickly heading downstairs. She had forgotten Francesca had said she was calling round and really wished she wasn't here. She wasn't up to facing anyone right now.

She opened the door to her friend, who was dressed in sunny

yellow, a colour that complemented her deep-olive skin, and who was already gushing apologies. 'Sorry I'm a bit late. I was just getting Harry settled with Adam. He does love his dad, just not as much as his mum.'

'It's fine.' Emily stepped back to let her in, and perhaps it was the fact she didn't make a joke back or her gaunt appearance – she knew she had bags under her eyes and that her hair was a mess – but Francesca's eyes were narrowing with concern.

'You're not coping well, are you?' she asked, as she followed Emily into the kitchen.

When Emily shook her head, Francesca pulled her into a hug.

'I'm so sorry I was away when your dad died.'

'You weren't to know.'

Francesca already knew that Emily had gone to her house that day, just as she was aware that Emily had caught Max and Leah together.

'Is he looking after you?' she asked. The 'he' in question being Max. Francesca had been on the fence there, wondering if Emily had forgiven him too easily.

'He's been great, to be fair. He helped me with all of the funeral arrangements this week and he's been trying to take care of everything.'

'So he should, especially after what happened.' Francesca pulled back, assessing her again as she tucked a strand of hair behind Emily's ear. 'Once the funeral is out of the way, you can take time to grieve properly and start to heal. I know you and your dad didn't have the easiest relationship, but sometimes that makes these moments more difficult. You're going to be okay though.'

It was those last words that undid her. How could she possibly be okay?

But Francesca wouldn't know that because Emily had kept

what had happened with Connor from everyone. Even her best friend.

She couldn't do it any longer, though, her face crumpling and fresh tears falling.

'Oh honey.' Francesca pulled her close again. 'I know your dad sometimes had a funny way of showing it, but he did love you a lot. He would hate to see you getting upset like this.'

'It's not my dad.'

'It's not? Is this about Max? If he's hurt you again, I'll bloody kill him.

'It's not Max,' Emily sobbed. 'Something else happened and I don't know what to do about it.'

This was when Francesca took charge. 'Okay, I'm going to put the kettle on and we're going to sit down so you can tell me exactly what's going on. Then we will figure out a way to deal with it together. Does that sound like a plan?'

Emily wiped at her eyes and nodded.

* * *

Half an hour later and Francesca knew everything, her eyes wide with shock.

'Emily, he didn't just take advantage of you. He raped you.'

There it was: the 'r' word that Emily had been so reluctant to use. Maybe because she had been attracted to Connor and she had kissed him, letting him ply her with alcohol.

She pointed out now that she hadn't been blameless, but her friend was having none of it.

'I don't care if you snogged his face off or even gave him a striptease, you made it clear that you just wanted to be friends and that you didn't want to sleep with him. And as for getting drunk, how many boozy nights have we had? You can handle your alcohol. A couple of bottles of wine and a cocktail isn't going to knock you out cold.' Francesca frowned. 'You said you had the cocktail last, right?'

'Yes. It was the drink that tipped me over the edge.'

'Did you see him make it?'

'No, I stayed in the living room.'

Francesca's tone was grave when she spoke. 'Emily. Do you think he drugged you?'

Was it possible? Emily tried to process that. She had been so convinced it was just the alcohol, but what if she was wrong? 'I don't know. I guess he could have.'

'You have nothing to feel guilty about.' Francesca reached for her hand, giving it a comforting squeeze. 'He drugged you and he raped you. And the solution is simple. We need to report it to the police.'

'I can't.' Emily's tone was panicked.

'You can't let him get away with it, Em.'

'But I can't prove anything. It's my word against his. And if Max finds out, he'll leave me.'

'Max will be horrified, just like I am. He's not going to judge you for this. Besides, Max doesn't exactly have the moral high ground here after what happened with Leah.'

'I don't want to go to the police.' Emily was crying again now. 'I can't and I won't. I have enough to deal with at the moment. I can't do this as well. I just want him to go away.'

'Okay, okay,' Francesca was backtracking, maybe because she could see how vulnerable Emily was right now. 'So no police.'

'And Max can never know. Just you.'

'He will support you.'

'You don't know him like I do. His mum cheated on his dad and he doesn't speak to her.'

'Jesus, Emily. This is completely different. You didn't cheat on him. You were raped.'

The use of the word again sent a shudder through her. 'Promise me you will never tell him.'

Francesca held her hands up. 'Okay, fine. I won't say a word. Connor has that photo, though. What are you going to do if he shows it to Max?'

This was still the sticking point. Emily had to make sure that never happened.

In the end, with Francesca's help, she decided to send another message to Connor, a strongly worded one to try to call his bluff.

Go ahead and send Max that picture. He already knows what happened that night and wants to knock your head off. You raped me and I'm pretty sure you drugged me too. If I ever hear from you again, I am going to the police.

She looked at Francesca after she composed it and when her friend nodded, she hit send.

Now she had to hope she had made the right decision.

27

Emily had no idea if her threat to go to the police had worked, but she didn't hear another word from Connor over the following days.

Francesca kept in regular contact, telling her that if he came back to Emily and refused to back off, to let her know. They would figure out a way to handle the threat together. Meanwhile, she kept dropping strong hints that it wasn't too late to go to the police or to tell Max what had happened.

Emily was steadfast, though. She just wanted Connor to go away.

Perhaps she was being cowardly and she should report him, but it had happened over a week ago. If she had been drugged, there would be no trace of it in her system now and she had gone to Connor's house voluntarily intending to spend the night, so it would end up being his word against hers. Given how highly emotional she had been that day and the fact that Connor volunteered at a hospice, a pillar of society for giving up his time to help care for the sick, there was every chance she wouldn't be believed. It just wasn't worth the risk.

Instead, she lived from day to day, fearful whenever she was in Max's company and his phone pinged. After talking things through with Francesca, she realised now that it had been rape, but that didn't make it any easier to accept. If anything, Connor became more of a monster in her eyes. He had abused her and then threatened her. She despised him, but she was also terrified.

Eventually, the day of her dad's funeral arrived and Emily sat in the crematorium holding tightly onto Max's hand, while looking straight ahead at the coffin, her brain trying to comprehend that her dad's body was inside.

She hadn't gone to the chapel of rest to see him, having said her last goodbyes that day at the hospice, and while she was happy with her decision not to, it felt surreal that this moment was finally here.

There were more people at the service than she had expected. Some she knew and others were strangers. People he had worked with or friends, she guessed. It was a reminder of how little of his life her dad had shared with her. When Aunt Cathy had died, Emily had known nearly everyone there.

Francesca and Adam had come to support her, leaving Harry with Francesca's mum, and Max's sister, Charlotte, had taken Scout for the day.

Eyes focused ahead, Emily didn't see the latecomer who slipped into a seat at the back of the crematorium just as the service was starting.

It was afterwards, when her dad's coffin had disappeared behind the curtain and it was finally over, Emily and Max heading out of a side door at the front of the building, where they could accept people's condolences, that she saw him. Her breath catching as he hovered at the back of the line.

He had shown up here at her dad's funeral. She hadn't even considered that he might do so and seeing him standing there as if nothing was wrong, stirred both anger and panic. How dare he show his face after what he had done to her?

Under different circumstances, it would have been perfectly natural. He had been a volunteer at the hospice and had spent time with her dad in his last weeks. But given everything that had happened after, his presence here was wholly inappropriate.

He wasn't going to approach her to offer his condolences, was he?

The idea of coming face to face with him, of having to look him in the eye, filled her with dread.

Or was his plan to talk to Max, to show him the photo?

Would he have the gall to do that? At her dad's funeral?

Emily knew she couldn't trust him at all. He had already proven to her that he was capable of unspeakable things.

She tried to catch Francesca's attention, but her friend was busy talking to Adam.

Although she had seen the photo of Connor and Emily, it had only been briefly. Would Francesca recognise him?

The words of the mourners as they offered their sympathies mostly went unheard. Emily was trying her best to focus, but it was difficult when she knew Connor was so close by.

'I feel unwell,' she whispered to Max, and it wasn't untrue. Nausea was churning in her belly, sweat pooling in her armpits, and she was a little unsteady on her feet. With the combination of the warm day and the trauma of the funeral, it wasn't unbelievable that it had taken its toll. 'I need to sit down. I think I'm going to pass out.'

He took one look at her and acted quickly, apologising to those waiting to give their condolences, then guiding her over to a bench and sitting her down.

'Wait here a moment. I'll go and get you some water.'

The line had dispersed now, Connor disappearing, and Emily

looked for Francesca. Her friend was viewing the floral tributes and hadn't noticed what had happened.

Emily focused on her breathing, trying to steady herself.

'That was a nice service.'

The voice came to the left of her and she glanced up in shock as Connor moved into her line of vision.

He smiled, seeming pleased to see her. 'I think Simon would have approved. Low-key and intimate.'

'What are you doing here?' she managed to squeak.

He was acting as if the text exchange hadn't happened between them. That he hadn't threatened to show Max the picture and Emily hadn't warned him she would go to the police.

'I came to pay my respects to your dad of course.' His tone was carefully neutral, giving nothing away. 'You didn't think I would miss this, did you?'

She had no idea what to say in response. Her mouth dry and she was so scared, she thought she might pass out in fright. She tried desperately to catch Francesca's eye.

Connor leaned in close and she tensed. 'You've made a big mistake, Emily. I could have given you everything. We could have been happy together.'

Was he insane? She wanted to scream at him, make him realise the trauma he had put her through, but he seemed to be in complete denial that he had even done anything wrong.

'You raped me.' She managed to get the words out. The first time she had said them aloud. Her voice was shaking badly though.

He didn't flinch at her accusation, his gaze steady on her face. 'No. I made love to you. Your word against mine.'

'Please go.' Emily couldn't cope with this. Especially not today. His presence here had her nerves in shreds. 'Please just leave me alone.'

'And miss being introduced to Max? I don't think so. I've been looking forward to meeting the man you chose over me.' Connor's tone lightened. 'Here he comes.'

Fear skittered through her as she looked up and saw Max striding towards them, a glass of water in his hand, and her heart started beating out of her chest.

She had told Connor that Max knew everything. A bluff that was now about to blow up in her face.

Max brushed past him, giving Emily the glass, but her hand was shaking so badly, water splashed everywhere. Noticing, he knelt down beside her, talking quietly. 'Take it steady, okay. You're panicking.' He placed his hand over hers on the glass and helped her take a couple of sips. 'Okay?'

Emily nodded, not trusting herself to speak, and he gave her knee a squeeze in a sign of comfort, before straightening up again.

Realising he had ignored Connor, he offered his hand. 'I'm Max Hunter, Emily's boyfriend. Did you work with Simon?'

Connor glanced briefly at Emily, a smile on his face, seeming to bask in the realisation that Max didn't know who he was, before returning the handshake. 'No, I volunteered at the hospice where he spent his last few weeks. Connor Banks. It's nice to meet you, Max. Emily's told me a lot about you.'

'She has?' Max sounded surprised as he glanced between the pair of them.

Oh God. This couldn't be happening. Emily was frozen in fear, aware there was nothing she could do except watch this moment play out.

'I spent a fair bit of time with Simon, so Emily and I got to know each other quite well,' Connor continued, his tone warm. 'It's always tough seeing a loved one reaching the end of their life. I just hope I was able to offer her a little comfort too.'

Max offered his hand again. 'Well, thanks for everything you've done. Both for Simon and for Emily. It's appreciated. It was kind of you to show up for the funeral.'

'I wouldn't have missed it.'

Emily couldn't bring herself to even look at Connor. It was enough that she caught a whiff of his aftershave. The familiar lemon and peppery cologne had been appealing when she had first met him, but now it only conjured bad memories, taking her straight back to the night at his house. It was a wonder she didn't throw up.

She was relieved when he didn't linger. Taking Max's subtle hint and wandering off to mingle with the other mourners, and luckily Max didn't dwell on his appearance, seeming more concerned about how she was feeling.

'You look really pale, Em. I think I should take you home.'

'I will be okay. Just give me a minute.'

'People will understand if you're not at the wake.'

'I just need the nausea to pass.'

'As long as you're sure.'

'Emily, are you okay?'

Looking up, Emily saw Francesca and Adam approaching. The chalk and cheese that always seemed to work. Adam in skinny black jeans and trainers, a black blazer his effort to glam up his usual boho style, while Francesca was elegant as always in a fitted black dress that skimmed her knees. It would have been one of her eBay finds. She had this knack of always finding the right thing that flattered. Meanwhile, Emily had given little thought to her outfit, dragging the one black dress she owned out of the wardrobe and hoping for the best.

Relieved to see friendly faces, she nodded. 'Just a bout of nausea. Max is looking after me.'

'It's a stressful day,' Adam commented. 'A warm one too.'

Francesca sat down on the bench and nudged her shoulder against Emily. 'How are you holding up?'

As Max and Adam started talking, Emily leant in close. 'He's here.'

Francesca's eyes widened. 'Who? What, Connor? Where?'

Emily glanced at mourners, realising he had disappeared. 'I don't know, but he was here. He spoke to Max.' She fought to keep the panic out of her voice.

'Shit, Em. What did he say?'

'Nothing bad. But he was getting off on it. And he knows I never told Max what really happened.'

'Okay, that's not good.'

'I'm scared he's gonna show up at the wake, Fran.'

Francesca placed her hand over Emily's and squeezed. 'If he does, I'll kick him in the fanny.'

As it turned out, she didn't have to. It seemed Connor had made his point and he stayed away. Still, Emily struggled through the afternoon send-off, and sensing she wasn't in a good place, Max insisted on getting her out of the pub room they had hired as soon as possible.

It was on the drive home from Scarborough that he raised the one topic she really didn't want to talk about.

'Connor seemed like a nice guy. I'm surprised you never mentioned him.'

'There were a lot of people looking after Dad. I remember him being nice to me, but not well enough to stand out.' She kept her tone casual, hoping Max hadn't picked up on any vibes.

He didn't appear to, changing the subject.

It seemed Emily had been given a lucky escape. She just worried about what might come next.

28

WEDNESDAY

Emily had been about to call the police when there was a knock at the front door, making her jump. Momentarily, she panicked, her mind immediately going to the figure she had seen standing on the jetty, but then she spotted Max and, relieved, she rushed over to open it.

His expression was stoic, giving nothing away of his mood, as she turned the lock, letting him and Scout inside.

'I was getting worried about you,' she told him, her heart sinking when he nudged past her without acknowledgement, unclipping Scout's lead and hanging it up before disappearing upstairs.

She had hoped he might have worked off some of his aggression, but apparently not.

Locking the door again, she went through to the kitchen and poured herself a generous glass of wine. Max had brought all of the earlier tension back in with him and she needed a drink, her earlier worry over whether he had been okay now turning to annoyance.

She contemplated getting a glass out for him too, before

deciding against it. The obstinate man would probably intentionally ignore it, just as he had the tea she had made him earlier. If he wanted a glass, he could get it himself.

Emily took a large sip, trying to steady her nerves as she heard his footsteps on the stairs, glancing his way as he came into the kitchen and opened the fridge, pulling out various ingredients and setting them out on the chopping board.

He was completely blanking her and she couldn't bear it.

They weren't sulkers and if he was still mad at her, which he clearly was, she would rather he started yelling than this awful silence that was creating such an uncomfortable atmosphere.

'Are we going to talk, Max?'

She didn't particularly want to, because she knew he would go straight back to the note, demanding to know what it was she had done, but, honestly, she didn't see that she had a choice.

She supposed she should have tried to devise an excuse or a reason to explain the note away while he was out, but she simply hadn't been thinking straight. Besides, if she lied and he later found out the truth, it would make things ten times worse?

No, she had to be honest with him.

At least as much as she could.

When he didn't answer her, instead starting to chop carrots and onions, and looking very focused on the task, she took another glug of wine and cut straight to the chase.

'I wasn't honest with you earlier. I do know who was following me.'

There. It was out in the open now and couldn't be taken back.

Max paused chopping just for a few seconds, and she watched her words sink in.

'Who?' he asked eventually.

'His name is Connor. He was a volunteer at the hospice.'

'The guy who showed up at the funeral?' He sounded annoyed.

'Yes.'

'He was stalking you?'

'Yes.'

'So why couldn't you tell me?'

When Emily was silent, unable to bring herself to say the words, Max found them for her.

'Did you have sex with him?'

'What?'

Why had he suddenly made that connection? 'Did you have sex with him, Emily?' Max repeated the question.

Her long pause was enough to confirm her guilt. How the hell was she supposed to answer? A simple yes wouldn't convey the nuances of what had happened.

Still, there was no point in denying it any longer. 'It's not like you think it was.'

'So that's a yes?' He sounded resigned.

'I'm so sorry, Max.'

She waited for him to react, but it was almost as if she hadn't spoken.

She watched as he resumed chopping, the aggressive strokes of the knife as he attacked the vegetables the only sign that he had heard her. He didn't speak or attempt to look at her and she could already feel him shutting her out.

She couldn't stand it.

'It was the day Dad died,' she blurted, suddenly needing to tell him everything. To somehow try to fix the mess she had caused. 'After I came home and found you and Leah, I drove back to Dad's... Connor, he had been kind to me. I went back to his house. He said he would look after me, but I didn't want to have sex with him.' Emily's voice was cracking, aware she had rushed through the words, eager to get them out, and hadn't explained things properly. 'Max, please say something.'

She watched his shoulders tense and his knuckles whiten as he tightened his grip on the knife. Eventually, he turned to face her.

'So you went back to his house?' he asked, his tone calm, but cool. 'And you had sex with him, but you didn't mean to? Have I got that bit straight?'

'Yes, but—'

'So how did that work, Emily? Did you trip over and land on his dick?'

His tone shocked her. He was so angry. 'No. It wasn't like that. I was upset about Dad and seeing you with Leah.'

'Oh yes. Leah. I've been trying to make things right with you over that for months. I know I let you down over your dad and that I wasn't there for you when you needed me, and I wish I could change things. Of course, I didn't realise that while you were judging me, though, you were carrying on with someone else behind my back.'

'I wasn't carrying on with anyone,' she snapped.

'This explains why you wouldn't have sex with me after your dad died.' Max spoke bitterly. 'I thought you were grieving, but you were thinking about fucking another man.'

'That's not fair. We hadn't had sex in weeks before Dad died and that wasn't just my fault, Max.'

He sighed, his frustration clear. 'We were supposed to be having a fresh start, Emily. No more secrets.'

'We were. This wasn't supposed to happen. I never wanted it to.' Emily's tears were falling now. 'He promised he would take care of me. We were drinking, but just as friends, then I passed out. I woke up in his bed, but I don't remember anything about what happened that night.'

There was a moment of silence as Max stared at her, his eyes wide with shock and his face paling. 'What?'

Emily's voice dropped to a whisper. 'I don't think it was just the alcohol. I think he might have drugged me.'

Max was still staring at her and she could see his shock had turned to horror. His anger had evaporated, though. 'Emily, that's rape.'

Unable to say the word herself, she nodded, biting into her bottom lip, desperate to stop the tears from falling.

'You didn't go to the police?'

'I didn't think to. I was so scared and confused when I woke up. I just wanted to get out of his house. At first, I didn't understand what had happened.'

'Why didn't you tell me?'

That was a loaded question and one she could only partly answer.

'I know how angry you are at your mum for cheating on your dad. I didn't think you'd forgive me.'

Her answer seemed to floor him. 'But you didn't cheat on me. If everything you're telling me is true, he took advantage of you.'

Connor had taken advantage of her, but it was something Emily had struggled to process. There had been a while when she had been attracted to him and she felt guilty about that. Rapists weren't supposed to be men you fancied. Were they? And she had gone to his house voluntarily, kissing him back when he had first kissed her. In the aftermath, she couldn't help worrying if she had somehow led him on. If she had perhaps asked for what had happened.

Of course she couldn't say that to Max. She had thought he wouldn't understand and that he would judge her like he judged his mother, but it seemed she had him wrong. Where she had expected to see disgust, he was upset and angry on her behalf.

But then, he still didn't know the full truth.

Would she be able to keep that from him?

She looked at him, realising that now the initial shock had sunk in, he had more questions. He was about to speak when Scout gave an ominous, low growl. As they both looked at her, a thump came from below the boat house.

Seconds later, all of the lights went out, plunging them into darkness.

29

In the days after the funeral, it seemed that Connor was everywhere that Emily went.

She would catch glimpses of him in the supermarket before he disappeared round the end of the aisle or he would pull up alongside her at traffic lights, raising his hand in a brief wave when she made eye contact, and she became afraid to go out of the office on her lunch break, knowing that she would inevitably bump into him at some point.

Occasionally, he would speak, though only to acknowledge her with a 'Hi, Emily'. Other times, he pretended he hadn't seen her, though she knew he was following her. She just didn't know what the hell he wanted. He hadn't made any attempt to contact her again. Nor had he sent to the photo to Max. It was clear he was toying with her, but what kind of game was he playing?

She became fearful walking Scout when Max wasn't with her, sticking to populated areas and grateful that it was summer and the evenings were still light.

Why was Connor even in Leeds? He lived and worked in Scarborough.

She remembered his job was in cyber security, though, and that he worked remotely. As he wasn't tied to a desk, it meant he could show up anywhere, and due to the nature of his work, she dreaded to think what information he might be able to access. Could he tap into her phone and her emails?

Why was he doing this to her? Was it not enough that he had drugged and raped her?

She needed time to properly grieve her father and come to terms with the trauma of what Connor had had done to her. She couldn't cope with him stalking her as well. And of course, she couldn't tell Max.

There were points where she considered following Francesca's advice and going to the police, but time had passed and they would surely wonder why she hadn't reported him sooner. Besides, Connor was right. It would be his word against hers. Even if she just reported him for the stalking, it could open a can of worms. And Connor wasn't stupid. He would probably say it was a coincidence. She couldn't prove he was following her.

No, she couldn't put herself through that.

Instead, she focused on living day to day, gradually retreating into herself.

Max noticed the change, but assumed it was grief for her father, and although he was patient with her and didn't say it, she knew he must be wondering why she was struggling so hard when she had spent much of her life estranged from her dad.

He tried to persuade her to have counselling sessions and encourage her to get out more, and she knew as the days passed, he was growing frustrated, unsure how to help her.

Emily understood she had to somehow pull herself together, and get her life back on track, and she resolved to make more effort.

It was while she was out for work drinks, celebrating one of the partners' retirements, that things reached a head and she realised things with Connor couldn't continue.

She hadn't wanted to go out, but everyone from work was going and it would be frowned upon if she wasn't there. Max was insistent that it would be good for her too, giving her a lift into Leeds city centre and agreeing to pick her up when she was ready to come home.

'Just give it a chance, okay?' he told her, leaning across to kiss her before she got out of the car. 'I promise I'll come and get you as soon as you've had enough.'

Emily spotted some of her colleagues as soon as she walked into the bar and they beckoned her over. A couple of drinks later, and her tensions had eased, though she was wary about having too much alcohol, remembering what had happened the last time.

When the rest of the group arrived, they moved on to another pub where they had booked the outside beer garden, and as soon as Emily walked in, she could smell the burgers and kebabs grilling on the barbecue, but instead of making her hungry, the smell had her feeling slightly nauseous.

As the large group took seats, waiting on the food to cook, Rob Bristow got up, his glass raised in a toast. He had been knocking back the beers and was swaying slightly, already well on his way to being drunk. 'I just want to raise a glass to Gordon. It's been good working with you, mate.'

Everyone joined in and as Emily raised her glass of Coke, having made the decision to move on to soft drinks, Rob glanced over, catching her eye and grinning lasciviously at her.

A heavy sensation sank in her stomach, remembering the last time they were out and he was drunk. How he had hit on her.

Sober Rob had despised her ever since, but the grin suggested that drunk Rob still fancied his chances. Luckily, he was on a different table to her.

Emily tried to relax as it was announced the food was ready, waiting at the table as others got up to fill their plates, wanting to be sure Rob was back at his table before she went to get her food. Not particularly hungry, she opted for salad and a vegetable kebab.

Back at the table, she picked at her food, trying to make an effort to join in conversation, but not liking that every time she looked in Rob's direction, he was staring back at her. In the first couple of days after she had returned to work, he had mostly stayed out of her way, but it hadn't taken him long to slip back into old habits, looking for little ways to make her life difficult.

As the evening progressed, he was becoming louder and more obnoxious, and she discreetly looked at her watch, wondering if it was too early to call Max.

It would take him about twenty minutes to get here.

Seeing that it wasn't yet 9 p.m., she decided she had better stick it out for a little longer, but excused herself to go and use the ladies'.

As she entered the pub, the man standing at the bar, a pint in his hand, turned to face her and she stumbled on the step, almost losing her footing.

Connor.

A ball of dread caught in her throat. It was the same every time she saw him and each time, it seemed to get worse.

Not giving him the chance to say anything, she hastily made her way to the loos, locking herself in one of the two cubicles and sinking her head into her hands. She was aware she was trembling, knowing she would have to walk back out past him. Would he be waiting for her?

How long had he been here? Had he been watching her with her work colleagues?

She honestly wasn't sure how much more of this she could take.

Pulling out her phone, she WhatsApped Francesca.

He's here in the pub.

She didn't need to say more. Francesca knew she was out with work and would know exactly who was referring to.

Her reply came almost instantly.

This has to stop, Em. Call Max, get him to come and pick you up. Tomorrow we're going to figure a way to put an end to this. xx

Acting on her friend's advice, she messaged Max next. She just wanted to go home and was relieved when he came back straightaway, saying he was leaving.

As she was washing her hands, taking her time, wanting to delay going back out into the pub, the door pushed open and a woman stepped into the room.

Emily gave her an acknowledging glance, her stomach dropping when she realised it was Leah.

Fuck!

Leah looked just as shocked to see Emily, her eyes widening, before settling her face into a scowl. 'Well, isn't this a lovely surprise.'

Just what was the correct reaction when you bumped into the woman who had tried it on with your boyfriend? Perhaps Emily should have been angry with her and given her a piece of her mind, but she was so stressed about Connor, she could barely think straight, let alone form a sentence.

'You'd think you would look a bit happier seeing as you won,' Leah was continuing. 'Though I honestly don't know what the hell he sees in you,' she added cattily.

Emily didn't need to stand here and listen to this. Finally, she found her voice.

'Just fuck off, Leah.'

She didn't give the other woman a chance to react, instead shoving at her so she could get past her to the door and making her way back into the bar.

Her gaze immediately went to where Connor had been standing and she was relieved to see that he was no longer there. Had he left? She really hoped so.

She couldn't wait for Max to arrive. She still had twenty minutes to kill, though, and with the appearance of first Connor and then Leah, her nerves were shot. She needed a stiff drink.

After buying a double gin and tonic, Emily headed back outside. Deciding she couldn't face more small talk, she made her way to the area set up for smokers and vapers. Although she was neither, it was currently empty and was far enough away from the crowd to give her privacy, though close enough that she could still see everyone.

She took large sips of the gin to try to calm herself down. Not wanting Max to see how rattled she was when he picked her up.

Francesca was right. This needed to end. She couldn't carry on living this way.

'Steady on, you won't have any drink left.'

Emily glanced up, dismayed to see Rob Bristow in her line of vision. He was looking amused at his unfunny comment, even more unsteady on his feet than earlier. A fresh pint sloshing in his hand.

She wanted to tell him to fuck off, like she had with Leah, but she had to work with him, so she said nothing, instead giving him a simple nod of acknowledgement.

'What you doing tucked away in the corner? You know this area is for smokers, right? I didn't have you pegged as a girl who likes to smoke.'

'I don't.'

'Come back to the party then. It's lonely over here.' He grinned at her, raising his eyebrows suggestively.

'I'm fine, thanks. My boyfriend is picking me up in a few minutes.'

'Tell him not to bother. The night's young, Emily. Get a cab instead, then you can stay and dance.' Rob was slurring his words and stepping into her personal space, which had anxiety gnawing in her gut. Her internal alarm was going haywire, and she was aware of sweat beading on her forehead and top lip as her body temperature escalated.

'I'm sure you'll have fun without me,' she told him, trying her best to stay calm and keep her tone pleasant as she took a step back.

'I'd have more fun if you stay.' He winked at her, closing in on her again. 'You know I like you, Emily. We could have a good time together, you and me.' He was leaning over her now and showering her with beer spittle as he spoke, and her chest tightened, making it difficult to breathe. 'That's a pretty dress you're wearing.' His voice dropped an octave. 'I'd like to see what's under it, though.'

He caught hold of her arm and tried to pull her against him, and panic took over as she tried to wrench herself free. 'Get off me. Let me go!'

Instead of doing as she asked, he tried to hush her, and as she struggled against him, the glass of gin slipped from her fingers, smashing to the ground.

Rob was red-faced with anger now, though his tone was low and threatening when he spoke. 'You crazy bitch. What the fuck is your problem? Calm down.'

As his fingers tightened their grip on her arm, she blindly hit out at him.

For a moment, she thought she had caused his stunned gasp, but then she realised Connor had grabbed hold of him. As Rob released hold of her, starting to tell Connor to fuck off, Connor's fist smashed into his face and he collapsed to the floor.

Emily stepped back in horror, watching as Connor started to kick Rob in the gut repeatedly. Someone was screaming and people were rushing over. A couple of the people she worked with were pulling Connor away as Rob tried to get up. His nose was bloody and he was lying in a puddle of broken glass and alcohol.

One of the other PAs was with Emily now, looking at her in concern. 'Are you okay? What happened?'

She couldn't answer, numb with shock as she tried to register the scene in front of her.

As a small crowd gathered around Rob, trying to help him to his feet, Connor pulled free of the two men holding him, rushing over to Emily and cupping her face in his hands.

'Are you okay? Did he hurt you?'

She flinched away from his touch, stumbling as her heel caught in the decking. She managed to catch her balance, looking at him warily, her heart hammering again and the sound thundering in her ears.

What the hell was he doing?

'Get away from me.'

'Emily.' He sounded hurt and confused, as if he couldn't understand why she would treat him like this.

'Just leave me the hell alone!'

People were staring now and she felt like a cornered animal. From the back entrance of the pub, she could see Leah watching her. The smirk on her face turning to one of shock as, needing to get away from everyone, Emily charged towards her, heading for the door.

This time, Leah had the sense to step back as Emily ran into the pub. It was more crowded now and she fought her way through the crowd.

Out on the street, she leant against the wall as she sucked in deep breaths.

'Emily?'

She heard Max calling her and glanced up, realising he was parked on double yellows across the street, waiting for her. He was out of the car now, jogging across to the pub.

'I messaged you to let you know I was here five minutes ago. Didn't you see it?' As he reached her, realising things weren't right, concern took over. 'Em? What the hell happened? Talk to me.'

From across the road, she heard a bark, and realised from the ajar window of the Audi that Scout had come along for the ride.

'I want to go home.'

'Has someone upset you?'

Two of her work colleagues appeared from the doorway of the pub. Grace, one of the younger conveyancers and gossipy Pam, who was the PA to the senior partner.

'Are you okay?' Grace asked, looking worried.

'You had us worried, running off like that,' Pam added.

Not getting any answers out of Emily, Max turned to them. 'Can someone please tell me what's going on?'

They were quick to share the story. Two men fighting over Emily. How creepy Rob from the office had been drunk and latching on to her, then another man showed up, knocking him to the ground.

'He is such a perv,' Grace said of Rob.

There was another bark from Scout, sounding almost as if it was in response to Grace's words, the dog agreeing.

'Was the man who stepped in a friend of yours?' Pam asked Emily, her close-set eyes looking hungry for gossip.

Emily shook her head. 'No. I don't know him,' she lied. She was still shaken by what had happened. The incident with Rob had made her uneasy, but Connor coming to her rescue had shocked her. What the hell had he been thinking?

'Funny. He seemed to know you.'

Max wasn't interested in what Pam had to say. His sole focus on finding out about Rob. 'Did he hurt you?' he demanded of Emily.

She shook her head again, the prick of tears against the back of her eyes tightening her throat.

'Where is he?' Max growled. 'Still inside?'

When Emily realised he was intending to go into the pub and find Rob, her panic sparked again. 'Please Max, leave it.'

She could see his temper was flaring and that he wanted to ignore her.

'Please. I just want to go home.'

When he made another move towards the pub, she pushed her way into his arms, hugging him tightly. As his hands came up to hold her, one stroking her back, the other smoothing over her hair, the warm and reassuring presence of him overwhelmed her and she gave into her tears, sobbing against him.

That was enough to have him backing down.

'It's okay, Em. We'll go. I'll take you home.'

She heard him mutter thanks to Pam and Grace, and then he

was guiding her across the road back to the safe familiarity of his car and their dog.

Emily was subdued on the ride home and Max didn't push her for conversation, instead turning the radio on, the music of the evening show providing soothing background noise.

She kept replaying in her head the moment when Connor had showed up in the beer garden, swinging a punch at Rob and then attacking him as he lay on the ground.

He had gone from stalking her to trying to play some kind of white knight hero, one she didn't want, and that really scared her.

She had made it clear she didn't want him in her life, yet he wouldn't leave her alone.

Francesca was right. Things couldn't carry on this way. Somehow, they needed to put an end to this.

30

WEDNESDAY

Scout had gone from growling to barking her head off, and the shock of the lights suddenly going out had Emily's stomach dropping.

'Max?'

'It's okay. Just a power cut,' he reassured her, his voice sounding close.

She had never been good with the dark, but out here in the boat house, it was even more oppressive, and as her heart hammered, she took a step towards him, comforted when she hit the solid wall of his chest and his arm went around her.

It didn't stay there for long, though, his hand giving her shoulder a quick squeeze before letting go. Moments later, his phone torch flicked on and she was relieved that they could again see one another.

'Do you think it's a power cut everywhere?' she whispered.

'I don't know. I need to go check the fuse box.'

'Down in the storage room?'

'Yes.'

The idea had her panicking again. 'I don't want you to go down there.'

'Emily, I need to if you want the lights back on.'

'But the noise. It came from below us. What if someone's down there?'

She thought of the threat that had been written on the mirror of her vanity case and the figure who had been standing on the jetty. Was it all connected?

'It was probably nothing. I'll take Scout with me. She'll soon let me know if we're not alone.'

'No. I don't want to wait up here by myself.'

'Fine.' There was a hint of impatience in Max's tone. 'She can stay up here with you.'

'I didn't mean that. I meant I don't want to be alone without you.'

'Okay, we'll go together.' He turned away from her, the phone torch moving with him, and Emily caught hold of the back pocket of his jeans, refusing to let go as she followed him into the kitchen.

'What are you doing?' she hissed as he opened one of the cupboards, using his phone light to see inside.

'Getting the torch. Why are you whispering?'

'I don't know. I'm scared.'

Max found what he was looking for and the bright beam had Emily blinking as he tested it, swinging the light briefly in her direction before dipping it again. As her sight readjusted, she heard him open a drawer, then the jangle of keys. To unlock the storage room, she guessed.

'Look, there's nothing to be afraid of,' he said, turning to face her. The movement had him pressing up against Emily again when she refused to let go of his back pocket. 'It's just a power cut.

We're out in the sticks. I'm sure it happens all the while. Stay close behind me, okay?'

She followed him down the outside steps, the beam of the torch cutting an eerie path ahead as they made their way along the side path to the door that led to the storage room and the boat tunnels.

Was it really a simple power cut? Emily had heard the noise coming from below the boat house seconds before the lights went out, and she knew both Max and Scout had too, even if Max wasn't letting on.

Trying her best to quash down on her fear, she followed him inside. Her stomach churned as the torch lit up the two dark tunnels, the beam flickering over the stone walls, showing her, to her relief, that they were empty. She looked at the dark mass of water Although it wasn't deep, it still looked creepy in the shadowy light.

They still had the storage room to check and she wouldn't be satisfied until she knew it was empty.

Despite downplaying it, she knew Max had heard the noise too and she suspected he too thought the power hadn't gone off by accident.

Her heart lurched as the door creaked open. It wasn't locked.

If it was Connor, how did he get down here and into the storage room without a key?

'Max?'

'Shh.'

He flashed the light into the room as Emily clung on to him, terrified of what he might find waiting. Her mouth was dry, fear tightening her chest and gripping her throat, her legs trembling as Max stepped forward, pulling her along with him.

'No one's here.'

They were in the room now and he flashed the torch around to show her the small space was empty.

'Someone was in here, though,' she whispered. 'How come the door was unlocked?'

'I don't know, Emily,' he said impatiently. 'Look, hold this.' He handed her the torch. 'Shine it on the fuse box so I can see what I'm looking at.'

Emily did as asked, nervously glancing around the dark space while he studied the switches. She was freezing cold down here without a jacket, but although the air was damp and cool, the chill going through her was probably in part down to fear.

Max hit a switch, glancing towards the mouth of the tunnels, a faint light now glowing over the river. 'Everything should be back on now.'

'What was wrong?'

'The master switch had been turned off.'

'Intentionally?'

'Let's just get back upstairs, okay,' he muttered, seeming unwilling to discuss what had happened.

Emily flashed the torch around the room as she followed him to the door, the beam landing on a spiral staircase in the corner. She looked to the ceiling, wondering where it went, surprised to see what appeared to be a loft hatch.

'Max, did you know this was here?'

He turned to face her. 'Know what is where?'

Emily shone the torch on the stairs again. 'Look. Where do you think it goes? It has to lead up to the first floor somewhere.'

'It's under the kitchen, I think.'

An unwelcome thought occurred. 'You don't think this is how he has been getting in, do you?'

Max was staring at the steps, considering. 'Here, give me that,' he said, taking the torch, and she crossed her arms as she watched him climb the staircase. He twisted the lock and pressed on the hatch.

'It's not opening. No one is getting up into the boat house from down here. I think it must lock on both sides,' he told her. 'I'll leave it unbolted and we can check when we get back upstairs. See if I'm right.'

He led the way back out of the storage room. Making sure the door was locked before making his way back round to the house. Emily followed, still a little jittery. Not liking that they still didn't know why the power had gone off. At least Max had been able to get the lights back on, which was a relief.

She wasn't sure how much more she could take of this, though. What was supposed to be a restful break and a chance to reconnect had turned into a nightmare. All she wanted to do was to go home. Something they should have perhaps done a lot sooner. As soon as they were back in the boat house, she would tell him she wanted to leave.

She followed Max back up the steps, realising as she saw the front door that in their rush to go down to the storage room, they had left it open.

If Max noticed, he didn't comment, stepping inside with Emily and Scout following.

The collie didn't seem agitated, but as Max paused to lock the door, Emily's attention was drawn to the middle of the room and the doll that was hanging from one of the overhead beams.

'Oh my God.'

Her hand went to her mouth, for a moment convinced she was going to be sick.

'What?' Max briefly touched her arm, but then he saw it, moving quickly to the centre of the room. Emily following on rubbery legs.

The doll was a similar size to a Barbie or Sindy, with dark hair that appeared to have been crudely cut in a bob that fell around its shoulders, in replica of Emily's own hairstyle. A noose was tight around its neck and a piece of paper was attached with a drawing pin through the doll's hand.

Striding into the kitchen, Max found a pair of scissors in one of the drawers and used them to cut the doll down. He ripped the paper free of the drawing pin, opening it up. The words were printed. Just like on the note Max had found earlier on the doorstep.

You can't hide from me.

Emily's eyes widened and she let out a sob. Adrenaline had her heart racing, anger mixing with the fear. She was scared, but she was also mad. How dare he try and destroy her life like this? She couldn't take it any more.

Ignoring Max when he went to catch hold of her arm, she marched to the door, twisting the lock, pulling it open and storming outside.

'What the fuck do you want?' she yelled the words into the darkness. 'I know you're out there and I know you can hear me. Please, just tell me what you want?'

She stopped and waited, aware Max was behind her and had caught hold of her hand, trying to pull her back into the boat house.

Just as she relented, turning to go, there was a rustle of twigs in the bushes up ahead and Emily swore she heard the soft sound of laughter.

Shuddering, she choked down on a sob and quickly followed Max inside.

—————

31

'When I get my hands on him, I'm going to kill him.'

Max was pacing, the anger rolling off him.

Emily didn't like seeing him so worked up, but at least his aggression was no longer directed at her.

She understood now that she had made a terrible mistake not telling him about the rape and then the stalking. If only she had been honest from the start. And yes, if she had gone to the police, perhaps everything would have worked out differently.

She hated that she had hurt him so badly.

'I'm so sorry I didn't tell you,' she told him now, going to him and pausing his pacing by hugging him tightly. For a moment, she worried he wasn't going to reciprocate, but then his arms went around her.

'You should have trusted me, Em. We've been together for three years. I thought you knew me better than that.'

Guilt stabbed her. She didn't even know how to answer him, other than to repeat, 'I really am sorry.'

He drew her back, looking down at her. 'No more secrets,

okay? We have to be honest with each other about everything going forward.'

She nodded and reached in her pocket for a tissue, blowing her nose. Now would be the time to tell him about the abortion, to come completely clean. She couldn't do it, though. Instead she nodded. 'I want to go home.'

She had told Max about the figure she had seen standing on the jetty and she knew he was desperate to confront Connor, but she really couldn't stand spending another minute here.

'I know you want to leave, but we need to call the police.'

'No.' Emily felt a stab of panic. 'No police.'

'Why not? He needs to be in fucking prison.'

'Please, Max. I can't cope with having to deal with the police. Not over this. I just want to go home.'

She thought he was going to argue the point, but then he backed down.

'Okay. We can go. I do want to knock his head off, though. It kills me knowing what he put you through.'

They both fell quiet, still holding on to each other. Scout watching them from where she had curled herself up on her bed.

'I just don't understand why he has suddenly started doing this again,' Emily murmured. 'He has been quiet for months. Why now?'

And how was Connor managing to get inside the boat house? Okay, Emily and Max had left the door unlocked when the power went out, so it would have been easy enough to sneak in and plant the doll, but the other times when they had been inside and everywhere had been secure, yet no locks had been tampered with.

Her thoughts went back to the Airbnb owner.

'Did you ever manage to get hold of the guy who owns this place?' she asked Max now.

'No. I didn't.'

'You said you were going to see if you could find a number and give him a call.'

Max eased back from her and rubbed his jaw, looking for the briefest moment like he had been caught out. He quickly collected himself. 'Yes, I did. There was no answer, though.'

Really? Emily had been with him for much of the day. There were only a few moments when he could have made the call. Was he lying to her?

'When?'

'Sorry?'

'When did you try to call?'

'This morning, before you got up.' He narrowed his eyes. 'What's the big deal, Em? This has nothing to do with the owner of the boat house. You know that.'

'No! I don't know that. How is he getting in? And how did he know where the electricity circuit was?'

He gave her a steady look. 'Honestly, I don't know. But the two things aren't connected.'

'You can't be certain of that.'

'Emily, please. Listen to yourself. What you're proposing is ridiculous. It's obvious Connor is behind this. You've said so yourself. Are you suggesting he just happens to know the owner of the boat house that we have rented for a week's holiday? I know coincidences exist, but that's a fairly big stretch, don't you think?'

Perhaps it was, especially when Max put it like that. It didn't stop her brooding over it, though. Her instincts hadn't been great through any of this, but still she couldn't shake the feeling that something about this whole situation was off.

Max didn't want to talk about it further, though, and a little annoyed, she headed upstairs to start packing.

Eventually, needing to satisfy her curiosity, she reached for her phone and clicked on to the Airbnb site, wanting to see the listing for herself. Max had been insistent that he be the one to have any contact with the owner, though at no point had he acted like it was a priority.

She put in the criteria and searched for the property, frowning when the boat house didn't come up. Going back to the home page, she did a broader search.

By the time she had completed it, a tiny ball of dread had knotted in her belly.

The boat house wasn't listed on the Airbnb website.

Think, Emily.

There had to be an explanation.

She typed the name of the property into Google, relieved when she saw it come up as a listing with another rental company. There was obviously just a blip on the Airbnb site.

As the page opened, her eyes widened.

No longer available.

What? That simply wasn't possible. How could they have rented the place?

She thought back to what the waitress had said in the restaurant. She had been surprised that the place was being rented out again.

On a whim, Emily typed *Boat death Wroxham* into the search engine.

It took a little while, but eventually she found an article.

Iris Butterworth, 52, had died on the river after her boat flipped.

She read on.

Iris and her husband, Peter, owned the Stone Boat House as a second property that they let out to holidaymakers. The couple, from Scarborough…

Emily sucked in a breath, double blinking at the screen. Scarborough? What were the chances of that?

Max was right about coincidence. It could only be stretched so far, and wondering if he had lied to her, had every muscle in her body tensing.

What if…

No, she wasn't going to even entertain the idea that Max was somehow involved in this. She loved him and trusted him. Apart from one slip-up with Leah, he had never given her cause to doubt him. There was going to be a simple explanation.

Her eyes scanned further down the article.

Leah Butterworth said, 'My aunt was an experienced rower. We are all devastated.'

Emily's stomach churned with nausea as she recalled Leah being upset over her aunt.

Max had said she was struggling to come to terms with the woman's death.

So this boat house belonged to Leah's family? Exactly what kind of twisted game was Max playing?

It was time to find out.

32

'We need to talk.'

Emily found Max down in the kitchen sorting out dinner for Scout.

She knew he could tell from her tone that she was annoyed, as he looked a little worried as he turned to her.

'What's the matter. Has something else happened?'

'Nothing's happened. We just need to talk.'

A frown creased his brow and she could see he was wary. 'Okay. What about?'

'Why didn't you tell me that Leah's aunt owned this place?'

He studied her silently as her words sank in, and for a moment, Emily thought he was going to deny it, but then he rubbed a hand across the back of his neck and sighed.

'How did you find out?'

'Airbnb. The property's not listed, Max. What the fuck is going on? I thought you no longer spoke to Leah.'

'I don't.' His eyes widened at Emily's look of disbelief. 'I swear. I did it directly with her uncle. He pulled it from the Airbnb site after Iris died, but he was still letting it out to friends and family for a cheap rate. I booked it as a surprise months ago, but then your dad got sick and I knew you wouldn't be able to go. Peter agreed to hold on to the deposit and let me transfer it to later in the year.'

Was he telling her the truth?

'If it was that simple, why not just be honest with me? You were the one who said it earlier. No more lies!'

'I know, I know.' He reached for her and Emily took a step back.

She wasn't letting him off the hook that easily.

Max sighed, looking frustrated. 'Look, yes, I should have told you the truth, but I was worried that after all the Leah stuff, you'd have a hissy fit and wouldn't want to come here. I knew it had been on Airbnb, so it was easier just to let you think that. I'm sorry, Em. I wasn't trying to deceive you. It was just a white lie.'

Just a white lie. Emily bristled.

'Does she know we're here?'

He shrugged. 'I have no idea. You know we don't speak any more.'

'Really?'

'Yes, really.'

Even though he was looking her dead in the eye, the brief hesitation before his answer and the slight tic in his cheek had her doubting him.

'Look, I'm sorry I didn't tell you this was her aunt and uncle's place, but it doesn't change anything.' He held out his hand. 'Come on, Em. She has nothing to do with this.'

'What if she does though?'

'Sorry?'

'What if everything that's been happening is to do with Leah?'

The more she thought about it, the more it made sense. Emily

218

KERI BEEVIS

had never seen the intruder's face and whoever it was seemed to know their way around the boat house.

Max's expression turned from incredulous to faintly amused. 'You think Leah is behind what's been happening?'

'It's possible. She hates me and I know she blames me that you two no longer speak.'

'Why would you think she's behind this, Em? It's obvious it's this Connor prick. You said it yourself.'

'Leah's uncle lives in Scarborough. You do know that, right?'

Emily's mind was working overtime and, yes, perhaps jumping to conclusions, but the dots were there as far as she could see, so she was linking them. She hadn't seen Connor in months and how would he even know they were here? No, it had to be Leah.

The woman hated her. That was a fact. And she had been besotted with Max. If she hadn't moved on, then Emily was still in her way. Max had no idea how far his crazy ex-friend might take things, but Emily didn't trust her.

The figure at the door, the break-in, the doll. It could have easily been a woman.

She thought back to the backpack in the cottage across the river. The hoodie she had found, she had assumed it belonged to a man, and she hadn't paid close enough attention to the underwear. Was it possible the items belonged to a woman?

Another scenario occurred to her.

What if Leah and Connor were in this together?

She remembered back to the bar where she had been for work drinks. Connor had been there and so had Leah. Was that a coincidence or did they know each other already?

They had a shared interest in wanting Emily and Max to break up.

Was it really that big a stretch?

She put that idea to Max now, not liking that his reaction was to laugh.

'You're getting carried away now and sounding ridiculous,' he told her. 'Look, I know you're scared and I get it, I really do, and I'm so sorry I lied to you about who I hired the boat house through. But I promise you Leah has nothing to do with this.'

'How come you're so sure?' Emily challenged. 'You said you never see her these days.'

'I don't.' Max hesitated, seeming to consider his answer. 'Okay, I'll be honest. I've seen her once since.'

Emily's mouth dropped open. So he had bloody lied again! And after they had sworn to be honest with each other going forward.

Given everything she had told him about Connor and how he had reacted to the secrets she had been hiding from him, she decided to go easy on him. After all, she hadn't told him everything, so it wasn't as though she was leading by example.

'Did you sleep with her?' she asked quietly.

'God, no.' Max looked so genuinely appalled at the idea, she was tempted to believe him. 'I swear nothing has ever happened with Leah and me apart from that day in the kitchen when you walked in on us. But that was her. I swear on Scout's life.'

Scout's ears pricked up and she glanced up from her food bowl.

Emily knew he adored the dog. She didn't think Max would say it unless it was true.

'So when?'

'I said to you I told her our friendship was over. I never lied about that. But, truthfully, she didn't handle it well. She kept messaging me and trying to call me, begging me to reconsider. I never said anything to you because I knew you had enough on your plate with your dad.'

'You said you saw her,' Emily pushed.

'I did. It was a few days after your dad died. She called me one afternoon. She was drunk and crying, saying she had taken a load of pills. I went over there to check on her. I wasn't sure if she was telling the truth or if it was just a ploy to get me round there. Turns out it was the latter. She'd just been knocking back the vodka. I swear I left as soon as I realised and I haven't been back since.'

Emily absorbed what he was telling her. He sounded contrite, but was it all the truth? He had no reason to make this up. 'Have you heard from her since?' she asked.

'A few times,' Max admitted. 'I've never answered or responded to any of her messages, though. You can check my phone if you don't believe me. The last time I heard from her was that night you were out with work. The night that twat, Rob, hit on you. Leah said she had seen you in the pub and that the guy who punched Rob had been acting like he thought he was your boyfriend. I thought she was stirring shit, so I blocked her.' He was quiet for a moment. 'The guy she was talking about, it was Connor, wasn't it?'

Emily nodded. It suddenly made sense why, when she had confessed Connor had been following her, Max had immediately jumped to asking her if she had slept with him.

'That's it, Em. I've told you the truth about everything. No more lies.'

'No more lies,' she repeated, knowing she would take her last secret to the grave.

'I know Leah. She has nothing to do with what's been happening here. I promise. It's not her style.'

No, Emily supposed it wasn't. Leah was the kind of girl who would lose her shit over a broken nail. It was difficult to picture her camping out in an abandoned cottage.

Max was right. She was just trying to make things fit. She was still annoyed with him, though, that he hadn't told her.

Emily knew Connor was behind all of this. It was because she was so frightened of him, she was doing everything possible to try to pretend it was someone else.

Francesca had promised her it was over, so why was Connor back on the scene?

33

BEFORE

'I know you're not going to like what I have to say, but I think we should tell Alex.'

Emily was sitting in Francesca's kitchen, her cold hands wrapped around a hot mug of tea. Despite it being a sunny June day, she just couldn't seem to warm up.

It was the shock of what had happened the previous night.

Connor was now interfering with her work life and he had given the impression to her colleagues that he knew her well. Rob had been a dick, but he was more senior than Emily, and Connor's attack had been unwelcome and vicious. Would she even have a job to go back to tomorrow?

That was why when Francesca mentioned her older brother, Alex, Emily didn't immediately baulk at the idea.

Alessandro Mancini had been in trouble with the police on more than one occasion when he was younger, and although he had long ago cleaned up his act, he still knew people who could get things done. Emily knew she could trust him. He had always looked out for her when she was a kid as well as Francesca.

'We can't kill him, Fran.' She figured she had better point that out before the conversation turned too dark.

Francesca let out a bubble of surprised laughter. 'Of course not. Don't be silly. I know Alex had done some dodgy things in the past, but he's never killed anyone. I was thinking more along the lines of a visit, a warning. I am sure he will have some friends who can persuade Connor to leave you alone.'

Would it work?

Generally, Emily was as straight as an arrow. She had never come close to breaking the law, but at this point, she was desperate.

'You'd better warn your brother. Connor's not stupid and he was in the army, so he can take care of himself too.'

'I will tell Alex, but trust me, he will know what he's doing. So, what do you say: am I telling him? I will swear him to secrecy.'

Emily nodded. 'Okay, if you think it will work, give Alex a call.'

* * *

It didn't take long for Alex to get back to Francesca and within twenty-four hours, everything was in place, not even allowing Emily time to object or to backtrack.

Francesca had showed up at the house the following day after Emily had arrived home from work. She was Harry-free and suggested they take Scout for a walk, not wanting Max to over-hear their conversation.

'How was work?' she asked as soon as they were out of the door.

'It went better than expected, actually.'

Emily had been dreading seeing James. He had always been so good to her as a boss. What was he going to think of her following Saturday's nights antics? She had knocked on his door as soon as she'd arrived, planning on apologising, but he had beaten her to it, telling her he was embarrassed by Rob's behaviour. It seemed one of the other conveyancers had been close enough to hear how he had drunkenly come on to Emily, and after she had spoken up, a couple of other women in the office had admitted he had behaved inappropriately with them too. He had been suspended, pending investigation.

Nothing was said about Connor or what he had done. That in itself had been a huge relief, but knowing she didn't have to face Rob either had meant Emily's day had turned out to be a good one.

'Finally, good news,' Francesca commented. 'And I have more of that for you right now.'

She explained how Alex had been outraged when he'd learnt about Connor and he intended to take care of things straight-away. By the time Francesca showed up on Emily's doorstep, he had already contacted a friend and they were just waiting on a few details that they needed from Emily.

'I don't know where he's staying in Leeds or if he's been going back to Scarborough,' she said when Francesca asked. 'And I don't know his address.'

'Can you describe where it was?'

Emily nodded, doing her best to provide as much information as possible. She also passed on details of the car she had seen, as well as both numbers Connor had used to message her.

'Right, Alex is insistent. No phone calls or messages breathing a word about any of this. As far as you're concerned, the less you know, the better it will be for you.'

'Okay.' Emily was nervous now. What was she getting into? If it went wrong and anyone was badly hurt, could she live with that on her conscience?

She stewed over it that night, her sleep even more interrupted than normal, and she was bleary-eyed and grumpy when Max brought her in a cup of coffee, placing it beside the bed.

'I'm taking Scout to Charlotte's. Are you okay?'

He had been keeping an extra close eye on her since Saturday, still worrying about what had happened and feeling guilty because he had persuaded her to go.

Of course, he had persisted with questions, wanting full details about what had happened and about the mystery man who had come to her defence. Emily had answered them as truthfully as she could, but there had been parts where she had changed details. Just when had she become such an accomplished liar?

What would Max's reaction be if he realised she had now involved Alex and his shady friends to threaten Connor? While Alex had promised Connor's life wouldn't be in danger, she knew their actions would be breaking the law.

'I'm fine,' she told Max now. 'Tired, but I'll be okay once I've had a shower. Thank you for the coffee.' She kissed him goodbye and watched him and Scout go.

And wondered just what the hell she had set in motion.

34

WEDNESDAY

Max was wracked with guilt learning everything that had happened to Emily. He kept going over everything in his head. Replaying the last few months and wondering how he had missed all the signs.

Emily had been so withdrawn after her dad's death, crying all the time and reluctant to leave the house, but he had put it down to grief. He remembered the panic attack she had suffered at the funeral. Connor had been with her at the time.

Now it all made so much sense.

How fucking dare he have the nerve to rape her and then show up at Simon's funeral? Knowing that Connor had forced himself on her made him sick to his stomach.

Max was desperate to get his hands on him, but he needed to get Emily away from the boat house. She had suffered through enough and he knew he was partly responsible for that. If he had been more supportive. If Leah hadn't been there that day Emily came home from the hospice. If he had managed to stop her from storming out of the house... He should have figured out sooner that she would head back to Scarborough. And he never should have encouraged Leah.

The pair of them had been friends for years and he had always known she liked him, even though she had been in a relationship herself until shortly before he met Emily. Leah and Emily had never seen eye to eye, but Max had kept Leah around because his ego liked the attention.

He had been stupid and selfish and fucking inconsiderate, ignoring how snipy Leah was towards Emily, and doing nothing to discourage her when she kept showing up at the house after Emily's dad became sick.

Leah had caught him off guard that day she kissed him, but, truthfully, he hadn't been quick to stop her.

It was all his fault that Emily had fled to Scarborough, that Connor had taken advantage of her, and that she had been dealing with all of this alone. But not any more. He would figure a way to sort this out.

'Are you ready?' he asked her now.

She nodded, looking exhausted and frightened.

This week was supposed to be a break for them to enjoy. Instead, it had caused a whole heap of stress, all because of that twat.

'I just need to pee,' she told him. 'Take the bags down. I'll meet you outside.'

'Okay.'

Max caught hold of her hand as she passed him, giving it a squeeze, and she glanced up, the pair of them exchanging a brief look of solidarity. His heart beat faster when her lips curved with the smallest of smiles that told him they were going to be okay. And they would be, but not while Connor was still hanging around.

He left her to go upstairs before switching on the porch light and stepping out of the boat house, Scout charging ahead, leaving him to bump their luggage down the steps.

It wasn't until he got his fob from his pocket and went to click it at the car that he spotted the front tyres. Both of them flat.

Fuck.

He dropped the bags, going to the car to survey the damage and could see that they hadn't just been let down. Both had been slashed. And that was just fucking great since he only had one spare. First the graffiti, now the tyres. Was there anything else this prick wanted to do to his car?

Swearing under his breath, Max went to the rear of the Audi to see if the back ones were damaged too, unsurprised to see they were in the same state, his temper rising.

They weren't going to be heading back to Leeds any time soon and he was scared about how Emily was going to react when he told her. She was already fragile, and that made Max even more furious. He wanted to kill Connor. What the hell was he playing at?

Fuck it, he would call a cab. Get them booked into a hotel for the night.

Tomorrow, he would get the car sorted.

At this point, he didn't care about cost; he just wanted to take his girlfriend and his dog and get them both the hell away from here before anything else happened. Maybe once he knew Emily and Scout were safe, he would head back to the cottage across the river for another look.

He hadn't been concerned when they had first found the backpack and sleeping bag. It could have belonged to anyone. Emily had freaked out about the mask, and yes, perhaps it was an odd thing to have. But it was just before Halloween.

She had seen the figure standing on the jetty tonight, though, looking across to the boat house. Was it Connor? Max would like to find out, and deal with him once and for all.

The crunching of twigs up ahead had his head snapping up.

Maybe he wouldn't need to go to the cottage to find him.

Was he loitering around here again? Probably enjoying the fact that he had just prevented them from leaving.

Well, he wasn't going to get away with it this time.

Seeing red, Max charged towards the trees.

35

She looked a mess.

Emily studied her reflection in the bathroom mirror as she washed her hands. Her eyes bloodshot and her cheeks paler than usual, while her choppy, bobbed haircut was in disarray, probably because she kept running her fingers through it.

She left the tap running, turning the water to cold and leant over the basin to splash it over her face. She was tired and panicky and so, so sick of being scared. All she wanted to do was get home. Norfolk was beautiful and so was this boat house, but the week itself had been hell on earth. She couldn't wait to leave.

If Connor showed up again in Leeds, she would have Max by her side this time, as well as Francesca and Alex. She still didn't understand why he had reappeared after Alex and his friends had warned him to stay away. She hadn't seen hide nor hair of Connor, so why was he here now? What had happened to make him target her again?

As she turned off the tap, reaching for a towel to dry her face, she heard Max return to the bedroom and guessed he must have forgotten something.

'I'm almost done,' she told him, smoothing her fingers over her hair and taking a moment to suck in a deep breath. She exhaled slowly, relaxing her shoulders and feeling just a little of the tension ebbing out of her.

He hadn't responded to her, but he must still be in the room as she hadn't heard him leave. Glancing towards the doorway, she wondered if perhaps he hadn't heard her.

'Max?'

Still there was no answer and, curious, she stepped back into the bedroom, surprised to find it empty.

Maybe it had been her imagination. Either that or he had left the room. The bedroom door was wide open.

The sound of crying abruptly cut through the silence and she froze.

What was that?

Scout? Was she okay?

Emily rushed out onto the landing, realising it wasn't the dog before she had even reached the top step. It was a human cry. In fact, it sounded like a baby. Her heart caught in her throat.

What the hell? Was this some kind of sick joke?

And where was Max?

The baby sound had to be recorded. There was no child in the house. But who was playing it? Was Connor in the house?

Fearful to go downstairs, Emily ran back into the bedroom and over to the window.

She could see Max's car, and their luggage standing a few feet away, bathed in the light from the porch, but she couldn't see any sign of him or of Scout anywhere.

She wanted to call out to them again, but the sound of the baby crying was still playing, and she didn't dare.

Her shoulders were knotting and her heart thumping as she tried to figure out what to do.

Her nerves were already on edge because of this bloody place and everything that had happened since they had arrived and now this? She was struggling to think straight.

The sound of the bedroom door slamming shut had her jumping out of her skin and swinging round. Her eyes widening as everything inside her froze, including the scream on her lips.

'Hello, Emily.'

Finding her voice, Emily screamed.

36

Connor Banks had known there was something special about Emily Worth the first time they met.

Her head had been in her hands when he saw her as he had walked into her father's room at the hospice and at first, he had thought she was crying. But then she had glanced up, looking at him with wide, golden eyes that were such a perfect contrast to her creamy skin and almost black hair, it had sent a kick of lust straight to his groin. With her hair cut in a short choppy style that swung around her shoulders, he was reminded a little of the Disney princess, Snow White. Up close, he'd noticed a smattering of freckles across the bridge of her nose and two anxious little lines between her eyebrows that deepened whenever she frowned.

She was perfect and he decided in that moment that she was the woman he wanted to marry.

Unknown to Emily, she wasn't the first woman he had felt this way about.

There had been others before her.

His first infatuation had been with Louise Noakes, a girl who had lived across the street when he was sixteen. Louise hadn't been very good about drawing her bedroom curtains when she got undressed and Connor had become besotted with her ample breasts, even going so far as to buy a pair of binoculars so he could spy on her.

She never knew of his crush, her family moving away a year later and breaking his teenage heart. But he was quick to move on, finding a new obsession in Kelly Carpenter, who worked in the local newsagents.

By this point, he was growing into his looks and working out too and he wasn't forced to steal Kelly's knickers off the washing line as he had done with Louise. She happily took them off for him in the back of his Citroen.

Connor and Kelly dated for a while, but then she grew bored and he learnt she had a roaming eye. When she dumped him, he had been unable to handle the rejection. She was the one he wanted to be with and he wanted to spend the rest of his life looking after her. He started following Kelly, begging her to take him back, and things became messy.

She had a new boyfriend who didn't appreciate his attention, and where Kelly had previously looked at Connor with adoring eyes, now whenever he saw her, she seemed scared.

The night he forced her into his car, driving her to a secluded wooded spot – just to talk, of course – had backfired badly. Kelly had managed to run away, flagging down a car, then calling the police.

Connor had received a caution and was told to stay away from her.

At first, he hadn't listened, but he had tried to be more discreet, until eventually his head was swayed by another woman, Jessica, and he lost interest in Kelly.

So the pattern continued.

Emily wasn't the first woman he had become fixated on, but the connection he felt towards her was perhaps deeper than with the others. They had both lost their parents – not that Connor had ever been close to his dad – and they were both alone in the world. Emily understood him and, in turn, he understood her.

For a moment, everything had been perfect and had felt so real, but then he'd started to suspect that perhaps she was too good to be true.

His suspicions had been alerted when she'd showed up at the hospice one night driving a different car.

His job allowed him to easily check the owner as being Max Hunter.

Emily had said she had borrowed the car from a friend, but that was a lie. It didn't take much detective work to find out that Max was Emily's boyfriend.

Realising that she was perhaps going to be more trouble than she was worth, Connor had tried to do the right thing and stay away her, but she was addictive and he couldn't stop thinking about her. Then, of course, she had sought him out, needing his protection the night she had gone to her dad's, thinking there was an intruder.

She was like a siren, luring him in, and he was powerless to resist her.

After Simon Worth had passed away, he had gone to the man's house, hoping he might find Emily there and realising when he did, that it was a sign. She was supposed to be his.

Max had cheated on her and she swore she wouldn't take him back. The universe was lining everything up for Connor and Emily to be together, yet she was holding back, seeming reluctant to move forward with him. He had to put an end to her indecisiveness.

Yes, she kept saying she just wanted to be friends, but he

knew she didn't really mean that. She was there with him in his house and getting drunk. He knew exactly what she really wanted.

Women like Emily could be easily confused. She wouldn't come willingly to him, so he needed to take a firm hand with her and take her control away.

That was why he kept a dose of ketamine in the house. He had learnt over the years that it came in handy on occasion.

As he had helped her upstairs to bed, he knew he was making the right decision for her. He would worship and adore her. And he'd realised, as he made sweet and tender love to her, that he would do anything for her. Emily would eventually understand that she was too good for Max, and that she and Connor were destined to be together.

He had planned to keep her in his house until he had talked her around, made her realise he was the one, but she had been intoxicating, and fully satisfied from the taste of her, he had fallen asleep. When he awoke, she was already gone.

Guessing she had gone back to her father's house, he had taken flowers for her.

He had arrived just a little too late, though, horrified when he saw Emily through the living-room window. She wasn't alone and had her arms wrapped around a man.

Although Connor couldn't see his face, he'd recognised Max Hunter's Audi parked out front, next to Emily's little Polo.

She had promised she wouldn't take Max back. What the hell was she thinking of? Especially after spending the night with Connor.

Initially, he had been upset, returning home, the flowers going in the bin. He had made a mistake. Emily wasn't the girl he had thought she was and she was undeserving of his affection. She had hurt him badly.

Of course, you can't choose who you fall in love with, and Connor gradually understood that she had wormed his way under his skin to an extent that he couldn't bear the idea of life without her. He needed to win her back.

Except it didn't go to plan. His friendly message had met with a demand to leave him alone.

As he'd continued to plead with her, her messages became more aggressive and she began accusing him of awful things. He'd tried to take control back, sending her one of the pictures he had taken of them in bed, suggesting that perhaps he should show it to Max, but she had been angry, threatening to go to the police.

Was she testing his boundaries?

He'd decided he would start to push them and see how she reacted.

Unfortunately, he had underestimated Emily Worth and the cruelty she was capable of.

37

WEDNESDAY

Emily tried to find her voice, wanting to question what Connor wanted, even if it was pretty bloody obvious, but for an awful, long moment, they simply stared at each other. The hunter and the prey.

Where was Max? Had Connor hurt him? And Scout?

React, for God's sake. React.

In the end, she wasn't sure who moved first, and she was only aware that she was running into the bathroom as the door slammed shut. She managed to lock it with shaking fingers, anxiously stepping back as he turned the handle, trying to force his way in.

'Come on out, Emily.'

She found her voice, sounding so scared, she barely recognised herself. 'Leave me alone! Please go away.'

'I just want to talk. Now we can do this the easy way or the difficult way. Your choice.'

He sounded so reasonable. As if he was trying to explain to a naughty child.

She glanced at the door handle. The lock wasn't going to hold. It wasn't strong enough.

She looked around anxiously. The window was too small for her to climb though, so she needed some kind of weapon. But what? She opened the bathroom cabinet. Although they had already packed their own things, there were still a few complimentary items in there, and she pulled everything into the sink.

'I'm going to count to five, Emily. If you haven't come out, we will do this the difficult way. You won't like that so much.' There was a moment of silence. 'Five. Four. Three.'

Shit, shit, shit. What the hell was she going to do?

'Two. One.' There was another dreadful pause. When Connor spoke, his tone was taunting. 'Okay, Emily. Coming. Ready or not.'

She grabbed a mini can of deodorant, finger ready on the nozzle as he hurled himself against the door and it buckled under his weight.

Where the hell was Max? Why hadn't he heard her screaming?

As the door almost flew off its hinges, she cried out again, stepping back and taking aim with the deodorant can, before squeezing the nozzle at him. She caught him off guard as he was still straightening up. The spray going directly into his eyes.

He yowled, putting an arm up to protect them, and she tried to barrel past him.

She almost made it to the bedroom door. Almost. But he was quick, catching hold of her and pulling her towards him.

'What do you want? Let me go! Get off of me. Max? Max!'

She fought like a wildcat, determined not to make things easy as she screamed for help.

Max had only gone outside to load the stuff in the car and she was making enough noise to wake the dead. Why wasn't he helping her?

Had Connor attacked him? Hurt him, even?

Oh God. What if he was dead?

And Scout? Was she okay? Where was her baby?

Worry for both of them slammed through her, scaring her half to death, but it also gave her the extra burst of strength she needed, and as Connor's forearm came up to lock around her neck, she sank her teeth deep into his flesh, earning another yowl of pain as he briefly loosened his grip.

Taking advantage of the moment, Emily managed to pull herself free, charging out of the bedroom and down the stairs, stumbling and almost losing her balance in her eagerness to reach the bottom before he caught up with her.

She had no idea what was happening and what his plans for her were. He had followed them to Norfolk and been watching them, trying to scare her, but what the hell did he actually want?

She wanted to stop and challenge him, but she was too afraid.

'Max!' She screamed his name again, willing him to answer, spotting the door to the boat house was open and fleeing outside.

Behind her came a thump, that was followed by a yell. Had Connor fallen? She didn't spare the second it would take to look back. Instead, she raced out of the door and down the outside stairs, running for the safety of Max's car.

He wasn't there and neither was Scout. And she could see from peering inside the driver's window that Max's fob wasn't in the ignition either.

Her own fob was in her jacket pocket, hanging up by the front door. There was no time to return for it, though, and she cursed, realising she should have grabbed it before leaving.

Of course, she had been in too much of a panic to do so.

She tried the car door, anyway, choking down on a sob when she found it locked.

Think, Emily.

With no other choice, she ran for the trees. Even though the woods were creepy as hell in the dark, they offered more immediate shelter than the lane leading down from the main road.

Just as she reached the safety of a large oak tree, Connor reappeared at the top of the steps outside the boat house and she froze to the spot, aware that the slightest crunching of twigs would reveal her location.

He appeared to be limping slightly. He definitely must have fallen and hurt himself, which was good for Emily, if it slowed him down.

She considered her options, realising there were only a few.

She could get back into the boat house and lock the door. Retrieve her phone and call the police. It all sounded easy enough, but she already knew locks wouldn't keep Connor out. Plus she didn't have the luxury of waiting for the police to arrive.

Alternatively, she could continue into the woods. Hope to bump into someone and raise the alarm. Though would she find her way in the darkness? If anything had happened to Max and Scout, she needed to locate them quickly.

There was one final choice. She needed to get her key fob. With it, she could leave this wretched place and raise the alarm within minutes.

It seemed like the best idea until she glanced at the car again. Even in the low light coming from the porch, she could now see the flat tyres. Her heart sank. She wasn't going anywhere.

Was this why Max's stuff was on the ground and the boot was open? Had Connor attacked him while his back was turned or had Max realised about the tyres and gone for help?

No. He wouldn't do that. He wouldn't just leave her here. Not without first telling her where he was going.

She watched Connor head over to the car and knew he was trying to figure out where she had gone, and her heart was almost thumping out of her chest, sounding so loud to her ears, she was certain he would hear it. Which was ridiculous.

As he glanced around him, she ducked her head back behind the tree, hoping there was no way he could see her. She kept as still as possible, afraid to barely breathe.

She couldn't risk him finding her.

While she waited, she tried to kick her scrambled brain into action.

With no clue where Max and Scout were, she was on her own.

She left it a couple of minutes, then, unsure where Connor was, she plucked up the courage to peer out from behind the tree again. This time, he had his back to her and was looking towards the lane.

Did he think she had fled that way?

It seemed so, as suddenly he had made a decision and was heading decisively away from the woods.

Emily watched and waited. This was it. Her opportunity.

She needed to get back inside the house and find her phone.

Leaving her hiding place, she realised her legs were trembling badly, she feared they might collapse. Trying to hold herself together, she crept cautiously towards the boat house, hoping to hell that he didn't come back.

Head back to the house. Find your phone. Call the police.

The instructions sounded so simple but were anything but, and as Emily snuck past the car, she continued to watch the lane, terrified in case Connor reappeared.

It took only seconds, but felt like much longer, and then she was climbing the steps and back towards the safety of the boat house. She honestly never thought she would be so happy to see the place.

But the sob of relief as she pushed down the handle quickly turned to one of anguish when she realised the door wasn't opening.

What the hell! Had he locked her out?

Disbelieving, she pushed down on the handle again, his actions flustering her.

Think, Emily.

Her options were quickly being narrowed down. The car and the boat house were both off limits, and she didn't want to follow him out onto the lane.

That left only one choice.

She was going to have to try to follow the path through the woods.

Knowing she didn't have time to waste, she turned to leave the veranda, screaming when she realised Connor was right behind her, standing at the top of the steps.

38

Whoever or whatever Max had heard had disappeared.

He had charged into the woods, Scout hot on his tail and liking this new game, and for the briefest of moments, he had caught the flash of a blue jacket in the distance. He must have imagined it, though, because he had followed the path all the way to the road before doubling back on himself, even straying into the undergrowth in case anyone was hiding, only to come up empty-handed. It seemed he was the only person in the woods.

He had been so convinced that whoever had slashed his tyres was in the woods watching, and he had acted without thinking, his anger spurring him on. Now he was calmer and thinking clearly, he realised that he had left Emily alone.

She wasn't going to like that and, given everything that had happened, he couldn't blame her. Had he even bothered to close the front door to the boat house?

As he whistled to Scout and they started to make their way back, a scream pierced through the tunnel of trees. One that chilled him to the core.

Emily.

Fuck.

Without hesitation, Max picked up pace, breaking into a run.

If anything happened to her, he would never forgive himself.

Emily stared at Connor, neither of them moving, and in that split moment of panic, all she could think about was that she was trapped and couldn't get past him. He clearly realised that too, because he was suddenly moving towards her, and with nowhere to go, she found herself backed up against the veranda wall.

She briefly considered jumping over the edge. It was only a storey up, though the embankment the other side was a steep incline and covered with nettles and brambles as it led down to the river, and it was pitch black down there. If she judged it wrong...

Instead, she did the only other thing she could think of. Charging at him in an attempt to knock him down the steps.

Unfortunately, she misjudged his strength and as she slammed against him, he realised what she was about to do and decided to play her at her own game, lifting her off her feet and swinging her around. He gave her a little shove as her feet hit the ground and she went tumbling down the steps, her body catching every bump and sharp edge along the way, though, fortunately, she didn't hit her head. Only when she landed on her back at the bottom did she realise how much agony she was in.

Seeing Connor slowly descending the stairs, Emily watched him warily, the face she had once considered handsome now looking so sinister, and panic kicked in.

'Please don't hurt me.'

She tried to shuffle away from him, whimpering as each movement sent fresh pain skittering through her. He didn't answer her or react and she was unnerved by his apparent calmness.

He had purposely pushed her down the stairs, so he wanted to hurt her. Was he now going to kill her?

She thought of Max and of Scout, and of the secrets she had kept. How she would do everything differently if she had a second chance.

Connor knelt down beside her, his movements careful and almost tender, as he reached down to smooth her hair away from her face.

'Please,' she begged. She was trembling so badly, she thought she might actually pass out from the fear.

His fingers tightened in her hair, his words a whisper against her ear. 'Why don't we go back inside?'

She wanted to lash out at him and hurt him, but her body painfully reminded her that she had just fallen down a flight of stairs. And he was bigger and stronger.

She knew he was a stalker and a rapist, but was he a murderer?

She honestly had any idea what he was capable of and that scared her half to death.

He stood up and reached down a hand to help her up, which Emily refused to take. Instead, she rolled over onto side, the pain shooting through her left leg and hip, causing her to grimace. She tried to pull herself up from the ground, crying out in agony and falling back down.

Connor huffed impatiently. 'I need you on your feet. Take my hand.'

'You did this to me.'

'Then perhaps you shouldn't have run. Take my hand, Emily.' He sounded angry. 'Now.'

He wasn't leaving her with any other choice. There was no

way she was going to be able to get up by herself. Grudgingly, she did as asked, her skin crawling at the contact as he heaved her up onto her feet.

'Now can you walk or do I need to carry you back up there?'

Every part of her body ached and the pain was making her want to puke, but the idea of him picking her up was revolting. Touching his hand had been bad enough.

'I can walk.'

She took it slowly, limping badly and wincing each time her left foot took the pressure.

The stairs were the hardest to negotiate, but aware that Connor was close behind her spurred her on. She didn't want his help.

He took hold of her arm anyway when they reached the top, and when she struggled to pull herself free, he held on tight, positioning himself so he was behind her, his free arm going around her throat, forcing her into a chokehold.

'I warned you if you can't behave, we will do this the hard way.'

Emily wriggled frantically and tried to kick out, but her movements were restricted, his arm pulling tighter across her throat so she was struggling for air. She tried to talk, to reason with him, but even speech was difficult and he held her easily as he unlocked the door. She was so busy trying to breathe, scared she was about to black out, that it took her a moment to realise that he had used a key.

Had he taken it from inside the boat house?

He dragged her inside, throwing her down on the floor, the hard wood making for an uncomfortable landing mat, and she spluttered and coughed, greedily sucking for air, and for a moment too disorientated to move.

When she eventually managed to roll over so she was facing

him, her eyes went to the knife he was holding and a chill of terror skittered through her.

Where had that come from? And what was he planning to use it for?

'Connor. Please don't.' She choked out the words, trying to pull herself back along the floor as he took a menacing step towards her.

'Where's your boyfriend?'

'I don't... I don't know.'

Why was he asking where Max was? Had he not attacked him too?

Emily had been certain that the reason Max had vanished was because Connor had hurt him. If he didn't know where Max was, that meant Max – and Scout – were still alive. Even through her fear, a tiny spark of hope ignited in her belly.

But why hadn't he come to help her? She had been screaming for him, but both man and dog had just disappeared.

'You don't know?' He didn't believe her. She could tell from his tone. 'I guess we'd better wait for him to come back then. I don't want him to miss this.' The smile he gave Emily was cruel. 'Get on the sofa.'

Not wanting to give him a reason to use the knife, she managed to crawl up onto the cushioned seat. At least the sofa was more comfortable to her aching body than the floor.

'What are you going to do to me?' she managed, terrified what the answer might be, but still needing to know.

He had locked the door to the boat house, which limited her chance to escape, so she didn't attempt to move when he started to circle the sofa, a predator watching its prey.

When he came to a halt behind her, she hoped he wasn't going to put her in a chokehold again. Instead, he smoothed his fingers through her hair. Although it didn't hurt, it was creepy and she wished he would stop.

It was something Max was fond of doing. If they were watching a movie, he would often play with her hair as she snuggled up to him on the sofa. The motion was soothing and usually made her spine tingle. But not now. Now her skin was crawling as she waited for Connor to answer her question.

'I think you know why I'm here,' he whispered against her ear.

No, she really didn't. Why, after all this time, was he back? What else did he want from her?

His tone darkened, making her bowels knot as he brought the cool, blunt side of the blade around to caress her cheek. 'You did a bad thing, Emily, and I am here to punish you for it.'

Tears slid down her cheeks and she desperately tried to keep her teeth from chattering. Was he talking about the threat from the men Alex knew? Emily had never been given any details of what had happened, being told it was better that she didn't know. Whatever had happened, it had been effective, though, as Connor had left her alone. At least for a while.

So why was he back now?

'I don't understand. What did I do?'

Connor didn't get an opportunity to answer, because there was suddenly a commotion as someone tried to open the front door.

Max?

Emily glanced up and saw him through the glass. His expression wide-eyed with shock as they made eye contact and he spotted the man behind her.

For a split second, she forgot about the knife, wrenching away from Connor and screaming.

'Max! Help me.'

Despite her injuries, she attempted to run for the door. She didn't get that far, Connor catching up to her and knocking her to the ground.

As she tried to roll over, doing her best to shake him off, she was aware of banging at the door.

It was impossible to wriggle free – Connor was much stronger than her – but she continued to fight valiantly, determined not to make things easy for him. She couldn't see the knife. He wasn't holding it as he was using both hands to try to pin her arms down.

Emily was aware of the door almost flying off its hinges as Max practically fell in the boat house and of Scout's bark as she charged in after him, but her attention remained focused on Connor.

And it was clear from the look on his face he wanted to kill her.

39

Max didn't allow himself time to think when he spotted Connor in the boat house, standing far too close to Emily for his comfort. He simply acted. Hurling himself against the door when he found it locked, while an agitated Scout barked her head off.

Emily had been on the sofa, and at first glance she seemed unharmed, but the fucker was touching her hair, and he had a knife.

What happened next was so fast, he barely had time to react. Emily realised he was there and was suddenly charging – well, more like limping – towards him, but getting knocked to the ground, grappling with Connor.

Max hit the door with renewed force, this time successfully knocking it open, and barely staying on his feet as he tore through it, the dog hot on his heels.

But then Connor was moving fast, taking advantage of the moment before Max could reach them. Managing to retrieve the knife that he had dropped when he had tackled Emily to the floor and yanking her up with him now, the blade pressing against her throat.

'Stay back!'

Max came to a halt before them, as Emily's eyes widened in fear. She knew as well as he did that just one slip of the blade and it would be over for her.

'Let her go.' He somehow managed to keep his voice calm, as anger and fear waged a battle inside him. He couldn't lose her.

'I don't think so.'

When Max took a testing step forward, Connor warned, 'I mean it. Stay back. I will kill her if I have to. '

He might be bluffing, but it wasn't worth the risk. He assessed the other man. Connor might be a little taller and wider, but Max was certain he could take him if he was unarmed. The knife changed everything.

'Why are you doing this to me?' Emily asked, her tone steady, though her face betrayed her nerves. Her wide, golden eyes in a face even paler than usual, stayed focused on Max as if he was her lifeline.

Connor ignored her question. Pressing the blade tighter, he briefly let go of Emily with his other hand, reaching into his coat pocket. The handcuffs he threw on the floor in front of Max landed with a thud.

'Cuff yourself to the staircase.'

And leave Emily vulnerable to whatever this monster did next? Max didn't think so.

He held Connor's gaze. 'Let Emily go. You don't want to hurt her. She's done nothing to you.' Max kept his tone reasonable and his movements calm as he chanced another step forward.

It was the wrong move.

'Back the fuck up.'

Connor pressed the knife tighter again and Max could see Emily was wincing, the blade leaving a mark where it pressed against her skin.

'Max,' she begged. 'Do what he says.'

Sensing the aggression and seeing that Emily was upset was working Scout into a frenzy. She had been whining since the discovery of an unfamiliar man in the boat house, but now was alternating between growling and barking, which seemed to agitate Connor further, and Max was worried about what she might do He couldn't risk anything happening to her either.

For now, he knew he didn't have a choice. He would have to figure another way out of this situation.

Reluctantly, he reached for the cuffs and went to sit on the stairs, slipping one bracelet around his left wrist and the other around one of the balusters. He wondered if he could chance leaving the second one unlocked, but he was being watched. Connor wasn't stupid, he realised. He was waiting for the recognisable click.

This was far from ideal, but at least he had his right hand free.

He whistled to Scout, relieved when she obediently came to sit by him.

'Good girl,' he told her, ruffling the fingers of his free hand through her soft fur. He gave Connor a hard stare. 'Now what?'

Connor smiled, seeming pleased with how things were going. 'Now we have a chat.'

40

'I take it from the spectacular fight I witnessed earlier that you found my note?'

Connor addressed the question to Max, who sullenly glared up at him, though refused to answer.

Instead, Connor goaded him. 'I know you were angry, Max, but you really shouldn't have left our poor Emily alone in the boat house. You have no idea who could be lurking around in the woods, waiting for the perfect opportunity to strike.'

He laughed at his joke, more relaxed now he was in control. This was better. There had been a couple of little hiccups along the way, but now he had Emily and Max both exactly where he needed them.

He looked at Max Hunter, aware that if he wasn't cuffed to the staircase, he would likely be trying to rip his head off.

The dog was out of the way, locked in the broom cupboard. It had barked and whined at first, but had fallen mercifully silent.

Emily hadn't moved from the chair he had positioned in the centre of the room, head down and studying her hands. He had sat her so she was facing Max, wanting to be able to see both of their reactions as they talked.

He had left her untied for now. Having her boyfriend and dog subdued seemed to be enough of a threat. She did flinch each time he touched her, though, seeming to find his touch repulsive.

Connor hadn't expected her reaction to sting so much and it only fuelled his desire to see this through. By the time he left the boat house, she would have fully paid for what she had done.

'So, are we both sitting comfortably?' he asked, pacing between them and keeping the knife visible.

Again, no response. But that was fine. He didn't mind doing most of the talking.

'Are you both ready for a chat?'

'Why are you here?'

A response at last. That was from Max and it was a relevant question.

'All in good time. We don't want to skip straight to dessert, do we?' He made a show of rubbing at his belly. 'And talking of food, do we have anything to eat? Setting up this little get together was hard work. I think I've earned a snack.'

This time, he looked at Emily, wanting her to interact with him, and was at first surprised when she answered. He had assumed she was going to continue with the silent treatment.

'There's some bits in the fridge, but Scout needs water and you have to let her out to pee.'

She was trying to negotiate. It was cute.

'She's not going out to pee, but depending on how our little chat goes, I might give her some water. How's that?'

Obviously less than ideal from Emily's scowl. 'You can't leave her locked in there.'

'Actually, I can do whatever I like. I'm the one holding the knife.' He stroked his hand over her hair, just because he could, feeling her flinch again, but catching the satisfying flare of Max's nostrils.

Although there had been moments of aggression and enough looks to kill, the cuffs were keeping him under control and he had mostly been measured in his responses.

Connor wasn't stupid, though. He knew that Max was biding his time, trying to figure out a way to escape. He needed to make sure that didn't happen.

'So, food. What have we got?

'What do you want? I'll make you a snack.'

He laughed, immediately sussing her out. 'That's a lovely offer, Emily, but I don't think I'm going to leave you alone in a room that has so many potential weapons. I'll go look myself.' He bent down so his mouth was close to her ear, close enough to realise she was trembling. Good, she was scared. 'Don't even think of running for the door. If you do, I will gut your boyfriend and your dog.'

She didn't answer him, but he caught her sharp intake of breath and knew she wasn't going to try anything.

It had been straightforward getting into the boat house. Emily's passwords had been her downfall. The foolish girl kept them written down in a little notebook, and it hadn't been difficult to hack into her email and iPhone. That was how he had learnt about Norfolk, seeing the message that Max sent her surprising her with the week away.

Initially, Connor had hated the idea of knowing they would be having a romantic break to get their relationship back on track, but then an idea began to form. He had the date and the location, which he saw was completely isolated, from the Google Street View search he did. It was the perfect spot to take his revenge.

Emily had no idea he was back in her life. That for the last seven weeks, he had been watching her, reading her messages, going through her bins, sneaking into her house when both she and Max were out.

It had been so easy tapping into her life and keeping tabs on things, and now, out here in the middle of nowhere, he could take his time.

The love he had once felt towards her had now morphed into hatred and the need to make her pay for her cruel act was burning through his veins. After realising the extent of what she had taken from him, she had once again become his sole focus.

It was all so simple. The keys for the boat house left in an outdoor safe. Max had sent a copy of the passcode to Emily, which Connor had jotted down. He had made sure he arrived before they did, planning to get a copy of the keys cut, but he didn't even have to go to the trouble. The owner had left two sets. Emily and Max had just never realised.

He took his time fixing a sandwich and making himself a cup of coffee, though he kept regularly glancing over to check Emily hadn't moved from the chair.

She hadn't and it was a good test to see how compliant she was going to be.

Taking his plate and mug over, he set them on the floor while he pulled over a chair, sitting down between the happy couple.

'So, what Emily did,' he said, picking up the sandwich and taking a bite. 'Any ideas, Max?'

'You raped her,' he snarled in response. 'I know she didn't deserve that. So nothing she has done could be worse.'

The 'r' word rankled. Okay, so Emily hadn't been conscious when he had made love to her, but she had been leading him on all night. She had been asking for it, and yes, he might have made the decision a little easier for her, but it wasn't rape.

He ignored the comment, staying focused on what he wanted to talk about.

'Has she told you what she got her friends to do to me?'

Max didn't answer, instead holding Emily's gaze. She was looking nervous and more than a little apprehensive.

Good. She fucking deserved to.

She had put him through hell.

41

The four men wearing balaclavas, who cornered him one night as he was leaving her house, having spent an hour spying on her and the arsehole boyfriend, Max, through their windows, had caught him off guard.

He had been making his way back to his van, which had recently been serving as his home away from home. A sleeping bag and a few supplies were all that he needed while he focused on trying to win back the love of his life.

The van was parked on a quiet residential street with wide pathways, houses with high hedgerows and long front gardens, and there were few street lamps about.

It was a nice area. The kind he could see him and Emily living in eventually. A great place to raise their children. Connor already had it planned out.

As an only child, he had longed for siblings and his mother would have liked more children. His father, though, was dead against it. Even telling Connor when he was being particularly cruel that he wished he had been aborted.

The marriage hadn't lasted. Connor's mother had suffered

depression when she did indeed fall pregnant again and his dad had forced her to terminate it.

Maggie Banks had never really recovered from that and although she had led a lavish life, thanks to a generous divorce settlement, Connor knew that losing her second child had badly hurt her.

Although his mother had passed away, he was determined to have children to help keep her spirit alive.

Emily would be the perfect mother.

He had almost reached the end of the road, could see his van parked near the street corner, when a car had turned into the room slowing down as it neared him.

At first, he didn't take any notice. Assuming it was someone returning home. But then the doors had opened. Men with masks on piling out and grabbing hold of him.

Connor worked out and he knew he could hold his own against most people in a fight, but these men were similarly built and he wasn't in a position to take on all three of them. As they bundled him into the back seat of the car, the driver, who had had been waiting and ready, put his foot down.

At first, Connor was panicked. He was sat in the middle of the seat with a man either side, ensuring he couldn't jump out, and he had no idea what they wanted or where they were taking him.

'What's going on?' he had demanded. 'What do you want?'

Was this a robbery? He didn't have anything of value on him.

None of the men answered and, moments later, a hood was forced over his head. The blackness suffocating. They had then forced him forward, binding his hands behind his back.

They had driven for probably an hour before stopping, not saying a single word, despite Connor trying his best to reason with them from beneath the hood.

He was sweating and nervous, his bowels knotting, wondering what the hell they were planning to do to him.

After the car had stopped, he was forced to walk, hood still on, for about a mile. The terrain was bumpy and he'd tripped a couple of times, his heart thumping uncomfortably as his mind conjured up all kinds of fates.

None of them were as horrific as the one they had planned for him, he realised, when they eventually stopped walking.

The hood was pulled from his head and, sucking in a breath of fresh air, he blinked, looking around him. A couple of them had torches and he understood they were in a forest.

What were they doing here?

The rope around his wrists was cut, then one of the men pointed a gun at him, speaking for the first time.

'Strip down to your underwear.'

Connor had started to protest when something hard hit him in the back, knocking the wind out of him, and he stumbled to his knees.

'Strip down to your underwear,' the man repeated.

He was surrounded and didn't have a choice, and as he'd complied, removing jeans and hoodie, shoes and socks, he almost gave into the urge to cry.

He wasn't someone who gave into fear easily, but right now he was terrified, especially when one of the other men threw him a shovel.

'Start digging.'

They wanted him to make his own grave.

His mouth was dry as he tried to rationalise with them. He had money. He would give it all to them. He would do whatever they wanted. Just not this.

There was no reasoning with them.

'Dig,' the order was repeated.

He was out there for hours working, the muscles in his shoulders aching and drenched with sweat, as the men stood around him watching. As dawn broke, it was about three foot deep and he could see what an isolated location they were in. No one would be coming to help.

'That's deep enough.'

Connor's heart sank, knowing what came next. He tried to put up a fight as the shovel was taken from him, but he was too weak from the digging, and they easily held him down, retying his wrists.

'Get in the hole.'

That was when he did start crying. Begging and pleading with them to let him go. He didn't understand how to reason with them because he didn't know what he had done.

When he'd refused to move, they had hit him with the shovel again and he lost his balance, tumbling into the grave.

It was while he was lying on his side on the damp soil, bawling like a baby, that they finally revealed why they were there.

'This is for Emily.'

What?

She was behind this?

Connor had tried to protest, dirt going in his mouth and choking him, as the grave was filled. They couldn't do this to him. They couldn't bury him alive.

He squeezed his eyes shut, begging and praying, barely daring to open them again when the men stopped.

One of them knelt down by the grave, with a warning to deliver. One he was to take heed of.

'Leave Emily Worth alone or next time, we will fill the hole in.'

They had left him then. Alone in the woods in his underwear, bound and covered in dirt.

He managed to wriggle out of the hole, eventually freeing his wrists, and scrambling around for his clothes. His wallet and phone were there also – though he didn't have a signal – and the screen was broken where it had been flung on the forest floor.

Filthy, thirty and exhausted, Connor had stumbled through the forest, trying to find a way back to civilisation.

He was still reeling that Emily could be behind this, but now he understood what kind of woman she was. Overnight, his love for her had manifested itself into hatred, but he knew he had to heed the warning. He was too scared of the repercussions. Fully believing that next time, he would be buried alive.

He had tried to move on, to forget about her. And for a while he did, happy that he was slowly erasing her from his mind.

But then a chance meeting a couple of months ago revealed that she had betrayed him in an even deeper way. And that was when he realised he couldn't let it stand.

Emily Worth had to pay for her sins.

42

Francesca had told Emily it was best that she didn't know what had happened to threaten off Connor. She only knew that it had worked and for that alone, she couldn't regret it.

It was awful hearing the details now and he must have been terrified, but she understood they had needed to scare him badly to get him to leave her alone. And for a while, he had.

Was this why he was here? To get revenge on her for what Alex's friends had done to him? But why leave it for so long?

Max had been quiet while Connor spoke and it was hard to gauge his reaction. She managed to catch his eye, bolstered a little when he gave her the hint of a smile.

At least he wasn't disgusted with her. She suspected he thought Connor was deserving of much worse for raping her.

It was obvious Connor had been affected by what had happened – he had even neglected his sandwich and coffee while talking – but he appeared to have channelled it into rage, and Emily's lack of remorse was not going to help. If he wanted an apology, she would give it to him. Anything to get out of this bloody nightmare.

'I'm really sorry,' she told him, hoping she was injecting the right note of shame in her tone. He needed to believe she genuinely meant it.

Connor didn't look impressed. 'It's all good and well apologising now while I'm holding the knife, but your actions were calculated. You knew full well what you were agreeing to at the time.'

'No, I didn't know. I swear. They wouldn't tell me. They just said they would take care of things for me. I had no idea what that meant.'

'Really?'

'Yes?'

Connor wandered over to her. 'You had no idea at all, but you gave them the go-ahead?'

Her heart thumped as he reached up with his knife, poking the point of the blade against the tip of her chin, the sharp pain making her eyes water.

'Is that right?'

'Get that knife away from her,' Max demanded and she heard the rattle of the cuff against the iron baluster.

His reaction only seemed to provoke Connor, who pressed deeper.

'Is that right? Answer me, Emily.'

'Yes.'

'So by taking care of things, you knew that they could have killed me. But you were okay with that?'

'No.' She squeezed her eyes shut, realising she was digging herself into a hole. 'That was not what I meant.'

To her relief, he withdrew the blade and she saw her blood was on it. Reaching up to her chin, her finger came away red.

'You're a terrible liar,' he commented, sitting back down.

'You raped me.' Her eyes filled with unshed tears.

'No, I made love to you.'

'How the fuck did you do that? I wasn't awake.'

She could see her question had upset him and feared for a moment he would come back over with the knife.

'Talking of making love. I almost forgot. Emily, I brought a present.'

He pulled something from his pocket, throwing it over to her.

Emily caught it, glancing down, her stomach clenching in horror.

It was a white pair of baby bootees and she immediately twigged the relevance.

Finally, she understood why he was here.

43

BEFORE

A few days after Emily had agreed to accepting Alex's help, she woke up with an upset stomach. Max was on day shifts and had only just left for work when she had to rush into the bathroom, needing to throw up.

Had she eaten something or was it a bug?

Or perhaps it was nerves at what she had set in motion.

Although she did start to feel better as the day progressed, she spent much of it in bed, reading and catching up on sleep.

It wasn't until later that night that her mind started to connect dots. Her period was late, though she had put that down to stress. It wouldn't be the first time it had happened. She had skipped an entire month after Aunt Cathy died, so she hadn't been alarmed. But this time she had been sick, and there were other things too. Her breasts were still very tender from the rape, and, of course, there was the tiredness.

Much of her exhaustion could be put down to everything that had been going on, but was it also because of another reason?

Was it really possible she might be pregnant?

Just the thought was enough to send her into a tailspin.

She hadn't had sex with Max in over two months, so she knew it couldn't be his. Which meant if she was pregnant, it was with Connor's baby.

What the fuck was she going to do?

* * *

Although she was well enough to go into work the following day, she still called in sick again. This time nipping to the shops when Max had left for the day and picking up a pregnancy test kit.

Back home, she peed on the stick and waited, hoping and praying that the line wouldn't appear.

Francesca WhatsApped her at lunchtime, asking if she fancied another dog walk that evening as the weather was nice. Emily guessed it was because she had news.

She messaged her friend back, telling her she was off work sick, but she could come over now if she wanted, and half an hour later, Francesca stood in Emily's kitchen breastfeeding Harry, while telling Emily that it was over and Connor wouldn't ever bother her again, speaking as if it was the most natural conversation to have.

Emily didn't ask any of the details. She didn't want to know and in truth, she couldn't think about anything other than what she had discovered. She must have looked worried because Francesca narrowed her eyes. 'You didn't have a choice, Em. We had to do it this way.'

'I know we did. It's not that.'

'Then what's wrong? Is it something else?'

She nodded.

'I'm bloody pregnant.'

44

Francesca took Emily to hospital the day she had the abortion. Leaving her in the waiting area, at Emily's insistence, and arranging for her to call when she was ready to be picked up.

Emily had hoped she would be able to have the abortion pill as she was only seven weeks pregnant, but her GP was concerned that her blood pressure was too high. No doubt it was to do with the recent stress she had been under.

Instead, she found herself waiting to have surgery. Something she was dreading.

She had lied to Max, telling him that Francesca was whisking her away for a spa day. He had been relieved that she was up for going, convinced it would do her good.

If only he knew the truth.

The procedure was done with a local anaesthetic and, afterwards, as she waited for Francesca to arrive, Emily couldn't stop crying.

She was wracked with guilt at what she had just done, but the idea of Connor's baby growing inside of her was unthinkable. She simply couldn't keep it.

'Emily? Are you okay?'

Hearing the familiar voice, she glanced up, shocked to see Jeff, the nurse who had helped treat her father, standing before her. No one was supposed to know she was here apart from Francesca.

He was wearing scrubs and she realised he must be working in the building.

'I moved jobs,' he explained, seeing her confusion. 'Are you waiting for someone?'

She shook her head, struggling to get the words out. 'No... it's... me.'

He smiled sympathetically, taking a seat beside her. 'Would it help to talk about it?'

No. She couldn't. Not with Jeff. He knew Connor. Though he had just said that he was no longer working at the hospice.

Of the nurses who cared for her dad, Jeff had always been the kindest. A friendly ear, ready to listen when things became too much. Suddenly, she had an overwhelming need to confide in someone. He was an understanding and familiar face.

Would it really hurt to talk to him? It wasn't as if he knew Max at all.

'I've just had an abortion,' she whispered.

'No wonder you're upset, love. Were you very far gone?'

'Seven weeks.'

He didn't pry into the circumstances, instead asking, 'Do you have someone to collect you and who can perhaps stay with you?'

Emily nodded. 'My friend is coming to pick me up. I'll be with my boyfriend when I get home, though he doesn't know about any of this.' Fresh tears started to fall as she thought about how badly she was deceiving Max.

'It's your body, Emily. If you're not ready for a baby with him, you're not obliged to go through with the pregnancy.'

'I do want his baby. But this one...' Her voice dropped to a whisper. 'It isn't his.'

Jeff was good with her, staying with her for a short while, telling her she had done nothing wrong and that she shouldn't feel guilty. Of course, he had no idea whose child it was or the circumstances of how it was conceived.

He managed to help Emily get her tears under control and by the time Francesca arrived, she was in a slightly better place.

She needed to get herself together before she saw Max.

'How did it go?' Francesca asked, pulling her into a hug.

'Horribly.'

'I'm so sorry, Em. You don't deserve any of this. It is over now, though, I promise. Connor won't ever be able to hurt you again.'

Emily let out a shaky breath and tried to shake the tension out of her shoulders.

She hoped to hell her friend was right.

45

———

WEDNESDAY

'How did you find out?' Emily practically squeaked the words.

She had been so discreet, going to the hospital with Francesca under the guise of a spa day. No one else knew, apart from her doctor and the hospital staff.

She didn't dare look at Max, who hadn't said a word since Connor had blindsided her.

No more secrets. They had both promised each other. Getting pregnant with her rapist's baby and having it aborted was a pretty big one.

Again, if she could turn back the clock, she would change everything. Well, except for the abortion.

'I bumped into Jeff Caldwell from St Edmunds,' Connor told her, his voice cold. 'He doesn't work there any more, but you know that, don't you, Emily? Because you saw him when you went in for the abortion.'

'I can't believe he told you.' Emily was appalled. She had trusted Jeff and had always liked him. How could he have breached her confidence in this way?

Connor seemed amused by her apparent outrage. 'Relax,

don't blame poor old Jeff. He slipped up. Lucky for me. Unlucky for you. He was in Scarborough, visiting family. Apparently he had already seen you that day.'

Emily remembered. She had been there with Max, Francesca and Adam, clearing out the property before it was sold, and she had nipped to the corner shop for sandwiches and sodas.

'We got chatting,' Connor continued, 'And your name came up. He said how much better you looked than the last time he had seen you, when you were at the hospital. I made out I knew what he was talking about and it only took a couple of leading questions for him to let on about the abortion. Of course, I wasn't sure if it was mine or his at the time.'

He pointed the knife at Max and Emily finally chanced a look at him. He looked more shocked than angry and again she knew she had badly hurt him.

She mouthed the words *I'm sorry* to him, willing him to react in some way, to let her know they were okay. If Connor was going to kill them, she couldn't die knowing Max hated her.

Finally, he gave the faintest of nods. One that told her he was still processing everything, but it would be okay. Her heart hitched. He looked so miserable that she hadn't trusted him and she desperately wanted to go and give him a hug.

He shouldn't even be here, caught up in all of this. It was her choices and mistakes that had led them into this mess.

'You need to start getting better with your online security, Emily. That little book you keep with your passwords in the drawer beside your bed, it reveals everything about you.'

She gaped at Connor. He had broken into their home?

'The trail of messages with your friend, Francesca, was interesting. I wasn't in any doubt who the father was after that. And the NHS account you have, it told me exactly how far along you were when you terminated *my* baby. How fucking dare you?'

Until now, Connor had been calm and conversational. It was unnerving. But suddenly, she saw the anger heat up his cheeks. Dark eyes flashing with temper as he got up again, moving behind her chair and suddenly yanking her head back by her hair, exposing her throat.

As the cool blade of the knife grazed against her skin, she swallowed. Her mouth dry with fear.

'Leave her alone!'

She heard the rattle of cuffs sliding up the baluster and was aware that Max was on his feet, even if she couldn't properly see him.

Connor took no notice. 'You killed my child. Give me one good reason why I shouldn't slice your throat open right now.

Emily squeezed her eyes shut, ice chilling her veins.

'Please,' she begged, barely able to think straight. She couldn't stop trembling, her heart threatening to beat out of her chest.

She had no idea how much time passed with that knife to her throat. She could hear Max trying to reason with Connor, the sound of both their voices thundering through the panic.

Eventually, he withdrew the blade, giving a bitter laugh. 'You didn't think I would make it that easy on you, did you? You murdered my baby. I have bigger things planned for you.'

As he spoke, he wandered over to the window. It was too dark to really see anything, but he appeared lost in thought, giving them a few blessed moments alone.

Max caught Emily's eye.

Run, he mouthed to her.

She couldn't. For starters, she had hurt herself falling down the stairs. Connor would easily catch her. But also she wouldn't leave Max and Scout. Connor would kill them without hesitation. She had to try to save them.

If they were going to escape, though, she needed to get Max

out of the handcuffs, and she had been trying to figure out a way to do that while Connor had been talking.

There were potentially things that could be used in the kitchen, but he was keeping a close eye on her, and there was no chance of her getting close enough to lay her hands on anything.

Unless she could get away for a few minutes, how could she find a way to help Max?

And Scout. Her poor baby was still trapped in that cupboard. She had been intermittently whining and barking, but the long periods of silence were worrying. Connor hadn't given her any food or water.

Max and Scout were both counting on her.

Emily caught Max's eye again. The brief exchanged look between them conveying more than any words they could have spoken. They were in this together and needed to figure a way out.

Relief at knowing that made her want to sob. She had hurt Max so badly, yet he was still standing by her side. She had misjudged him so badly.

She hugged her arms around herself, trying to keep warm. Beneath the woolly fabric of her jumper, she could feel her bra and the underwire that ran below the cups.

She had heard that handcuff locks could be picked with a kirby grip or a paperclip. Would her underwire work?

Of course, it was irrelevant unless she could somehow get it out of the bra and over to Max.

Seeing that Connor was still distracted, she discreetly moved her hand beneath her jumper, finding the end of the wire. If she could work a hole in the fabric to get to it, she should be able to thread it out, but she would need to be careful. She couldn't risk Connor seeing what she was trying to do.

She concentrated on pulling the nylon material taut against

the end of the wire, trying to work through it. It was hard going. The fabric was doubled up and she had to be careful not to draw attention to herself.

It was a work in progress and she had to keep stopping whenever Connor wandered back over. He had fallen quiet, not saying too much, helping himself to more food and drink and looking pensive as he ate. She suspected he was playing over the abortion in his head and his plan for what he intended to do to her and Max.

She assumed he had a plan. It seemed he had thought this all out carefully. Unless, of course, he was adapting it.

Quiet Connor was unsettling. At least when he was talking, she knew what he was thinking.

He finished the second sandwich he had made, washing it down with a glass of water.

'That's better,' he announced, coming to stand in front of her. 'I've been living off cereal bars and McDonald's for the last few days. Not ideal, though needs must.'

Remembering the rucksack they had found, Emily understood.

'It was you in the cottage. You've been watching us.'

He didn't answer, instead grinning at her and holding out his hand. 'Come on.'

Come on where? Was this the moment where he was going to kill her, or did he have something else planned? Both options filled her with dread.

She was about to ask, even though she didn't want to know the answer, but Max beat her to it.

'Where are you taking her?' he demanded.

A wide smug smile tipped Connor's lips as he addressed Max directly. 'I'm taking her upstairs.'

Emily was pretty sure her heart stopped for a moment. He was going to rape her again.

The idea scared her witless. She couldn't let it happen.

'No, you're fucking not.' Max was furious, tugging at his cuff. If he wasn't chained to the banister Emily knew he would be trying to rip Connor's throat out.

'Please don't do this,' she begged.

'This isn't a request, Emily.' Connor's tone was hard.

'I still hurt from where I fell earlier,' she protested. It wasn't a lie. Every part of her ached and she was pretty certain she had sprained her ankle. 'I don't know if I can get up the stairs.'

'In which case, I will carry you.'

'No!'

'Fine. Then get up. I don't have to remind you what happens to that lovely dog of yours if you don't do as you're told.'

He didn't and Emily despised him for the threats he kept making against Scout and Max.

She pulled herself up, ignoring his outstretched hand, just as she was trying to ignore the fresh blast of pain in her leg.

As she limped towards the stairs, Max got up, blocking the way. He looked murderous.

'She stays down here,' he demanded. His right hand was balled into a fist, but his cuffed wrist was pulled taut against the top of the baluster.

Despite his best intentions, there was no way he could stop Connor.

The other man simply laughed at his attempt. 'Very valiant,' he commented, not bothering to hide his smirk.

Emily didn't want this either, but Max needed to calm down. He wasn't in a position to make threats. Connor still had the knife and she knew he would use it.

She went to Max, taking his free hand between hers. 'Sit down. It's okay.'

When he didn't react, simply staring at her, she threw her arms around his neck, holding him close and whispered into his ear. 'I have a plan.'

'That's enough,' Connor snapped, pulling her away. He was being unnecessarily rough as he dug his fingers into the top of her arm, dragging her up the stairs behind him.

She winced, crying out as she stumbled, her bad ankle hitting the sharp edge of the step, and then they were in the bedroom, and before he closed the door, Connor shouted down to Max. 'I'll make sure she stays awake this time.'

As Max yelled back a string of expletives, Emily's stomach turned.

She took a step back. The bed in between them as they stared at each other.

'I need the loo,' she managed, heading towards the bathroom before he could stop her.

Once inside, she started to shut the door, but then Connor was there pushing it open and forcing his way into the bathroom.

Her heart nearly beat out of her chest. 'What are you doing? I want some privacy.'

Connor didn't answer, instead shoving his way past her and studying the contents of the bathroom cabinet that she had earlier thrown in the sink. He removed a pair of nail scissors and some nail clippers, and a couple more spray bottles, before glancing around the room.

He gave her a terse nod. 'Okay. But don't take too long about it.'

Emily watched him go, relieved when he shut the door after him.

She didn't waste any time, removing her jumper and then her

bra. She pulled at the wire again, but there was not enough tear in the fabric and she cursed him for taking the scissors. Instead she used her teeth, trying to rip at the material.

'Hurry up in there.'

'I can't pee while I know you're waiting out there,' she shouted back. 'It's making me nervous. Just give me a minute, please.'

Her second attempt was more successful and she created a hole big enough to feed the wire through. Quickly she slipped her bra and jumper back on, then she hid the underwire up her sleeve.

Somehow she had to get it downstairs to Max.

She flushed the chain and ran the tap for a few moments, then stepped back into the bedroom where Connor was waiting for her, his hands in his pockets and his feet spread apart.

'Are you done?'

She nodded, pausing by the bedroom door. 'I need some water though.'

'You don't have to go downstairs for that. I saw a plastic tumbler in the bathroom. You can use that.'

'My pills are down there, though.' When his frown deepened, she quickly added, 'I have a really bad headache.'

'Do you really think I give a shit if your head hurts?'

He had a point.

He stared at her for so long, she thought he was going to either call her a liar or tell her it was tough, but eventually he huffed out in frustration.

'Okay, come on. But this had better not just be a ploy to buy you time.'

This was good. He was letting her go back down. She hadn't been sure if he would but was counting on him not wanting to leave her alone in the bedroom.

It was harder work going down the stairs than up and she

clung on to the banister, ignoring Max's enquiring look as she passed him.

She found the painkillers, relieved she had left them in the kitchen and hadn't packed them away, and took a couple with a glass of water. She had been lying about the headache, but it might help her throbbing ankle.

'Are you done?' Connor demanded.

Emily nodded, carefully working the underwire out from her sleeve and into the palm of her hand, relieved when he started to walk up the stairs ahead of her.

She reached for Max's hand as she passed, pressing the wire into it.

His eyes widened as his fingers closed around hers and he nodded to confirm he understood. Emily gave his hand a brief squeeze before letting go and limping back up the stairs, unsure what awaited her.

It was down to Max now and there was nothing more she could do but wait.

46

———

Finally, something was going their way and Max worked as quickly as possible to pick the lock of the handcuffs.

If Connor had his hands on Emily, he was going to kill him.

He wanted to get his dog out of that damn cupboard too. Scout's pitiful whining and confusion at why she had been locked away had cut through him and he wanted to kill Connor for that alone.

Kill.

He had considered that word a lot over the last couple of hours.

Max had noticed the way Connor looked at Emily and he had seen the bitterness and resentment he had towards her. He was also certain that he had no intention of letting either of them leave alive.

If it came down to it, could he take another man's life?

He worked as part of a team who routinely saved people, whether it was rescuing them from burning buildings or cutting them out of crushed vehicles.

This was the other end of the scale.

But Connor had hurt Emily. He had drugged and raped her, and he had stalked her, all while she had been grieving for her dad. He had taken advantage of her in the worst possible way. And, even all these months later, he was still terrorising her and was now planning to rape her again.

Rage burned in Max's gut, and he knew if the situation came down to it, he couldn't afford to hesitate.

Emily's latest revelation about the pregnancy and abortion had left him reeling and, again, he couldn't believe she had kept it from him. Ultimately, it had him asking questions of himself, though. She had clearly believed he wouldn't stand by her.

Nothing was further from the truth and it almost broke his heart that she had felt she had no choice but to go through everything without him. Knowing she had suffered alone intensified his hatred for the man upstairs and he vowed that if they got out of this mess, he would prove to her that she could trust him.

He twisted the wire again, this time hearing the welcoming click of the cuff unlocking, pulling his wrist free.

Keeping his movements slow, he got to his feet.

* * *

'Get on the bed. I won't ask again.'

Connor gave Emily a warning look, one he hoped told her he was through messing around.

Although her eyes were shining with tears, there was a hardness in her stare that he hadn't seen before. She stood before him, her fists clenched and her chin jutted up, and although he could see she was trembling, she was holding her ground.

'No.'

She wasn't making this easy and that was a shame. Last time, she had been drugged and unresponsive and he really wanted to make sure she was awake this time. He wanted her to feel every-thing, but she wasn't playing along.

Instead, he tried the threat that had worked so well throughout the afternoon. 'Do I need to go and hurt your dog? Scout. That's her name, right? I'll give you a choice. I can either use my knife or leave her in that cupboard to starve to death.'

Emily's temper flashed. 'If you lay one finger on her, I swear I will find a way to kill you.'

This wasn't going according to plan and Connor was begin-ning to get irritated.

He had hoped she would be compliant if he made threats, but if that wasn't going to be the case, then he would resort to force.

* * *

After letting Scout out of the cupboard, Max grabbed the nearest weapon to him: Scout's leash.

If for no other reason, it seemed poetic justice for how the fucker had treated his dog.

Telling Scout to sit, not wanting to put her in any danger, and grateful that she was being obediently quiet, Max crept up the staircase, his hand closing on the bedroom door, wincing at the screams coming from the other side.

He slowly eased it open, partly hoping to have the element of surprise, partly dreading what he was about to walk in on.

Emily was on the bed, pinned beneath Connor, but he was relieved to see she was still fully dressed. And she was fighting him too. Clawing at his face as Connor tried to pin her arms down, and yelling and swearing at him to stop.

When he saw Connor reach for the knife, Max's belly dropped. Without thinking any further, he acted, wrapping the leather strap around Connor's throat and startling the hell out of him, watching his limbs frantically lash out as he struggled to break free.

Emily was wide-eyed, sitting up now and scooting back across the bed.

'Run!' Max yelled at her. 'My phone is downstairs. Call the police, then take Scout and get the hell out of here.'

'What about you?' She seemed reluctant to leave him.

'I'll come find you. I promise.'

He watched her leave the room before tightening his grip.

Emily had struggled to get down the stairs, focusing on Scout's eager face as she bit down on her pain. The dog was delighted to see her, jumping up at her and licking her face. The feeling was mutual and she wanted to make a fuss of Scout back, but she needed to locate Max's phone.

She had hated leaving him upstairs fighting with Connor, but he seemed to have the upper hand and she knew it was important that she call for help as quickly as possible.

They needed to get out of the boat house too, but she wasn't sure if her ankle would support her down yet another steep flight of stairs.

Seeing the phone on the coffee table, she snatched it up, but instead of leaving via the front door, she toyed with the idea of staying and hiding, suddenly remembering the hatch that led down to the storage room. She had forgotten all about it.

She recalled that she had intended to look for it, but had been distracted after they had found the doll. If she could find the hatch and lock herself inside, she could call the police, then wait for them to arrive.

She looked towards the kitchen now. There was a rug

covering part of the floor. Going over, she kicked it back, spotting the trapdoor in the floor.

Unlocking it, she pulled it open and peered down into the darkness, spotting the spiral staircase. It wasn't going to be easy with her bad leg, but she could sit down and shuffle her way to the bottom. This felt safer than heading into the woods.

She called to Scout, stepping down onto the top rung before helping the dog down, then she pulled at the rug, holding it against the edge of the door, hoping that when she closed the hatch door, it would cover it up again.

As Connor started to choke, Max fought against every instinct in his body to let go.

He wasn't a killer. But then he thought about Emily and everything this bastard had put her through, and as Connor gripped at the lead, thrashing out with his legs as he fought to free himself, Max tugged harder. He was simply doing what he needed to do to protect his family.

Still, he let go when the man's body eventually went limp, figuring he would get the cuffs from the stairs and restrain him, just in case he was still alive.

Heading back downstairs, he picked up the bra wire, using it to unpick the cuff that was locked to the stairs. There was no sign of Emily or Scout and he was relieved she had heeded his advice, getting the hell out of there.

Hopefully, she was already on the phone to the police.

He had just unlocked the cuff and was turning to go back upstairs when something smacked into him from the side, sending him flying to the floor. For a second, he was stunned, but then as he gathered himself, ready for a second attack, he realised Connor was back on his feet.

He wasn't aware of the knife until the blade penetrated his skin. The white-hot searing pain taking his breath away.

The fight ebbing out of him, his hands going to his chest, Max fell onto his back, sweat beading and gasping for air as his vision swam.

The last thing he saw before his world turned black was Connor's bloody, but grinning face.

* * *

'Emily!'

Connor called her name as he stood over Max's body.

Was she still in the boat house or had she run for the woods again?

She couldn't have managed to get far on her ankle and he was relishing her moment of realisation when she understood that her escape plans had been foiled and that Max had sacrificed himself for nothing. It was the first time he had ever taken a life. He had thought about it before, but until now, he had never crossed that line.

What Emily had done though, killing his child, it was unforgiveable.

They had talked about his desire to become a father and how important it was to him. How fucking dare she?

With Max now out of the picture, Connor could take his time with her.

One down, one to go. But he needed to find her fast. He couldn't risk her getting away.

He was about to head out of the boat house when he heard a muffled bark.

She obviously had the dog with her.

Where was the noise coming from? It sounded like it was from below him.

Grinning as he realised where she was, Connor headed out of the door.

47

Emily hadn't thought about the fact she might struggle to get a phone signal down in the storage room. Frustrated, she limped around the small space, the only light coming from the torch on Max's phone, holding it at different angles, but there was nothing.

Deciding to have one last attempt, she managed to climb the spiral staircase again, sitting on the top step and holding the phone as close to the hatch as possible.

The sound of Connor's voice calling her name as he paced on the floor above her filled her with both dread and worry.

If he was okay, then where the hell was Max?

Had Connor done something to him?

Tears threatened and she fought to keep them at bay. She needed to be strong. Max had made her promise. And he might be okay, Or he might need her help. She couldn't let him down.

She held the phone up again, this time managing to get a single bar. Hoping that would be enough, she dialled 999.

On the floor below her, Scout barked, frustrated she couldn't get up the staircase, and Emily shushed her.

Her call connected and she requested to be put through to the police.

A woman answered. 'Norfolk Constabulary. What's your emergency?'

'Please help me. He's going to kill me. You need to come now.'

'Where are you?'

'Wroxham. Or near it.' Damn it. Emily was flustered. 'We're out in the countryside.'

'Are you at a house?'

'Yes, we rented it.'

'Do you know the address?' the woman asked.

'The Stone Boat House. It's down a country lane, but I can't remember the name of the road.' Damn it, what was it called?

'Can you describe where you are?'

Yes, she could do that. 'There are woods and there's a jetty and an abandoned cottage on the opposite side of the river.' Above her, came the distinct sound of a door slamming. Had Connor gone into the woods to look for her? Or what if he was coming down to look in the tunnels? 'You have to come quickly. He's going to kill me. Please just help me!'

'Okay, help is on the way.' The woman sounded so calm. 'Are you hurt?'

'Please hurry. I'm scared.'

'What's your name?'

'Emily.'

'Emily. I need you to stay calm and talk to me.'

That was easier said than done.

'Help is coming,' the woman continued. 'Is there somewhere you can hide?'

'I am hiding. I managed to get down in the storage room.'

'That's good. Stay there and wait for the police to arrive. Do you know where this man is right now?'

'I don't know. He was upstairs, but I think he might have gone outside.'

Emily wondered if she dare chance opening the hatch slightly and having a look.

'Do you know who he is?'

She vaguely heard the question, but was too busy lifting the hatch lid to notice. Peering across the room, the first thing she spotted was Max on the floor. He was motionless and covered in blood. The knife that had been used to stab him on the floor beside him.

She choked down on a sob. Was he dead?

'Emily?' The woman was trying to get her attention. 'Are you okay? Are you still there?

'My boyfriend, Max. He's got a knife—'

Wound. That was the last word she had meant to say, but the storage door was suddenly flying open and seeing Connor standing in the dark entrance had her pausing in horror.

And that was when she started to scream.

48

It all happened so quickly.

Scout barking.

Emily raising the hatch door, trying to clamber up inside the boat house.

Connor charging for the spiral staircase in a bid to stop her escaping.

She had managed to pull her torso through, but her legs were still dangling, and feeling his hand grab her bad ankle, she squealed in pain, kicking out as best as she could and earning herself a grunt as he released her. But then he got a firmer grip, wrapping his arm around both her legs so she couldn't hurt him and dragging her back down inside the hatch.

Emily screamed as her head and chest bashed against the metal stairs, dropping Max's phone and plunging the room into darkness.

She struggled against Connor, but he firmly had hold of her now and she heard his low chuckle, hot breath against her ear stirring nausea in her gut.

'It's just you and me now, Emily. What do you say we get out of here before the police arrive and take this little party of ours somewhere private?'

'Please... let me go. I won't tell them you were here.'

'Now, where would be the fun in that?'

He pulled her tight against him so she could feel his hardness against the small of her back, and his arm banded so tightly around her waist, she thought it might crush her. Forcing his free hand between her jeaned legs, he rubbed his fingers against her.

Emily whimpered, and Scout started going nuts, barking and growling, sensing the hostile threat in the room.

'Shut up, you noisy fucking mutt.'

Connor kicked out suddenly and Emily heard a thump before Scout let out a pitiful whine.

'Don't hurt her. Please don't hurt her.'

'Then you'd better make sure you do as I say.'

Thankfully, he removed his hand and she felt him rummaging for something, probably in his pocket. Moments later, a tiny beam threw a low light on the room.

Emily looked for Scout, needing to know she was okay. The collie was keeping her distance, but was still riled up.

As Connor dragged Emily back towards the door, the dog followed, though was careful not to get too close.

She assumed he was taking her out through the door that led to the front of the boat house, but instead, he turned towards the tunnels looking out on the river. The two mouths like the letter M in the shadowy beam of his torch.

And then she spotted it. The old rowing boat moored along the side.

Was it the one they had spotted at the cottage? She had assumed he had a car parked close by, but had he been using this boat to come and go?

As they neared, she spotted the rucksack in the boat. It was open and she could see a bigger torch and a coil of rope poking out. On the floor beside it was another much smaller bag, some kind of hessian sack with a drawstring on it, more knives, and a shovel.

Panic clawed its way into Emily's throat as she remembered what Connor had said Alex's friends had done to him.

Did he plan on burying her alive?

'Come on, get in.'

'No. NO!'

She fought frantically to free herself as he tried to force her into the boat, dragging her feet and clawing out with her hands. He was far too strong for her, though, throwing her into the boat like she weighed nothing at all, then starting to climb in behind her, the boat rocking heavily back and forth.

Emily had landed heavily on her knees and as she tried to get up, she heard a ferocious growl and then a scream from Connor. As Scout attacked him, the torch fell to the floor of the boat.

He yelled and swore at her dog, trying to fight her off, and Emily took advantage of the moment, twisting herself around, catching the glint of the blade in Connor's free hand and realising that he had picked up one of the knives.

No. He couldn't stab Scout.

While he was preoccupied, the Collie having sunk her teeth into his arm, Emily reached for the shovel, throwing it onto the walkway between the two tunnels and managing to pull herself back out of the boat.

Connor had his back to her, his knife hand raised, and she clambered to her feet, swinging the shovel at him.

The metal cracked hard against his hand, the knife falling and clattering back into the boat.

As he turned in surprise, Scout still clinging on to one arm, Emily swung the shovel again, this time with as much force as possible. It smacked him hard across the face and, losing his balance, Connor toppled out of the boat and into the water.

As she waited for him to resurface, determined to hit him again if he did, she whistled to Scout. The dog jumped out of the boat, coming to stand beside her.

Emily's heart thumped as she stared at the water.

Where was he?

In the distance, she heard the sound of sirens.

As they drew nearer, she slowly backed out of the tunnel, Scout by her side, and the shovel still in her hand in case she suddenly needed it.

It wasn't until the first police car arrived that she dared to believe it was actually over.

49

THIRTEEN MONTHS LATER

Max had proposed to Emily while he was still in the hospital, recovering from the knife wound he had sustained – one that had luckily just missed his heart – and they had married two months later in a low-key ceremony, attended only by his family and a few of their closest friends.

The week spent in Norfolk had shown both of them just how precious life really was and they were in mutual agreement that they didn't want to waste another minute. Everything that had happened had brought them closer together, making them realise how much they wanted to be with each other.

Six months after the wedding, they put in an offer on a house just outside of Leeds that they had fallen in love with. A character property with high ceilings, bay windows and a generous, mature garden. It was the perfect place to start over and they were both thrilled when their bid was accepted.

Today was moving day and Emily collected the keys from the estate agent, sending a quick message to Max as she walked back to her car, saying that she was on her way and would meet him and the friends who were helping them move, over at the house.

From the passenger seat of her Polo, parked in the pay and display, Scout started barking, the sound carrying through the gap at the top of the window, and as was often the case over this last year, Emily's head shot up, as she glanced anxiously around the car park.

She was alone and it was broad daylight. Shoppers only a few yards away. Still, fear of what could be lurking chilled her skin and she quickened her pace, anxious to get back to the car. Once inside, she locked the doors, letting herself relax.

The overreaction was natural and the counsellor she had been seeing told her to be patient, that the panic of someone following her would gradually fade with time.

Determined not to let Connor Banks ruin her moving-in day, Emily held up the envelope with the house keys for Scout to see. 'Are you ready to go meet your new home?'

The dog whined, though this time picking up the excitement in her tone, and Emily started the engine.

As she followed the exit signs, the flash of something from the corner of her eye caught her attention. Was there a figure standing by the corner wall?

She wasn't quick enough to see, whoever it was disappearing from sight, and she tried to shake away the feeling of paranoia, turning on the radio for a distraction.

Connor had never been found, despite a thorough search of the area.

It would have been nice to have closure, but it wasn't to be, and although the case remained open, Emily and Max were advised to move on. If Connor was alive, as the police suspected, they didn't think he would bother them again. He would be in search of his next fixation and, sadly, a new victim.

Emily shook him from her thoughts as she and Scout joined Max and their friends at the house. Helping with the building of furniture, unpacking boxes, and keeping everyone supplied with cups of tea soon took over as priority.

Later, when everyone had been fed, courtesy of the fish and chip takeaway in the village, and they had thanked and said goodbye to the last of their friends, it was just the three of them.

While Max let Scout in the back garden for a late-night wee, Emily cleared away the wrappers and empty cans, taking them out of the front door to put them in the recycling bin.

It was almost Christmas and beyond the front garden hedge, she could see the twinkle of fairy lights adorning the houses across the road. It was so quiet and peaceful. The crisp, cold air biting at her face as the breeze picked up, one of the chip wrappers coming loose and blowing down the driveway before she could get it in the bin.

As she chased it towards the road, bending down to try to retrieve it, a booted foot stamped down on the paper, startling her. Emily glanced up the jeaned leg, unable to stop the grip of fear that was clamping down on her chest.

'You okay?'

Max.

She saw his face peering down at her in the dark and nodded, immediately feeling foolish.

He gripped her hand, pulling her up, and the brief look he gave her told her he understood. He pulled her close, his breath warm against her cheek.

'This is going to be good for us, Em. A fresh start.'

'It is pretty here,' she told him, hugging him back, and as they stood together in front of their new home, Scout wandering over to join them, she knew he was right.

EPILOGUE

NINETEEN MONTHS LATER

'Here. Let me get that for you?'

Nina Shannon thanked the man who held the front door for her, appreciating that she didn't have to negotiate opening it with her arms full. She had come straight from work and had her laptop and files with her, and hadn't wanted to leave them in the car.

She had seen him about before, which perhaps wasn't surprising. The seaside town of Portrush on Northern Ireland's north coast had a population of less than eight thousand. Faces became familiar.

And she would be a liar if she said she hadn't noticed him. Tall, with a shaved hair and a full beard, and kindly, dark eyes. For such a big man, he was gentle in his manner, and she liked that about him.

She hadn't seen him at the support group before, though she had only been twice herself. Needing somewhere that she could go and be with like-minded people who understood how she was feeling after the death of her beloved mother.

He didn't speak, other than to introduce himself when asked.

Connor Nicholson.

The name suited him. And he had an English accent. Not a local.

Tonight, Nina spoke, finally trying to put into words the grief she felt. There were sympathetic murmurs of support from the others. Connor said nothing, but she was aware he was watching her, and when she finally looked up, she picked up on an overwhelming sense of empathy. He understood her pain.

His timing was spot on again as they left the session, and he was there holding the door for her, then falling in step beside her as they crossed the car park.

'I'm sorry about your mother,' he told her and Nina's eyes welled up.

It was still all so raw. And she had no siblings to share the grief with. No father either, as he had passed away when she was a child.

'Thank you.'

'If you ever want to sound off to someone just one on one, I'm happy to help.'

When she looked at him, perhaps surprised by his offer when they still barely knew each other, he offered her a warm smile. 'I've been told I'm a good listener.'

'You've lost someone.' It wasn't a question. He wouldn't be in the group if he hadn't.

'Yes.' Now his brow furrowed and he looked troubled. 'It was a while back. Coming up to two years ago in November, but it's still very painful.'

When Nina waited patiently, a sign for him to continue in his own time, he opened up.

'It was my girlfriend. Emily. But I don't think I'm ready to talk about it yet. Though I want to move on and I do think it's time I tried.'

He sounded so earnest.

'It's okay. You have to do it in your own time. But if you want to talk, I will be here for you too.' It was an offer she didn't mind making. This was simply about supporting each other, but if anything else developed further down the line, would it really be such a bad thing? 'Would you like to grab a coffee sometime, Connor?'

Connor paused walking and turned to face her. His dark eyes lighting up.

'Yes. Thank you, Nina. A coffee would be great.'

ACKNOWLEDGMENTS

This story changed drastically while writing it, becoming something altogether more personal, and the person I have to give most thanks to is my editor, Caroline Ridding. She is the one who kept me in check and helped to guide me on the right path. This book was easier to write with you by my side. Thank you also to Jade Craddock and Emily Reader for their eagle-eyed copy-editing and proofing.

To Amanda Ridout, Nia Beynon, Claire Fenby, Sue Lamprell, and everyone else in the Boldwood family, thank you for everything you do. I love being part of Boldwood Books.

Usually I gush here about all of the fantastic people who have supported me. My wonderful friends, fellow writers and readers, the Beev clan, the bloggers, my beta readers, etc. Truthfully, I am exhausted after finishing this story. If I start mentioning names, I will forget some of you, so please know I appreciate every single one of you.

I did promise Angela Kane and Deb Day a mention in the acknowledgements. The story has changed since seeking your advice, but thank you both for taking the time to try to help me. And to the fabulous Tara Lyons. You have been so good, helping me with research questions on my last two books, and I realised I have forgotten to say thank you previously. Please know that your help has been really appreciated.

There are two Facebook groups I want to give a shout out to who have been super supportive of my books. They are the fabulous Psychological Thriller Readers and Bitchy Bookworms, run by our honorary Brit, Christina Cook. Thank you to all of the members in both groups. You are awesome.

Finally, a brief note to my readers. I am known for the twists in my novels and this one has fewer than usual, as the antagonist is revealed quite early on. It's a sad fact that predators like Connor Banks do exist and, although what you have just read is a work of fiction and the story has been embellished for this purpose, this one hit very close to home. I was able to draw on the personal experience of someone very close to me when it came to writing some of the scenes in this book.

My lead character, Emily, blames herself for much of what she goes through, but the truth is, she has done nothing wrong. She is sadly a victim of a predator.

For everyone out there who has had the misfortune of meeting a Connor Banks, this one is for you.

ABOUT THE AUTHOR

Keri Beevis is the internationally bestselling author of several psychological thrillers and romantic suspense mysteries, including the very successful *Dying to Tell*. She sets many of her books in the county of Norfolk, where she was born and still lives and which provides much of her inspiration.

Sign up to Keri Beevis' mailing list here for news, competitions and updates on future books.

Visit Keri's website: www.keribeevis.com

Follow Keri on social media:

twitter.com/keribeevis
facebook.com/allaboutbeev
instagram.com/keri.beevis

ALSO BY KERI BEEVIS

The Sleepover

The Summer House

The Boat House

Trust No One

Every Little Breath

THE
Murder
LIST

**THE MURDER LIST IS A NEWSLETTER
DEDICATED TO SPINE-CHILLING FICTION
AND GRIPPING PAGE-TURNERS!**

**SIGN UP TO MAKE SURE YOU'RE ON OUR
HIT LIST FOR EXCLUSIVE DEALS, AUTHOR
CONTENT, AND COMPETITIONS.**

SIGN UP TO OUR
NEWSLETTER

BIT.LY/THEMURDERLISTNEWS

Boldwood

Boldwood Books is an award-winning fiction publishing company seeking out the best stories from around the world.

Find out more at www.boldwoodbooks.com

Join our reader community for brilliant books, competitions and offers!

Follow us
@BoldwoodBooks
@TheBoldBookClub

Sign up to our weekly deals newsletter

https://bit.ly/BoldwoodBNewsletter

Printed in Great Britain
by Amazon